D0438087

CRAZY EIGHTS

CRAZY EIGHTS

A JAKE HINES MYSTERY

ELIZABETH GUNN

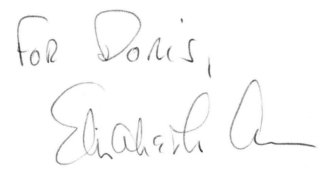

For Doris,

Elizabeth Gunn

A TOM DOHERTY ASSOCIATES BOOK
NEW YORK

CRAZY EIGHTS: A JAKE HINES MYSTERY

Copyright © 2005 by Elizabeth Gunn

This book is printed on acid-free paper.

A Forge Book
Published by Tom Doherty Associates, LLC
175 Fifth Avenue
New York, NY 10010

www.tor.com

Forge® is a registered trademark of Tom Doherty Associates, LLC.

Library of Congress Cataloging-in-Publication Data

Gunn, Elizabeth, 1927–
    Crazy eights : a Jake Hines mystery / Elizabeth Gunn.—1st ed.
        p.   cm.
    "A Tom Doherty Associates book."
    ISBN 0-765-30806-1 (alk. paper)
    EAN 978-0765-30806-1
    1. Hines, Jake (Fictitious character)—Fiction.   2. Criminals—Crimes against—Fiction.
3. Police—Minnesota—Fiction.   4. Minnesota—Fiction.   I. Title.

PS3557.U4854C73 2005
813'.54—dc22

                                                                                2004056321

First Edition: March 2005

Printed in the United States of America

0 9 8 7 6 5 4 3 2 1

ACKNOWLEDGMENTS

Many people helped me understand how law-enforcement agencies function and fit together so that I could write this book. Brendan McConnell, an attorney in the Office of the Commonwealth Attorney of Prince William County, Virginia, helped me with courtroom procedure and points of law. Mary Ann Hutchison, long a courtroom clerk in Superior Court of the State of Arizona, guided me through the Pima County courthouse and helped me find trials to watch. Investigator (now Sergeant) Jeffrey Stillwell and narcotics investigator Daryl Seidel of the Rochester, Minnesota, police department were generous with information about drug interdiction and arrest procedures. At the Bureau of Criminal Apprehension in St. Paul, Minnesota, I am greatly indebted to lab director Frank Dolejsi and to the following forensic scientists: David Peterson, a great storyteller about the art, as well as the science, of latent-fingerprint identification; Stephanie Eckerman, whose comprehensive knowledge of guns and ammunition shaped this narrative; and Ann Marie Gross, who has built her career at BCA in lockstep with the science of DNA and still has the patience to make this daunting subject approachable. John Sibley, retired deputy police chief of Rochester, Minnesota, has done his resourceful best to keep me out of Snicker City. If in spite of the best efforts of these kind, intelligent people there are errors in this text, they are entirely my own.

CRAZY EIGHTS

1

"What are we doing here," I asked Trudy, one hot Sunday morning in May, "raising potatoes for the whole town of Mirium?"

"Enough for us and the two Sullivan families for all winter, that's the deal."

The deal dominated our lives now, an unintended consequence of falling in love. We work eighty miles apart; I'm chief of detectives in Rutherford, Minnesota, and Trudy's a forensic scientist at the Bureau of Criminal Apprehension in St. Paul. When we were seized with the desire to live together we bought a small farm just outside the small town of Mirium, midway between our jobs. It seemed like a perfect solution till a winter in the antique farmhouse made us realize it lacked a few amenities, like heat and insulation.

Short on cash, we cobbled together a contract with two local carpenters that featured complex webs of barter and sweat equity. The Sullivan brothers got the use of our hayfields and barn, and on weekends I became their unpaid serf and gofer while they rebuilt the house. Trudy was raising a garden the size of a battleship, with the bulk of the produce committed to the Sullivan families.

I was free to help her in the garden this Sunday because my new slavemasters had gone fishing in what used to be my personal boat. It was still registered in my name, and I had paid the license, but they were using it more than I was. It was all part of the deal. Which after all, as Trudy had several times reminded me, was only going to last three years.

"And only in the summer at that," she said.

"Which is when you mostly use a boat in Minnesota."

"Well, granted. But by the third summer the house will be finished. Then you'll only have to help me with the garden and do two or three haying weekends."

"Ah, the haying weekends." Ozzie Sullivan had begun smiling at me in a predatory way whenever he mentioned his ripening hay crop. He was looking forward to breaking the city boy's balls, I figured. "Maybe I'll turn out to be no good at haying. Ozzie might have to fire me off that job."

"In your dreams." Trudy giggled. "Haying isn't complicated; it's just hard. Let's have a cup of coffee before we plant the carrots."

We sat in our torn-up kitchen with the door open, enjoying an odd kind of luxury. With the ceilings and most of the interior walls torn out, we couldn't keep the house clean so we didn't have to try. And we were working too hard to worry about calories, so we both put cream and sugar in our coffee and ate glazed doughnuts from Leonard's Cafe in town.

"I'd like to get the peas and beans planted this weekend too," Trudy said. "In case you get too busy to help me later."

"You don't have to worry about that," I foolishly said. "I'm already working all the time I'm awake—how could I get any busier?"

That question was answered at four the next morning, when Captain Russ Swenson's phone call woke me. "Heads up," he said, in his bugle-call voice.

"Glah?"

"Got a job for you. You awake now?" I could feel the phone vibrate.

"Mmm."

"Shelley Gleason's disappeared. Remember her?"

"Uh." I didn't.

"Big basketball star at Central High, three–four years ago, later on at the U? Works at IBM now, know who I mean?"

"Ah." I was looking at my watch. Too early to get up and too late to go back to sleep. Damn.

"Well, Greeley's just filing the report. She went out to do an errand last night about nine o'clock and she hasn't come back."

"Why are you calling me?" It was a reasonable question. My job carries heavy responsibilities but responding to street calls is no longer one of them. Besides, we hardly ever declare an adult missing in the first twenty-four hours. A high percentage of young women who don't come home when they're expected turn up in due time, embarrassed but unharmed.

"I think we're looking at a high-profile case here, Jake. Ten–twelve people already, got up outa bed to call and tell me Shelley Gleason's not the kind to get lost and she would never run away. Dispatch's been busy ever since the first call came in, and soon's all them IBMers get to work, it's gonna be a real cluster-fuck around here. Half the people in town know this girl, and they all want her found an hour ago. Her family's on the way in to talk to you."

"I hear you," I said. "I'll be right in, Russ." I slid out of bed as quietly as I could, trying not to wake Trudy, who had rolled onto her stomach when the phone rang and pulled a pillow over her head.

Coming out of the shower five minutes later, I stood by the bed, looking down at the sweet curve of her shoulder while I buttoned my shirt, thinking how it would feel to wake up and find her gone from there. I never quite get over the luck of it: I was rescued as a foundling from a Dumpster, an ugly duckling that grew into an ugly duck, with indeterminate brown skin and a mixed-race face that looks like it was made by a committee. But this smart, beautiful blonde likes me. Go figure.

Somehow she sensed me watching her, came out from under the pillow with her eyes open and said, "What?" I laughed and leaned down and kissed her. She smelled like raw potatoes and dirt.

I whispered, "I think you're the sexiest farmer in the Upper Midwest."

"Shee." She giggled, turned over and went back to sleep. She didn't even ask where I was going. We'd been living together nine months; she knew why cops get early calls.

Phones were ringing all over the second floor as I came through the door of the Government Center at five minutes to five. Shelley Gleason's family was waiting for me at the top of the stairs.

I remember it as the day I never did get a cup of coffee.

2

In school I remember reading that the wheels of justice grind slowly but exceedingly fine. I'm still not sure how fine the grind is, but in the fifteen years I've been a cop, either the wheels have slowed down some or I've lost a little patience. Getting Shelley Gleason's kidnappers into court, for instance, seemed to take, as Chief Frank McCafferty remarked one day when his lunch wasn't sitting right, "absolutely goddamn freaking forever."

Not really forever, but a year and two weeks passed before the first of the two killers was tried and convicted. And it was four months after that, the middle of August, by the time the county attorney finally got a firm court date for the second man.

"And this was such a simple case," the chief said. "What would we do with something complicated?"

A car-jacking that turned into murder, it did seem simple enough, at the time. We tracked Shelley's missing Ford Explorer through her credit cards, following ATM withdrawals and gas purchases to LaCrosse and most of the way back. When we stopped the car near the east edge of Rutherford five days after her disappearance, Shelley

Gleason wasn't in it. But nobody in Hampstead County law enforcement was very surprised to hear that one of the two men running away from it was Benny Niemeyer.

Recently paroled from Stillwater after serving half of a two-to-five for auto theft, Benny at twenty-two had changed woefully little from the hyper-thyroid, attention-deficit kid he'd been in seventh grade, when he quit terrorizing teachers and dropped out of school to devote himself to troublemaking full time. Since then he had racked up a consistent record as a small-time thief, hooligan, and pain in the ass.

The other fool wasting a beautiful May morning trying to outrun six law enforcement officers was Dale Trogstad, whose previous offenses were mostly break-ins and pilfering. Dale hadn't done any serious time—he even had a home address and a record of occasional employment—so initially my detectives and I were inclined to view him as the hapless helper in this crime. Shelley Gleason was still missing, and common sense argued against optimism, so we figured we were looking for one or more murderers, and Benny Niemeyer fit the mold.

The chief agreed. "Niemeyer's been a criminal all his life," he said. "He's never killed anybody before that I know of, but if he's crossed that line now we better put him away for good, because Benny never quits anything till we make him quit."

I didn't argue. The community was outraged that Shelley Gleason had been snatched off the street "Right here in Rutherford, Minnesota, for heaven's sake." Nobody wanted to hear about our low crime rate. "That didn't help Shelley any, did it?" my barber said peevishly.

So I put all my People Crimes staff to work, digging up incriminating evidence on Niemeyer. It wasn't hard to find; everybody we

CRAZY EIGHTS | 15

talked to told another Big Bad Benny story. Triple-B's, the People Crimes section began calling them, as Benny's three-ring binder fattened with tales of a gang fight that spread over three city blocks, a meth lab that smelled so bad the rats left the house, and a party that got so loud the prostitutes next door called the cops.

The Ford Explorer yielded fingerprints of both suspects, and we had two guns and a few DNA samples making stately progress through the queues at the state crime lab. Benny regaled us with hours of nonsense chatter before he finally asked about an attorney. "Seems like he's enjoying the visit, doesn't it?" one detective said.

Dale Trogstad made an immediate request for an attorney and lapsed into silence.

Once we found Shelley's body, though, most of the physical evidence pointed to Dale, so County Attorney Milo Nilssen wanted to try him first. Against our best instincts, the chief and I and four People Crimes detectives yielded to his judgment.

It turned into a solid home run for Milo, a conviction of Murder One after only four hours of deliberation by the jury. Perversely, instead of increasing his confidence for the second trial, the Trogstad win made Milo even more uneasy about how thin the evidence was against Benny.

"Come on," I said, "it's a lock. You already got a conviction on the partner everybody thought was innocent."

"Oh, yeah. Mr. Sweetface." Milo had built up a monumental grudge against Dale Trogstad in the course of his trial. It compounded the felony, for him, that Dale could sit there looking like an altar boy after murdering a blameless girl for no reason. Milo's resentment wasn't entirely irrational: Trogstad's unmarked, boyish features had made getting a conviction harder than it should have been. Milo used all his smarts and every bit of the fingerprint, ballistic and

DNA evidence my squad compiled for him, and in the end, despite the fact that two of the younger females on the jury wept while the verdict was read, Dale Trogstad got life without parole. The pre-trial hearing in the Niemeyer case was three months later in Judge Dotzenrod's courtroom. It was the kind of a session only a lawyer could love: long dry discussions about records and exhibits, and nearly inaudible wrangling over language and protocol that made me long to yell, "Who the hell cares?"

The session only caught fire once, over the defense attorney's objection to introducing the taped conversation in which Benny directed us to the body of the victim. I had urged the county attorney to use it, insisting it was a key piece of evidence.

"I don't think I'll ever get it in," Milo said, "because you got those directions after he asked for an attorney."

"He volunteered the information. What are we supposed to do, tape their goddamn mouths shut?"

I was blowing smoke, though, a little bit. While it was true no physical force was used, "volunteered" did not exactly describe how Benny gave us that information. What happened was, Rosie Doyle sat down across from him five days after his arrest, twirled a curl around her little finger and described Shelley's grieving family. "They're sure she's dead but they don't have a body to bury. I figure you're the kind of a guy who can understand that a family needs closure," she said. What she really figured, she told me, was that, "Ol' Benny likes to talk."

On the tape you could hear him chuckling over what a bunch of dumb shits we were, couldn't find our own privates if the directions were printed on the crapper wall. Then Rosie mentioned that we'd had this anonymous phone call from somebody who claimed to know about a body in a sinkhole just a few miles south of town. "But my boss and I think it sounds like some wannabe trying to get famous off of somebody else's crime."

A long interval of thumping and scraping followed, while Benny looked up at the ceiling and scratched himself and finally said, "Wha'd'joo say it might be worth to me if I knew somethin'?"

Rosie said something like, "Well I don't know, what do you want?" and Benny said quickly he'd like to be cellmates with Dale Trogstad. Rosie said she couldn't promise that but she could ask, no law against asking, and finally Benny mumbled, "How far south of town he say?" And little by little he gave her the directions we followed to Shelley Gleason's body.

Interestingly, at the pre-trial hearing Reese Newman, the public defender, didn't seem very interested in that piece of evidence until the judge stared down at him over the top of his reading glasses and asked, "Defense, have anything to say about this?"

"Well, um, yes, Your Honor, defense objects on the grounds it was obtained before counsel was present," Reese said.

"He volunteered the information," Milo said.

"My client dropped out of school in seventh grade, Your Honor. He can barely read and write."

"No reading or writing involved. He'd been Mirandized; he knew he didn't have to talk." Milo looked at me for confirmation. I nodded and held up two fingers. "Mirandized twice."

"And he'd asked for an attorney twice," Reese Newman insisted. "They had no business asking him about anything till I got there, Your Honor."

Judge Dotzenrod listened carefully to both sides of the argument for three minutes, cut Reese off in the middle of an elegant sentence and said, in that impersonal voice that stifles dissent, "All right. Niemeyer's directions to the body are excluded." Like cyclones,

Dotzenrod's quick decisions sucked all the air out of the room for a few seconds, leaving their victims dazed and staring. It's fun to watch when it happens to your opponents.

Milo gave me a black look. I gave it back. My division had been looking for badly needed information, which is what detectives do. We got plenty of "attaboys" the day we found Shelley Gleason's body. I wasn't going to apologize now about how we did it.

3

"**All rise!**" **Bailiff Marty** Burke's rich baritone caromed off the wood panelling of Hampstead County District Courtroom Number Six at ten o'clock Tuesday morning, and we all jumped up as if our seats were on fire.

"Helps to have a little belly on your bailiff," a judge told me once. "It gives him that resonance that makes people pay attention." Marty's ample midsection kept us standing at rigid attention while Judge Dotzenrod strode in, gave us a half-inch nod and said, "Be seated." His voice has the quiet crackle of a brush fire in a dry year. He never raises the volume; to hear what Merlin Dotzenrod has to say, lawyers lean forward in their seats and pay close attention.

Marty brought in the twelve jurors and three alternates. Milo and Reese made their opening statements, Milo assuring the jury the state would prove Benny Niemeyer guilty of this heinous crime beyond any reasonable doubt, Reese promising the defense would blow the prosecution's case full of holes. Opening statements don't prove anything but they warn the jury that the procedure is adversarial so they should stay awake.

Milo's poise had improved during two years at this job. He used to get a sneaky look and start shooting his cuffs and twitching when he faced an audience or a camera. He watched a couple of his interviews on the nightly news and realized he looked guiltier than the accused, so he hired a speech coach and shed most of his jittering habits.

Reese Newman's volunteering to defend Benny Niemeyer had come as an unpleasant surprise to Milo. A prominant attorney whose corporate clients paid him well to keep them out of court, he certainly didn't need any pro bono clients. Asked by a reporter why he took the case, Reese said, "Benny did some yard work for me a few years ago, and I took a liking to the kid. He's had a hard time growing up and I'd like to see him get a fair shake."

"Bullshit," Milo said when he read that. "Hell's he up to, anyway?"

Reese seemed to carry his own light with him as he paced thoughtfully in front of the jury, chesty and gleaming in his expensive threads, explaining that the burden of proof was on the state. "Benny doesn't have to prove his innocence," he reminded them—which considering his client's thuggish aspect, I thought was lucky for him.

Milo's new assistant, Chrissie Fallon, called her first witness. Vince Greeley was an experienced, confident street cop who maintained his appearance at spit-shine perfection every day, and projected authority and total recall on the stand. He and Chrissie had been over his part of the case until they knew it by heart, so his testimony had plenty of snap.

Chrissie led him through the initial call for service at Dan Frye's house and asked him, "What did you do there?"

"I interviewed Mr. Frye about the disappearance of his fiancée, who was living with him at the time. He said she left the house four hours earlier to run a couple of quick errands and never returned."

Chrissie Fallon: What other information did you get from him?

Vince Greeley: The make and model of the vehicle she was driving, plus her height and weight and a description of the clothes she was wearing. Then I interviewed the missing woman's parents, who were also there and who had actually seen her last.

CF: And did they substantiate Mr. Frye's account of the evening?

VG: Yes, and they gave me a recent photo of the missing woman.

CF: (showing him a photo) Is this the picture they gave you?

VG: Yes, it is.

Chrissie took it to the judge and then the courtroom clerk, saying, "Entering as people's exhibit number one, Your Honor." The jury seemed to enjoy watching her cross the courtroom, a tall, slender blonde who looked good in a pantsuit. She had a husky, carrying voice that reminded me of Kathleen Turner in *Body Heat*. Only the sulky pout was missing; her look was open and direct.

She came back and asked Vince, "What did you do next?"

"I told them a Missing Persons report had to be filed by our chief of detectives," Vince said, "but I'd pass this information along, with my urgent request that he contact them in the morning. I also told them I'd put the information into BOLOs—that's the 'Be On the Lookout' notices that are passed out by the shift captain at the start of every shift."

CF: What else?

VG: I told Dan Frye he should look up the numbers on any credit cards Shelley might be carrying, so the detectives could have them monitored.

CF: Did they say anything else?

VG: Yes. Shelley's mother said Shelley remembered just as she was starting home that she'd forgotten to drop the DVDs she'd rented, so she'd do that on the way home.

CF: Did she tell you which store?

VG: The one in the strip mall over by the Dairy Queen, on Fourteenth Avenue. I said I'd go by there on my way back to the station and look around.

Greeley then told how he went to the video store Shelley's mother described, looked around and found nothing. He went back to the station, filled out an Attempt to Locate form on Shelley's Ford Explorer and put all of Shelley's information into BOLOs for the next day's shifts.

CF: Did you do any other tasks pertaining to this case before your shift ended?

VG: Yes, I left a message for the detectives on the day shift to take a look around that video store in daylight. And I passed on all the family phone numbers.

Chrissie said she had no more questions, defense had none and the judge said we would take a ten-minute break before the next witness. We went outside and walked along the sidewalk till we got clear of the smokers.

"Nice job, Chrissie," I said. "I watched the jury—you kept them listening."

"Thanks. I thought Milo's opening went well too," Chrissie said.

"For sure. Keep it going like this, guys, and you got it made."

"Maybe." Milo's face took on that constipated expression he gets when he hears the sin of optimism being committed. "If the witnesses all show up. If they remember to say what they said before. If if if." Faced with any uncertainty, Milo goes straight to pessimism the way some people knock on wood. "Have you found Kylee Mundt yet?"

"No. But one of Bo's snitches thinks he saw her a few days ago." Kylee Mundt was a former schoolmate of both Trogstad and

Niemeyer who claimed she had seen them riding together in the victim's car on the day after the car-jacking. "They stopped at my apartment," she had said at the Trogstad trial. "My brother was there. He saw them too." We wanted her to say that again at Benny's trial, but she was gone from her apartment; nobody seemed to know where.

"I've got to have her testimony, Jake. This case is too circumstantial as it is."

"I know. All my guys are working on it." I dropped behind the two of them and counted backward from three hundred by elevens. Math tricks help me control my temper, which I often have to do around Milo during a trial. While he's trying a case, I think if you gave Milo a double scoop of chocolate ice cream on a fudge brownie he'd probably say, "What happened to the chocolate chips?"

"You'll be next up, Jake," Milo said. "Did you review your testimony last night? You haven't forgotten anything?"

"I'm ready." He made a little *hmmpp* sound which I took to mean, "Not likely."

Back inside, the courtroom clerk swore me in and Chrissie began plowing through the questions we'd rehearsed so many times.

Chrissie Fallon: Will you state your name, please?

Jake Hines: Captain Jake Hines.

CF: And tell us what your job is.

JH: I'm chief of detectives at the Rutherford Police Department.

CF: Describe your experience, please.

JH: I've been on the Rutherford police force for almost sixteen years, a detective for seven years and chief of detectives for two years. I have completed over eighteen hundred credit hours of law enforcement and criminal justice–related training during my career—

Milo wanted all my bona fides, to add heft to my testimony, so I gave them the full resumé, the courses in Constitutional Law, crime-scene techniques, collection and preservation of evidence, and topped it off with the eleven-week FBI National Academy program in Quantico, Virginia. A cop, these days, is a work in progress; law enforcement techniques are changing so fast, we train all the time.

CF: Thank you. Now please tell us, when did you first hear about the disappearance of Shelley Gleason?

I described the early morning phone call and the family group waiting for me when I got to the station. Dan Frye, desperately worried but struggling to stay calm, went back over the story of how Shelley left the house saying she'd be back in an hour or two. He had an early shift at Methodist Hospital, he said, where he worked as a physical therapist. "So I said I have to get up at five, I won't wait up. I went to bed as soon as she left and I fell asleep."

When Dan woke at midnight and found her not in bed, not in the house and her car not in the garage, he called her mother. Mrs. Gleason said Shelley had left for home shortly after ten-thirty. Since their houses were only twenty blocks apart, they were immediately alarmed.

"I said I'm going to call Annie and Grace," Shelley's mother said, "see if she maybe stopped to see one of them."

"But she never," her sisters said, shaking their heads in unison.

Dan said he was going to drive to Gleasons' house the way he figured Shelley would go, to see if she had broken down someplace. He didn't find her on the way, and took an alternate route home with no more success. He called everybody he could think of for a couple of hours and then called 911.

CF: Did you question him about her state of mind?

JH: Yes, I asked Mr. Frye if they had quarreled. He insisted they weren't fighting about anything, and her family agreed—she was happy, looking forward to her wedding.

CF: What else did you ask them?

JH: I asked Dan Frye if they had any joint bank accounts. He said they had a savings account and I asked him to use my computer to check the balance.

CF: And was he satisfied with it?

JH: Yes, he said it was just what it had been last time he checked it.

CF: What did you do next?

JH: I took them to the captain's desk to confirm that Shelley's description and the description of her car were already in BOLOs. I explained they'd be given to every Rutherford policeman and Hampstead County deputy on duty that day, and both crews would be looking for her. Then we went back to my desk where they helped me prepare a Missing Persons report.

CF: Do you always do that as soon as a person is reported missing?

JH: No. Usually we hold off a day or two. But in Shelley's case there were so many people in close touch with her, and they were so convinced she was in trouble that I decided not to wait.

CF: Describe, please, how the information is disseminated.

JH: I entered it in the Minnesota CJIS, the Criminal Justice Information System database that's shared by every police force in the state, and I sent it to NCIC, the National Crime Information Center.

CF: Very well. What happened next?

JH: I sent one of our detectives to the video store where Shelley had said she would drop off the DVDs. He searched the area and came back an hour later with a blue button that appeared to have come from a woolen garment. He showed it to Mrs. Gleason and Dan Frye, and they both said it looked like a button from the sweater Shelley was wearing the night before.

CF: Did Mr. Frye give you her credit-card information?

JH: Yes. Shelley had one gas card and one VISA. I called the 800 service numbers on them and they gave me the fax number to send the stolen-card report to.

CF: This is the regular protocol?

JH: Yes. In a few minutes they returned the phone numbers of the local banks that handle those accounts, and I filed the reports with them.

CF: With what results?

JH: We got reports of activity on both cards within hours.

CF: At this point, Your Honor, I'd like to ask that you excuse this witness, with the understanding that I might need to recall him later.

Judge Dotzenrod: Does the defense have any questions?

REESE NEWMAN: Not at this time, Your Honor.

The judge said we would break for lunch and resume at one-thirty.

"Ray is next after the two credit-card experts, and you know Dotzenrod, he's prompt," Milo said. "So tell Ray we could be ready for him by two-thirty."

"He'll be here." Now that Rutherford's in perpetual growth mode, it's faster to walk three downtown blocks than to drive them, so I trotted down the alley behind Second Avenue and jaywalked across Broadway, avoiding the glares of gridlocked motorists. Breezing through the front door of Denny Lynch's High Times Bar, I waved to the proprietor, walked briskly past the nine lighthearted malingerers trading lies with him at eight minutes before noon on a weekday and hurried out the back door to the RPD parking lot. My shortcut doesn't work if you slow down enough to get lured by Denny's jokes and lager.

Ray Bailey, head of People Crimes section, was coming down the front stairs of Government Center putting his coat on. "Ray, anything on Kylee Mundt?"

"I left a message on her mother's phone, she hasn't called back." He pulled his tiny spiral notebook out of his shirt pocket. "I found out she got laid of. Did I tell you that? I checked the unemployment

office; she hasn't filed a claim. Landlord said she didn't leave a for-
warding, paid three months' rent in advance and said she'd be back.
That was two months ago, give or take. I'll go by her mother's house
again after lunch, huh?"

"Good. Milo says he has to have her testimony. Tell Mrs. Mundt
if Kylee's out of town and can't get back by tomorrow, we'll take a
deposition by phone and try to get the judge to accept it."

"Sure." He squinted morosely through the glass doors into the
sunshine. Ray is no more deeply troubled than the average police detective, but he's a Bailey so his worries show up more. Born with
long, mournful faces, Baileys start to look downright funeral when
they're aggravated. "Damn funny she'd run off like this. She's lived
here all her life."

"Well, but the job market here really sucks right now."

"Sucks everyplace else too, what's the use moving? I'm sure her
mother really knows where she is. She just won't call me back because
she's pissed at cops since we sent her baby boy up to St. Cloud."

"You mean—are you talking about Roger Mundt?"

"Sure, the antiques burglar." Property Crimes detectives followed
Roger's trail for half of last year before they caught him with some
of the heirlooms he was looting from the best houses in town.

"That was Kylee's brother? I missed that connection. Well, be sure
you're in court by two o'clock. They're gonna put you on right after
the credit-card people. Milo would kiss your foot, though, if you
found Kylee Mundt; he wants her testimony bad."

"Milo never has enough, does he? Hell, half the people on that
jury must be ready to give him a guilty verdict right now. Everybody
knows Benny planned that highjacking. He bragged about it all over
the North End."

"I know. But that's hearsay and Milo's a lawyer."

4

Ray went off to lunch muttering to himself, and I went to see how Property Crimes was doing with the plague du jour, a rash of bike thefts and skateboard heists. It was worse than usual this spring because Nelson Aldrich, the old guy who made a fortune in pharmaceuticals in Rutherford and was now "giving back," had just added a skate park and bike path to Aldrich Park, the big green space he gave the city a few years ago. Juvenile daredevils loved the place, but they were making life easier for thieves by concentrating their sports equipment there.

"It's crazy this year," Kevin Evjan said. "Who needs six skateboards a day?"

"That's what was lost yesterday?"

"That's the daily average for the past ten days."

"You're right, that's crazy."

Kevin had been proud, a couple of years ago, to make lieutenant at only twenty-nine, and last year when I put him in charge of the Property Crimes section he wore a smile as bright as the new nameplate on his door. He sobered down some as he began to realize how many hard-to-find items get swiped every month in a town growing rapidly toward a population of a hundred thousand. A cop nine years, he thought he knew all about larceny, but he'd only been dealing with it one theft at a time. Lately the overview was beginning to weigh on him.

"Somebody's fencing them," I said. "Gotta be. Who is it?"

Kevin shook his head. "Nobody in town, I'm starting to think. My guys are sure it's not the pawn shops. And we haven't caught a secondhand store selling boards." He put down his list and gave a windy sigh. "How's the trial going?"

"Fine."

"We gonna lock up ol' Triple-B?"

"Yeah, I think Benny is toast."

In my office, I pulled up a screenful of e-mails and answered them while I gobbled my August sandwich. It was Trudy's creation, full of fresh lettuce, tomatoes, cucumbers and radishes. This year's Olympic-size garden was doing even better than last year's had, putting out more fresh produce than we and our carpenters could eat at dinnertime.

"I'm working on a breakfast salad," Trudy said. "Meantime, everybody eat your August sandwiches. Good witamins!" she added, in a hilariously accurate imitation of her Swedish mother. "Vaste not, vant not!"

The chief put his head in the door as I crouched over my baggie, wiping tomato juice off my chin.

"You sound like a hog," he said. "Why are you eating slops?"

"It's an August sandwich. Full of Trudy's good garden stuff."

"Ah, that garden." He'd been out, a couple of times, to get free compost and tips on raspberries. "Anybody ever tell you you're a lucky sumbitch? A sexy woman who can grow tomatoes, isn't that every husband's dream?"

"Pretty close," I said. "Now if I could just teach her to clean fish." We chuckled comfortably, knowing our significant others were safely out of earshot.

"What are you even doing here, come to think about it? I thought you'd be at the trial all day."

"I am. I just ran over here to check a couple of things. I'm mostly just sitting over there, Chief, but you know how it is with trials—I'm afraid to leave for fear they'll call me to the stand again or Milo will need something."

"Yeah. Don't worry about how much time the trial takes, Jake. Just hang in there with Milo and get the job done. We got Trogstad put away; now let's lock up Benny Niemeyer and show the taxpayers they get what they pay for." He'd won a fierce battle with the city council last winter, over their most recent effort to cut his budget. He saw the Trogstad/Niemeyer prosecution as bolstering his arguments.

Working my shortcut in reverse, I hurried past the shouted invitations of Denny's increasingly raucous clientele and got back to my chair at the prosecution table ahead of Milo and Chrissie. When they got there, Milo immediately started reading over, for the umpteenth time, the questions he intended to ask the witnesses that afternoon. Chrissie took a list across the room to the boxful of odd-shaped parcels by the clerk's table, and began reading her requests for exhibits to Mary Kinnear, the courtroom clerk.

Mary was a twenty-five-year veteran who knew more about how trials work than most lawyers. She began pulling exhibits out of the box, all the while trading muttered comments with Chrissie about a movie they'd both seen over the weekend. To watch her there, a comfortable granny schmoozing and smiling, you would never guess she had one of the most taxing jobs in the building. The clerk has to keep track of every item entered into evidence and stay current with that monster called the Minute Entry, the document that tells the story of what happens in court all day.

The camera likes to linger on the court reporter, who sits typing every spoken word into that nifty Stenograph machine. Most people hardly notice the courtroom clerk except when she's swearing somebody in—her easiest chore. But judges rely on her for a record of every move, and she has to maintain it in real time, surrounded by constant hullabaloo. I asked Mary once what it took to be a courtroom clerk; she said patience in the daytime and Jack Daniel's at night.

The sheriff's deputy brought Benny in from the jail, and he stood by the defense table, smiling confidently at Reese Newman while the deputy took his cuffs off. When his hands were free he picked up his belt off the defense table, handed it to the deputy and stood waiting while the deputy unrolled and inspected it. Benny watched him, moving his buffed-up shoulders inside his shirt, his smile conveying: "You think I'd be dumb enough to hide something there, fool?" When the deputy gave him back his belt he threaded it through his belt loops, taking his time, enjoying showing off his jailhouse tats. He had bulked up some in prison, pumping iron, and added some complicated facial hair, a pencil-thin mustache and a half-inch goatee just under his chin. When he was good and ready he sat down by his attorney, still wearing his leg chains.

He stood up again for the judge when we all did, and again with his attorney when the jury filed in, and he watched the jury carefully while they found their seats. Most of them wouldn't look at him, but there was one girl, surely not much over eighteen, who let her eyes wander toward the defense table casually, grew flustered when she met his eyes and looked away quickly. I made a note to tell Milo to keep an eye on her, as well as the young man on the end in the back row who was watching Benny with an expression I thought was a little awestruck.

Milo called Henrietta Flack, from the accounting department at the Farmers Bank & Trust, who explained electronic reporting for the benefit of those jurors who'd been off the planet and didn't know how it worked. Then she detailed how, on the morning of my request for monitoring of Shelley Gleason's credit card, she was able to report that just before eleven o'clock on the previous evening, two hundred dollars in cash had been drawn on Shelley's card at an ATM outside a convenience store on the south edge of town. At fifteen minutes after two on the following morning, the card was used again, at the freestanding ATM in the Mohawk shopping mall, east of town just off the Beltway. That time the request was for four hundred dollars, which was refused. Two minutes later a request was entered for three hundred dollars, which was paid. With that, Shelley Gleason's credit line was just about tapped out.

The family gave one big horrified gasp, that afternoon in my office when the news of the two withdrawals came in. The women listened with their hands over their mouths, tears running down their cheeks, while the men glared at their shoes. Somebody had Shelley's card, they all said when they could speak. Shelley was saving for the wedding; she wasn't going on any spending sprees in the middle of the night.

Milo showed Henrietta copies of the ATM withdrawals, got her confirmation that these were the records she was talking about, entered the exhibits for the jury and said he had no more questions for Henrietta Flack. Reese Newman stood up and asked her whether a signature was required to withdraw money from Shelley's account.

Henrietta Flack: Well, no, both withdrawals were at ATMs. You enter your PIN number when the machine asks for it. That substitutes for your signature.

Reese Newman: So there's no way to know who drew out that money?

HF: No.

RN: Specifically, there is no evidence whatsoever that Benny Niemeyer drew money out of Shelley Gleason's account?

HF: That's correct.

RN: Thank you, no further questions.

Milo Nilssen: Redirect, Your Honor.

Judge: Go ahead.

MN: The PIN number is known only to the cardholder, is that correct?

HF: Well . . . it's issued only to the cardholder, that's right.

MN: Isn't that the same thing?

HF: Well, it could be shared with anyone the owner wanted to tell it to, or it could be copied if . . . some people write it on the card if they have trouble remembering it.

MN: But normally, isn't its purpose to insure exclusive access?

HF: Yes. It's a control number, not printed on the card, that is given to the cardholder at the time the card is issued. It's supposed to assure that nobody can get money out of the account except the person to whom the card was issued.

MN: So when Benny Niemeyer used that card—

Reese Newman: Objection! Not established.

Judge: Sustained.

CF: So whenever *somebody* used Shelley's card to take the money out of her account that night, he or she had to get the PIN number from Shelley, isn't that right?

HF: That's right.

MN: Had to get the number from her at gunpoint and then make her sit there—

RN: Objection, Your Honor, this is pure supposition!

Judge: Sustained. The jury will disregard. Let's stick to the established facts, please, Mr. Nilssen.

Milo said he had no further questions, though he looked at Henrietta like she was a choice cut of tenderloin for a couple of seconds before he said it. At the Trogstad trial, Milo had mesmerized the jury with the image of the terrified girl forced at gunpoint to reveal her PIN numbers and then watch while her murderers proved they worked. Reese seemed to debate for a few seconds whether to emphasize the fictional nature of that story, but finally said he had no more questions either.

Milo called Adam Benson, the designated official at First Federal who had monitored Shelley's gas card. He looked young and nervous while he gave his name and short resumé, but when the subject turned to credit-card charges his confidence blossomed.

Milo Nilssen: In your capacity as a bank officer, did you monitor the activity on Shelley Gleason's gasoline credit card beginning on May eighth of last year?

Adam Benson: Yes, I did.

MN: Tell us what occurred, please.

AB: On May eighth, I received a charge for seven dollars and eighty cents. It was stamped eleven-oh-eight P.M. May seventh, for gas purchased at a Texaco station on the north edge of Rutherford. The next day, May ninth, a charge came through from a Mobil station in LaCrosse, Wisconsin, thirty dollars and fifty-three cents for gas, at six-fifteen P.M. on May eighth.

MN: Did you receive other charges later?

AB: Yes. Two days later we got a charge for seventeen eighty-seven, from a Shell station in Dover, on US-14, about twenty miles east of Rutherford.

MN: Thank you. No further questions.

Judge Dotzenrod: Defense?

Reese Newman: Did any of those gasoline charges produce a slip that required a signature?

AB: No. They were all at-the-pump purchases, which produce a charge slip but do not require a signature.

RN: So the charge slips furnish no proof of who was actually using the card?

AB: That's correct.

Milo entered the gas-charge slips into evidence and called Ray Bailey. Ray had taken over the hour-by-hour tracking of the Shelley Gleason search by midmorning of the first day, as soon as my interview with the Gleason family had finished. His testimony concerned not only the factual evidence he developed but the conclusions we drew from it, and what those conclusions led us to do. Milo knew Reese Newman wouldn't put up with any answers that began, "I concluded—" so he and Ray had composed the questions and answers of Ray's testimony as painstakingly as poets.

Milo Nilssen: When you got the credit card information, Lieutenant Bailey, what did you do next?

Ray Bailey: I called Dan Frye and asked him, do you know how much gas Shelley had in the tank when she left home?

MN: What did he say?

RB: He said she had filled up earlier that afternoon when they were out buying groceries.

MN: What was your next question?

RB: I asked him, was Shelley in the habit of topping off her gas tank every few hours? He said she wasn't.

MN: Did you ask him anything else?

RB: Yes, I asked him if he could think of any reason why she would have done that last night.

Reese Newman: Objection, calls for a conclusion.

Judge: Sustained.

MN: After the second gas purchase, did you call him again?

RB: Yes. I told him the card had been used again in LaCrosse. He

got very excited then and said there was no way Shelley would
ever—

Reese Newman: Objection, hearsay.

Judge: Sustained.

Reese wasn't letting Milo get any conclusions into the record, but
we knew the jury would see what we'd been thinking: obviously,
somebody other than Shelley was using the card. And everybody in
the room today knew we'd turned out to be right.

MN: The second charge—the sale for thirty fifty-three—what
did that tell you?

RB: Obviously, that the card was in LaCrosse, with somebody
who needed a full tank of gas.

MN: Would it take a full tank of gas for a Ford Explorer to drive
to LaCrosse?

RB: No, the math didn't come out right. The mileage to LaCrosse,
depending on which side of town you went to, would be seventy-five
to eighty miles. Explorers get something around twenty miles to the
gallon, so obviously the vehicle had gone some extra miles.

MN: What did you do next?

RB: I called the police department in LaCrosse and asked the duty
sergeant to put out an Attempt to Locate for the Explorer, and asked
them for drive-throughs of motel parking lots and so on.

MN: Why did you do that?

RB: It looked like they'd been driving around for some time, and
we were hoping they might settle down for a while.

MN: What were the results of your request?

RB: None.

MN: They didn't find the car?

RB: No. We got no news of it until two days later.

MN: What happened then?

RB: Adam Benson called from the bank and said he had a notice of purchase from a gas station over by St. Charles, twenty miles east of Rutherford. And the good news was, the time on it was just fifteen minutes earlier.

MN: What did you do then?

RB: Well, St. Charles is in Winona County, so we got in touch with Winona Dispatch, and he said they had two cars he could assign to locating the vehicle. We weren't sure which way the suspects were headed, of course, but in case they were travelling toward Rutherford we sent two of our squads, and Sheriff Grant Hisey detailed two deputies from Hampstead County. So by ten minutes after the report reached us we had six cars on the road, headed toward St. Charles from all directions.

Judge Dotzenrod leaned forward then and said, "It's almost five o'clock. We'll break here and resume tomorrow." Some of the jurors gave him glum looks, going out, like they thought the least he could have done after this long, tiring day was hang on a few more minutes and let them hear about the chase.

5

Rosie Doyle walked over to Milo's office with Ray and me at nine Wednesday morning. The four of us had to figure out a new way to explain to the jury how we found Shelley Gleason's body, since the judge had ruled we couldn't mention Benny Niemeyer's directions.

Ray got his bitching done first. "This is ridiculous. How in hell am I supposed to explain how we found that sinkhole if I can't say Benny told us where to look?"

"Aw, shit, Ray," Milo said, "you guys really screwed up! What were you thinking, you and Rosie, trying that stupid old trick?"

"He'd been Mirandized twice—"

"Oh, Mirandized my ass. You know as well as I do Benny Niemeyer has never been able to resist talking to anybody who'll listen to him. Hell, I've seen him talk for half an hour when *nobody* was listening."

"And all of it lies, almost without exception. This time by some crazy fluke he told the truth and we can't use it. Goddamn, jury trials are such a fucking farce."

I said, "Are we just going to sit here and swear at each other? I thought we came over to decide something."

"That's right," Ray said. "We have to decide how I go into court and make an ass of myself." The end of his nose kept getting redder and redder. " 'Your Honor,' I'll say, 'we ordered a helicopter up in the air and put dogs into the field because I had a vision.' "

"Not a vision," Rosie said, "an anonymous phone call. You can tell about that, can't you?"

"Aw, shit." Ray kicked the rug and then Milo's desk. "I suppose so. Jeez, it makes us sound like a real Mickey Mouse outfit, though, running a search off an anonymous phone tip with no confirmation."

"The jury won't care," Milo said. "Quit kicking my desk."

"Other cops will care." Ray went back to punishing the carpet. "Anybody with any brains will care."

"See, Milo, that's why we had to try talking to Benny," Rosie said, still trying to make things right between Milo and Ray. "We got the phone tip, we couldn't just sit on it, but you know what a search costs. We wanted to give Jake a little something more to go on before he ordered it. Dale Trogstad wouldn't talk at all, not even 'Hello,' so we said, 'Maybe 'ol Benny feels like having a chat.' "

"So you pulled your irresistible redhead act and got a great piece of evidence that we can't use."

"Not such a great piece," Rosie said, blushing a little at the backhanded compliment. "All he would say was stuff like, 'That sounds possible.' Then I'd guess another coordinate off what he'd already said plus what we'd heard from Mr. Anonymous, like, was it about so many miles from the blue silos? And Benny'd say, 'I guess that might be pretty close,' so I'd ask him, 'About three or four miles from County Road Seven, is that your best estimate?' and he'd say, 'That's about what I heard, yeah.' It was kind of like a game with him. He never did confirm or deny he was there. That little bit I got out of him; it's really not much to lose, Milo."

"Maybe not to you. But short of hard evidence as I am, I can't afford to lose *any*."

"Okay, come on, let's decide what to say." Hugging my briefcase hard, trying to get the zipper to close, I saw Chrissie Fallon struggling down the hall under an armload of documents that made my briefcase look like a manila folder.

"Welcome to the electronic age," I said, as she struggled past our chairs. "No more of those pesky old paper records, right?" She hurried toward Milo's console, giving me a brief glimpse of her nice smile in passing. She seemed a little hard to know, chic and self-confident in court, shy and quiet in private.

"Look, the tip turned out to be correct, so there isn't going to be much second-guessing about it," Milo said. "I'll ask what made you initiate the search, you describe the phone call and we'll move right on." Brooding over the wording of his question, he watched his new lawyer struggling to set down her load.

I started to put down my briefcase, saying, "Chrissie, can I help you?" She looked around, startled, and said, "Oh, no . . . thanks," as if I'd said something embarrassing. I wondered, were there issues about gender equality in this office? I hadn't heard Milo express anything but satisfaction with his new hire.

"Okay, here it is," Milo said. "I ask you, what made you initiate the search where you did? And you say, we got a phone tip about a body in that location."

"Good," Ray said. "That sounds good and dumb."

"That's it, then? We're all agreed on how to handle this—we can go?" I stood up. Milo was starting to shoot his cuffs and slick down the back of his hair the way he did when he was uneasy, and I wanted to get out of his office before he started that tie-smoothing thing that would make me feel like a basket case for the rest of the day.

We went back to the station and I held another hurried meeting, reassigning two or three pressing tasks so Bo Dooley, my vice officer, could stay on the trail of a meth lab he had been following for months.

"They must have a lab out in the country somewhere and they're bringing it to town with a setup something like a bookmobile," Bo said. "Plenty of evidence on the user end, tweakers are getting pulled out of ditches and culverts all over town. Doctors and nurses are yelling at me to do something, but I'm not getting noise complaints, or reports of stink and refuse in any certain neighborhood. So I'm looking for a mobile outfit."

"I should be able to give you more help by next week," I said, "once we get this damn trial out of the way."

"Hey, don't worry about it, Jake. Any week you put Benny away is a very good week."

6

Milo's first witness was Sheriff's Deputy Alvin Schoenfelder, who had organized the team and led the chase, after Shelley Gleason's vehicle was reported at a gas station in St. Charles.

"The four of us coming from the west agreed to meet at the Chester off-ramp," Alvin said, "and proceed east a few miles and then deploy in driveways along the roadside between Eyota and the county line. I was in the lead car."

Milo Nilssen: Why did you do it that way?

Alvin Schoenfelder: We were hoping that the Ford Explorer would continue coming west toward Rutherford. The two Winona County cars agreed to follow the car from the gas station and let us know if it took any other route.

MN: Is that what happened?

AS: Yes. The Winona County cars were just saying they had the Explorer in sight near the county line, when I spotted it about a half-mile east of my position, traveling toward me. So I told the Winona County deputies, "Okay, we got 'em in sight here. Thanks a lot," and they hung back, waiting to see if we'd need any help.

MN: What happened next?

AS: When the Ford Explorer passed the second squad in our group, me and the other Hampstead County car pulled onto the roadway behind them. The two squads from Rutherford pulled out in front of the Explorer, and we traveled some distance in that configuration till the road turned into four-lane, right there at Eastwood Park. The Explorer pulled into the left-hand lane then, trying to sprint around the two lead squads, and that's when we moved up from behind and got 'em in a tight box, one squad ahead, one behind and two alongside, and forced 'em off the road into the median.

MN: Was that according to plan?

AS: Exactly. We wanted to get 'em off the road before we got any closer to town.

MN: What happened next?

AS: The Explorer came to a quick stop and two men jumped out of it. The driver ran south, across the rest of the median and then across two lanes of eastbound traffic toward the ditch on the south side.

Amy Nguyen was one of the Rutherford officers assisting Alvin Schoenfelder that day. She is the smallest cop in Rutherford and the fastest, a marathon runner who teaches fitness training on her days off. She dodged through light eastbound traffic to catch Dale Trogstad just as he reached the shoulder, hit him in back of the knees with her Asp, and the baton sent him spinning into the ditch. She was kneeling on him, reaching for her cuffs, by the time Tim Casey arrived to help.

Benny Niemeyer jumped out of the passenger's side and ran east on the median, passing Deputy Fogarty's car door just as Fogarty was getting out of it. Using some of the muscle he'd put on in the St. Cloud Reformatory weight room, he hit the door with his shoulder and momentarily pinned Fogarty between the door and the body of the vehicle, gasping for air.

That left Alvin Schoenfelder as the lone obstacle to Benny's escape.

Benny dodged around the passenger's side of Alvin's car and ran north, across two lanes of heavy westbound traffic. "There were brakes squealing, cars pulling off the road and people yelling. I couldn't fire my weapon through all those cars so I hadda catch him. He kept dodging traffic and so did I, and I caught up to him just as we reached the ditch on the north side. I threw a running block on him and we both went down." It must have been quite a crash; Alvin has eaten a few doughnuts since he played tight end for the Dover-Eyota Eagles.

"Before or during the chase," Milo asked him, "did the suspect drop anything?"

"Yes. I saw him throw the gun away—"

"Objection." Reese Newman was on his feet, stern and self-assured. "It has not been established that my client ever had a gun, Your Honor."

"Sustained."

"Just give me a yes or no answer," Milo said, sweet as honey. "You saw Benny Niemeyer drop or throw something, is that right?"

AS: Yes.

MN: What did it look like?

AS: Looked like a handgun.

MN: What happened after you caught him?

AS: The prisoner wouldn't give up. It took considerable force, Fogarty and Longworth and me all together, to get him into restraints.

MN: And once you had him in restraints, what did you do?

AS: Well, some gawkers stopped, cars parked every which way, so I went out on the road and got the traffic moving. While I was doing that the other officers searched the prisoners, confiscated the VISA card Trogstad was carrying and found the other card—the gas card—in the glove compartment of the vehicle.

MN: Did you verify that the cards were the ones the detectives had been tracking?

AS: Yes. We got the prisoners into cars then, secured the scene and did a thorough search of it. That's when Winnie found the weapon under the car.

MN: That's Officer Nguyen?

AS: Yes.

Vietnamese names are tough for Minnesota people to say. Chief McCafferty, doing the best he could with Amy's, introduced her as Amy Win when she joined the force. She got nicknamed Winnie the first week, and has answered to it, unprotesting, ever since.

MN: What else did you do before you left the scene?

AS: We called for a tow for the Explorer. Casey and Winnie stayed behind to guard the vehicle and the rest of us took the prisoners into town.

MN: No further questions.

Judge: Defense?

Reese Newman: When Benny Niemeyer got out of the car, did he start to run right away?

AS: Yes, he did.

RN: And you began chasing him right away, is that correct?

AS: As soon as I saw him pin Fogarty in his car and start around me—yes, I did.

RN: How far away were you when you saw Mr. Niemeyer drop something on the ground?

As: Maybe thirty feet.

RN: And you were watching him and starting to run yourself?

AS: Yes.

RN: So you never really saw it clearly?

AS: I was pretty sure what it was—

RN: Will you answer the question I asked, please? Did you see it clearly?

AS: No.

RN: Were you sure whether it was metal or plastic?

AS: Not for sure, no.

RN: So you could hardly be sure it was a gun, either, could you?

AS: I was pretty sure.

RN: Are you aware that my client says he lost his Gameboy when he jumped out of the car?

AS: I know he said that later.

RN: How much later? Didn't he ask you to try to find it while you were on the road back to Rutherford?

AS: Uh . . . I believe he did say something like that, that he had some kinda gaming gadget that he dropped, and he wished he could get it back.

RN: And did you attempt to find it?

AS: You mean did we turn around and go back to where we found him in a stolen car and try to find his toy?

RN: Just answer the question, Deputy.

AS: No.

RN: So you can't be certain that he didn't have one, can you?

AS: We found a Ruger twenty-two-caliber revolver, is what we found.

RN: Your Honor—(Reese Newman favored the judge with a noble, tragic look.)

Judge: Right. Answer the question you were asked, please, Deputy.

AS: No. I don't know for sure he didn't have a Gameboy in the stolen car with him. Coulda had a Barbie doll, too, I guess.

There were titters in the gallery. Mary Kinnear dropped a pencil and took her time picking it up.

RN: Your Honor!

But Judge Dotzenrod's gavel had already crashed onto its plate. Holding his left hand aloft to shush Newman, he turned to Alvin

Schoenfelder and told him, in a voice that was neither harsh nor pleasant but simply indifferent, that he was "walking a fine line around contempt of court," and one more disrespectful answer would cross that line and win him a fine and some jail time. Then he turned to Reese with an expression that somehow suggested he was pretty sick of Gameboys himself, and said, "Proceed."

RN: Thank you, Your Honor. Will you tell us, please, Deputy, who was driving the Explorer when you stopped it?

AS: Dale Trogstad.

RN: And once again, who was carrying Shelley Gleason's VISA card?

AS: Dale Trogstad.

RN: And the gas card was in the car, is that correct? Mr. Niemeyer wasn't carrying it?

AS: No, he wasn't.

RN: Thank you. No further questions.

Milo called Amy Nguyen to the stand next. As she listed her experience and training credits, I watched several jury members getting that look that said, *What a cute cop.* Cuteness is Winnie's big problem. She weighs ninety-seven pounds and has the face of an Asian doll. She deals with her charming attractiveness by being an utterly straight arrow and letting people figure out in their own time that she's a real police officer. I don't have any trouble believing it myself, since the day in her rookie year when she saved my life.

Amy told the court about her part in the traffic stop. Milo asked her how she came to find the gun and she told how, after the suspects had been put into two cars in restraints, Deputy Schoenfelder had led a search of the median around the stolen vehicle.

Milo Nilssen: And where did you find the gun?

Amy Nguyen: Under the car. Deputy Schoenfelder was sure he

had seen one of the suspects throw away a gun, so after we searched the grass all around the car and didn't find it, I crawled under the Explorer, and there it was.

MN: Was it more on the driver's side or the passenger side?

AN: Well . . . it was really just about in the middle.

MN: In a holster?

AN: No.

MN: Was it loaded?

AN: Yes, it was; there were six cartridges in the cylinder.

MN: Thank you, no further questions.

Reese Newman got up and said, "Officer Nguyen," with a heavy note of condescending humor in his voice so everybody knew he thought Winnie was a joke as a cop. "Where were you when you began to run after Dale Trogstad?"

Amy Nguyen: I started from my squad, two car lengths directly ahead of the Explorer.

RN: There were four cars surrounding the Ford Explorer, is that correct?

AN: Yes.

RN: The man you ran after got out of the Explorer on the side away from you, right?

AN: No, the driver's side of the Explorer was directly behind me by the time he stopped.

RN: Had you drawn your weapon?

AN: Yes. But Trogstad jumped out and started to run, so I reholstered my weapon and gave chase.

RN: I see. So there was a period while you were putting your gun away and getting out of your vehicle when you weren't watching the suspect, right?

AN: No, that's not true. I was directly ahead of the Explorer, watching him in my rearview mirrow while I got out of the car, and then I turned and ran after him.

RN: But with all that was going on you can't be sure it wasn't Dale Trogstad who dropped the gun, can you?

AN: I'm ninety-nine percent sure. I had my eyes on him the whole time, and I never saw him drop anything.

RN: Dear me. You can holster your gun and get out of your car without ever once taking your eyes off a suspect? That sounds extremely difficult, Officer Nguyen.

Reese Newman leaned over Winnie and smiled, oozing benign tolerance, smiling like a fond uncle asking his adorable niece if she really needed popcorn with the movie.

Winnie turned into an ice sculpture with the face of her grandmother, the flinty boat person, looking out, and said, with perfect courtesy frosted by outrage, "It's somewhat easier when your life is at stake, Mr. Newman."

Reese stepped back, resettled his pricey jacket with a shrug of his shoulders, and asked her, "Yes or no, Officer, can you swear beyond a shadow of a doubt that it wasn't Dale Trogstad who dropped the gun you found under the car?"

"No," Amy said.

"Thank you. No further questions."

There was considerable stirring and coughing while Newman sat down and Amy returned to her seat in the gallery. Everybody had felt the quick flash of animosity between them, and felt relieved when their exchange ended. While the gallery whispered and scratched, Milo called Ray Bailey back to the stand, to tell about finding Shelley Gleason's body.

Milo Nilssen: How long had Benny Niemeyer been in custody by the time you found the victim's body?

Ray Bailey: Five days.

MN: What was he charged with at that point?

RB: Niemeyer and Trogstad were both charged with kidnapping and auto and credit-card theft.

MN: Had either of them confessed to those crimes?

RB: No.

MN: And had they admitted to knowing the whereabouts of the owner of the vehicle they were riding in?

RB: No. Trogstad indicated through his attorney that he had purchased the car from a stranger, that he'd lost the receipt but had no idea it was stolen. Benny kept saying he was just along for the ride, and that Dale offered him a ride so he took it.

Benny did plenty of talking during that long tiresome week but rarely said anything that made sense. All his answers were circular: I didn't do it, I wasn't even there, I don't know what you're talking about and besides I was someplace else that night. We'd say, "I didn't say it was night, Benny. How'd you know it was night?" and he'd say, "Oh, I musta misunderstood you. You know I have one bad ear from when my daddy hit me with a piece of stovewood, you believe that?" And out of all the sad and foolish things he said that week, I remember thinking maybe that one piece of information might be true, but it turned out even that was a lie—whoever fathered Benny had been long gone by the day he was born. Niemeyer was his mother's name, sort of; she got it from one of her several stepfathers, male abandonment being the one constant in a chaotic family history. Benny's origins were a lot like mine, hard to establish.

7

Dale Trogstad never said much of anything beyond, "I want an attorney." He said it every time I spoke to him till he got one. Somewhere in his recent past (he was only twenty-one), Dale had found out what his rights were. Since very little else penetrated the sociopathic dead zone that surrounded his brain, he was able to pay close attention to his rights.

"God, he's like *The Picture of Dorian Gray,* isn't he?" Rosie said, after a few hours of talking to people who knew Dale. "He looks like this perfect angel, and underneath he's just pure—" she reached out helplessly for the appropriate adjective, sighed and said, "Pussbag is much too mild a term."

Dale seemed to have trained up for this hateful crime. His North End neighborhood was crowded with tortured cats, bullied classmates, ex-girlfriends who looked away and said, "I don't want to talk about Dale." They would talk about each other though: Deanna said he got off on hurting; he always wanted it rough. Cami said he made her do it with the dog. After a couple of days of Dale research, we had a meeting at which I said, "Let's stick to the Gleason incident from now on. We've got enough of this background garbage," and four detectives, without looking at each other, said softly, "Fine."

We were pretty sure Dale and Benny had kept Shelley Gleason alive long enough to test out her PIN number and gas card. As we learned more about our suspects, we began to hope she had not lived long after that. I began to dread the sight of her family and fiancé, who came in frequently with their jaws set against any suggestion that she might be dead, while their eyes begged for this horror to end.

Now Milo led Ray Bailey through the story of how it ended.

MN: Tell us, please, what happened on the day you found Shelley Gleason?

RB: We got an anonymous phone call.

MN: Who took the call?

RB: I did. It came in through the front office, dialed in to the main police department number that's in the phone book, and whoever answered in the front office put it through to me.

MN: And what did the caller say?

RB: He said, 'Ask Benny Niemeyer why he put Shelley Gleason in that damn sinkhole south of town.'

MN: That was all?

RB: Yes. He said just those words and hung up.

MN: It was a man's voice?

RB: Yes.

MN: Were you able to trace the number it came from?

RB: No. Our front office phone doesn't record the numbers of incoming calls.

MN: I see. So, what did you do next?

Ray kept his eyes fixed firmly on Milo's shoulder while he told the bald-faced lie they had agreed on. "I talked to my boss, Jake Hines. He went to the chief and got authorization to mobilize a search."

"What did that entail?"

"We rented the services of a helicopter from Skycam, the company that does traffic surveys and weather. And we have our own K-9 team—we used that."

Now Milo had to ask the high-risk question, "How did you decide which sinkholes to look at?"

Ray, still lying like a bandit, said reasonably, "We figured it wouldn't be more than ten miles out of town, so we asked the Skycam guys and they said they had most of the nearby sinkholes pretty well spotted. They said there were two or three in the area we were talking about and they could look in all of them."

MN: When did the search take place?

RB: On Tuesday, May thirteenth, about nine o'clock in the morning.

MN: Tell us how it proceeded, please.

RB: The helicopter went up first. After about half an hour they said they'd spotted two anomalies—that's what they called them— two spots of bright color that didn't belong in the trees in a sinkhole, and they gave us the GPS coordinates for both of them.

MN: That's Global Positioning System?

RB: That's right.

MN: Tell the jury how that works.

RB: It triangulates radio signals off three or more satellites to pinpoint the latitude and longitude of any position on earth.

MN: Thank you. What did you do with the coordinates the helicopter gave you?

RB: Our K-9 guys took the dogs out to both locations, and I followed with Rosie Doyle in a department van.

His first impulse had been to take Darrell, but Rosie glared and said, "Who got the directions from Benny?"

"Rosie, this is not gonna be pretty," he said. "Are you sure?"

"Absolutely," she said, so he took her.

MN: Tell us how the search went from there.

RB: The K-9 team had a garment, a blouse of Shelley's that Dan Frye had given us, for the dogs to smell. They didn't seem much interested in the first hole so we tried the second, where they got very excited.

What the pilots had spotted from the air was Shelley's bright blue sweater, torn and blowing in the breeze. One of the small animals feasting on Shelley's body had snagged her sweater and pulled out a long tangle of yarn that was nearly worn through in several spots by the wind. If anything in this terrible scenario could be called lucky, it really was lucky that we found her when we did, before that scrap of wool blew away entirely. The rest of what was left of her had all but disappeared into the abundant undergrowth of the sinkhole.

MN: What happened next, please?

RB: I phoned Jake Hines and told him we needed the coroner and a team from BCA. The K-9 crew took the dogs back to town and Rosie and I stayed till the coroner and the folks from BCA got there.

MN: What did you do while you were waiting?

RB: We looked around, as much as we could without disturbing the crime scene, looking for a gun mainly. We didn't find that, but we did find other evidence.

MN: Tell us what that was.

RB: Well, first we found a spot, about twenty feet south of the sinkhole, that looked like a place where an injured person might have been lying down.

MN: Will you describe it?

RB: Yes. The grass was matted down there in an area about the size of a human body, there was considerable blood around and there was a kind of a trail, maybe I should say a track, of drag marks from that spot to the slope in the sinkhole where we found her body.

MN: How did you know they were drag marks?

RB: The grass was all flattened down one way, in the direction of the sinkhole. And there was blood along the track . . . looked like the blood in the matted spot. Aged about the same.

MN: What did you do when you found it?

RB: We went and had another look at the victim. It was hard to tell but we were pretty sure we could see a bullet hole in her forehead. So we came back and looked very carefully at the flat spot in the grass without touching it, and we thought we saw an indentation where a bullet might have penetrated the dirt.

MN: And did that prove to be the case?

RB: Yes. After BCA got there and photographed everything and took blood and DNA samples we got their permission to dig in that spot and we dug up a bullet.

MN: Was that the only bullet you found?

RB: No. The other thing we did while we waited for the people from town was string crime-scene tape around the sinkhole, and while we were doing that I found another bullet embedded in a silver maple at the edge of the hole.

MN: So that was actually the first bullet you found?

RB: Yes.

MN: What did you do with those two bullets?

RB: Gave them to the BCA crew to take to the lab.

MN: Are these the two bullets you gave them?

RB: Yes, that's my signature on the evidence tag.

Milo showed them to the judge but retained them to use again later, and said he had no more questions of this witness. Defense had none either. Milo had guessed right about Reese going along with our anonymous phone call story, since he was the one who wouldn't let us talk about Benny's directions. Everybody speaking for the record that day left the anonymous caller where they had found him: nowhere. Out there. What else could they do?

Milo called Adrian Pokornoskovic. His Ukrainian name does not roll easily off Rutherford palates, so most Rutherford laymen just call him the Coroner, and Rutherford cops call him Pokey. He stood smiling whimsically down at Mary while he took the oath, sat down and turned his foxy little face up to Milo.

MN: State your name, please.

AP: Adrian Andreyevich Pokornoskovic.

MN: And what is your job in law enforcement?

AP: Hampstead County coroner.

Pokey recited his bona fides and got on with the story of the crime. The victim being all too obviously deceased, his examination at the sinkhole had been cursory. Ray had called me soon after Pokey arrived and said, "Pokey says this body ought to go to BCA."

"He does? That's pretty amazing." Usually Pokey fights zealously to have Rutherford autopsies done locally, so that he can participate. He doesn't like certifying other people's conclusions. "Let me talk to him."

"Yah?" Pokey said, gutteral and quick.

"You want to ship this one out? How come?"

"Is gonna be damn hard to figure cause of death, Jake. So much exposure, and small animals been at it. You know how long she's been here?"

"I'd hafta guess."

"Probably still be guessing when autopsy's done. Be better to let St. Paul work this one. They got more experience at rough stuff." Pokey's English is directly translated from the Slavic, so it's pretty short on articles.

"Okay by me. Put Ray back on, will you?" When he got there I said, "You pretty sure about this ID?"

"The clothing all matches. Otherwise we wouldn't know." He sounded bleak. "I suppose we'll have to wait for a dental match to make it official, but yeah, everything's just what her mom described:

the blue sweater, the shoes, even her purse is here. Empty, but—"

"Engagement ring?"

"No. Bastards took that, too."

"One more thing to look for. How's Rosie doing?"

"She had a few bad seconds at the beginning but she's fine now. I showed her how to put Vicks in her nose, and a mask on."

"Okay. I'm gonna notify the suspects' lawyers so they can plan to be here tomorrow morning. We're gonna start the questioning all over."

We wasted another whole day trying to pry anything useful out of our prisoners. Benny told bigger, fancier lies as fast as he could dream them up, and Dale sat in surly silence while his attorney assured us her client knew nothing of these matters. From then on we relied on the physical evidence we could find for ourselves, and the scientists working for us in St. Paul.

Milo finished questioning the coroner and called Rosie Doyle, who looked uncharacteristically solemn, taking the oath for the first time. She had only been a detective for a couple of years, but she had five years before that as a street cop and had, besides, a rare pedigree: three generations of law enforcement work on both sides of the family, Doyles and Fogartys, Brennans and Manahans back to the turn of the last century. Her whole life had prepared her for this moment and as usual she was up for it.

"Sergeant Doyle," Milo said, "will you tell the court what part you played in locating the murder weapon?"

"Captain Hines called me and my section chief, Ray Bailey, to his office and asked us to look at the gun that Deputy Schoenfelder had brought in with the suspects."

Milo Nilssen: For what reason?

Rosie Doyle: He said, "Could this be the gun that killed Shelley Gleason—I thought you said you found nine-millimeter bullets?"

MN: What was your answer?

RD: We said no, this can't be the gun.

MN: Please tell the jury how you knew that.

RD: The bullets we found at the scene were nine-millimeter. The revolver they brought in was a twenty-two, which shoots smaller, less powerful ammunition.

MN: So then, what did you do next?

RD: We went back to the crime scene with new equipment for a different search.

MN: Describe that to us, please.

RD: Lieutenant Bailey asked Sergeant Betts—a detective who does spelunking as a hobby—if he could get down in the sinkhole and he said sure, easy, so Sergeant Betts went home and got his equipment, harnesses and ropes and so on, and he and I went back to the crime scene and climbed down in the hole.

A sort of shuffling noise came from the jury box. I looked over and saw that they had all uncrossed their legs and sat up, brought wide awake by the image of Rosie's red curls disappearing into the murky depths of a sinkhole. Most of those depressions are pretty shallow but some are not, and they're filled with trees and underbrush and sometimes snakes and badgers, and often have trash like old bedsteads and used tires in them as well. There are plenty of farmers in southeast Minnesota who plow around their sinkholes all their lives without ever going into them.

"Darrell talked me through it." Rosie shrugged. "I was never in any trouble." That was before they both got poison ivy.

MN: Tell us what you found.

RD: About twenty feet down, the hole got so narrow Darrell couldn't get into it and still see down, so he belayed for me and I went down another six feet or so, a little over the height of my body, shined my light straight down and there it was, a handgun wedged against a rock.

Milo brought a package from his table and asked Rosie to open it, saying, "Is this the gun you found that day?"

RD: Yes. This is my signature on the evidence tag.

MN: Will you describe the gun for us?

RD: It's a Sig Sauer P 226, a nine-millimeter semiautomatic hand-gun.

MN: Does this weapon shoot the kind of bullets you found at the crime scene?

RD: Yes. This magazine holds fifteen copper-jacketed nine-millimeter cartridges, which fire bullets the size of the two we found out there.

MN: Thank you, no further questions.

Reese Newman stood up and asked her, "Do any other makes of gun fire nine-millimeter ammunition, Sergeant?

"Oh, sure, plenty . . . all the Sigs come in that caliber I believe, and the Glocks like we use, and—it's a popular caliber for a handgun, yes."

"So the fact that you found a gun in the sinkhole that shoots the size of ammunition that killed Shelley Gleason, by itself that doesn't prove it's the gun used in that crime, does it?"

"No, the ballistics experts at BCA proved that."

"Objection!" Reese thundered. "Not in evidence, Your Honor!"

"Sustained," the judge said. They both looked at Rosie, who said meekly, "Will you repeat the question, please?"

"Yes or no, did the fact that the gun was in the vicinity of the body make it the only gun that could have been used?"

Rosie looked at him thoughtfully for fifteen seconds and said, "No."

The judge said it was time to break for lunch. I stood and watched the jury file out, turned and saw the BCA team standing two rows back. Trudy was on the aisle, smiling at me.

I walked back and said, "Glad to see you. Let's have lunch."

Her onetime supervisor, Fred Welch, the BCA fingerprint specialist, said, "She'll only come if you take me too, the girl is crazy in love with me." Fred's a large ebullient guy in his fifties who combines scrupulous technique in the lab with egregious lies about his prowess as a drinker and devastating letch. Trudy says he's secretly devoted to his wife and his model trains, a hobby that for some reason makes her snicker behind her hand.

Milo walked up behind me, saying, "Lunch is on me; all of you, come on." Ray and Pokey and Chrissie came too. We pushed tables together at Victor's and made a big, noisy group, snarfing up beef stew and baskets full of the crusty bread they make every morning. Milo tried to play jovial host with the county's expense account but kept lapsing into nervous twitches, smoothing his tie and checking his watch.

"Hell's the matter with Milo?" Fred asked me. "He got mange or something?"

"He's worried that the case against Benny's a little light."

"Hell, tell him not to worry," Fred said. "Time that jury's done listening to us brilliant scientists, they're gonna want to strangle Benny Niemeyer with their bare hands." He yelled down the table, "Quit playing with yourself, Nilssen. We're gonna save your ass."

"Good," Milo yelled back, "somebody should. Ray and his crew haven't brought me jack shit."

It was standard ragging, well within the bounds of allowable black humor on a trial day, but Ray Bailey gave Milo a humorless, brooding look. The Ray/Milo relationship, always cold, had been greatly stressed by the difficulty of getting the goods on Benny Niemeyer. And no matter how much boasting Fred Welch did now, I knew from their reports that they had not brought us much, because the physical evidence on Benny that we had sent them to test had been really quite scanty. I walked back to the courthouse beside Trudy, hoping that she and her clever colleagues had somehow turned Not Much into More Than Enough.

8

Dr. Jason Goodpastor took the stand after lunch to report on Shelley Gleason's autopsy. Jason Badpreacher, Trudy usually calls him, or sometimes Doctor Evilpriest. I asked her once why she always makes a joke out of his name; she said, "Because he's a pompous prick."

At lunch I began to understand. Pale and silent, with a condescending frown, Goodpastor's clenched jaw and taut shoulders clearly conveyed his dread of the next dumb thing you were probably going to say. He had a way of staring across the shoulder of anyone who addressed him, waiting tensely till he could bang out his answer like a burst from a nail gun, "Yes, I suppose so," or "No, of course not." Trading small talk with Goodpastor felt like conversing through an open car window with someone who kept goosing the gas pedal.

I figured he'd turn the jury off in the first five minutes, and nothing he said after that would matter. Chrissie seemed to have the same opinion of his potential; she quickened the tempo of her questions, stepping on the last word of his answers with the beginning of the next question, so the recitation of his long list of credits—prestigious medical schools and training hospitals, and two other crime bureaus before the one in St. Paul—went by too fast to make anybody very resentful, and she was soon bopping along to the questions that counted.

Chrissie Fallon: Did you perform the autopsy on Shelley Gleason, Doctor?

Jason Goodpastor: I did.

CF: When was that?

JG: (consulting his notes) On the fifteenth of May of last year.

CF: Describe the general condition of the body for us, please.

JG: The victim had been exposed to the elements for several days, and the body had been considerably damaged by predators.

CF: Did you find any other signs of inflicted damage, Doctor?

JG: Yes, there were six gunshot wounds, three entrance and three exit wounds.

CF: In other words, evidence of three gunshots?

JG: (Impatiently) Well, yes.

I glanced at the jury. Their faces were already turning cold.

CF: Will you describe those wounds for us, please?

JG: The first penetrated the right triceps brachii, the muscle along the inside of the arm here, a through-and-through wound that just nicked the humerus, the long bone of the upper arm. The second bullet entered through the left trapezius, the muscle of the shoulder and the upper back, went through the superior lobe of the lung, broke a rib and exited through—well it was hard to be sure, but given the wound track I would say it came out through the pectoralis major.

CF: Is that the chest?

JG: Yes.

CF: So both these gunshots appear to have struck the victim from behind?

JG: Yes.

CF: And was the third shot from behind also?

JG: No. It entered the skull here on the forehead above the nasal bone, making a hole about two-thirds the size of a dime, and smashed a somewhat larger exit hole through the occipital bone . . . that's back here, at the back of the skull.

CF: Please tell the jury how you know which one was the entrance wound, Doctor.

JG: Well, the exit wound will tend to be larger. The bullet expands as it passes through the body. Also, on the forehead, there was a starburst pattern of splitting in the skin around the wound, which occurs when the gun is pressed against skin over bone. There's no place for the gas that's exploding out of the gun to go, so it explodes under the skin and creates that stellate pattern.

CF: I see. Which if any of these gunshot wounds was fatal, in your opinion, Doctor?

JG: The shot in the arm wasn't life-threatening, certainly. The bullet that penetrated the upper back tore quite a hole through the lung and would have caused death eventually if left untreated, though not right away. But the gunshot that passed through the brain front to back and severed the cranial nerve would have caused death probably within seconds.

CF: And from the damage inflicted by the gunshot wounds, Doctor, were you able to infer the probable order in which they were administered?

Reese Newman: Objection, calls for a conclusion.

CF: Doctor Goodpastor has been established as an expert witness, Your Honor.

Judge: Yes, we brought him here for his expert opinions, let's hear them. You can produce your own expert later if you want to argue with his conclusions, Mr. Newman. Go ahead, Doctor.

JG: Very well. The two shots from behind, the shot that went through the arm was a clean shot that would have hurt but was in no way disabling. The target person could certainly still move after that injury. The one through the chest was also from some distance; neither of these shots left any soot or tattooing, such as you might see within eighteen inches or so, and the size of the wounds from the second shot indicates a bullet that was losing a little momentum. It was probably fired from five to ten feet, possibly even twenty feet behind the victim. This argues for the arm shot being first, aimed at a person walking or running away, and the bullet through the upper back and chest being fired second. The victim may have been gaining a little ground at first but the lung shot would probably knock her down, and would very likely be too disabling for her to get back up. It's reasonable to infer, then, that the head shot was the third and last, that the shooter turned her over while she was on the ground, put the gun against her forehead and shot her between the eyes.

There were soft but audible gasps from Shelley's family, seated behind us. Despite all the times they'd been over the sequence of events leading up to Shelley's death, I realized, they had probably not heard before exactly how she died.

CF: And your reason for concluding that the head shot would have been last . . . ?

JG: It was a contact shot, that indicates a disabled victim. And it would certainly have been fatal, so there would have been no need for the other shots if the head shot had been the first one.

CF: I see. Now, Doctor, despite these conclusions, you performed other standard tests on Shelley Gleason's body, is that correct?

JG: I did.

CF: With what results?

JG: Tox screen was negative, no trace of any drugs or alcohol. She was HIV negative, she was not pregnant nor suffering from any sexually transmitted disease. These results were in line with her re-cent medical records, which indicated a twenty-four-year-old woman in excellent health.

CF: Could you tell whether she had been raped?

JG: That would be difficult to establish on a body so degraded.

CF: But you didn't see any signs that she had been?

JG: No.

Chrissie had achieved a remarkable coup with Doctor Goodpas-tor: by pushing him along so fast, she had kept the jury's attention off his personality and fixed on his information, which had a repel-lant fascination. So they were all still wide awake when she said, "Thank you. Your witness, Mr. Newman."

Reese Newman: Nothing that you have said in any way implicates my client, is that right, Doctor Goodpastor?

JG: That's right.

RN: Did any of your tests give you any idea who killed Shelley Gleason?

JG: No.

RN: Thank you, no more questions.

The jury watched the next witness being sworn in with faces that said, Hey, technical evidence isn't so tough, we can handle this. And Willy Meeker, BCA's firearms and ballistics expert, started well, claiming a B.A. in chemistry and a master's in forensic science with-out any fanfare. A small, rabbity-looking man with thick glasses and a slight speech impediment, and a confusion between his Rs and Ls that made him sound faintly Japanese, he was famous around the bu-reau for knowing arcane details about guns and ammo, like who used which guns in famous robberies and ancient wars. "Don't let him get started on George S. Patton," Trudy warned me before she introduced us.

People who own and use guns enjoy firearms testimony. I spotted two of those as soon as Willy took the stand—they were Gun Men. The rest of the jury ranged as usual through several shades of mildly interested Neutrals all the way to the Hostiles, who hate guns so much they almost can't stand to hear about them. The Niemeyer jury, I quickly saw, had three Hostiles. That left seven swing votes, people who might absorb the information Willy had for them if it was presented in an interesting way.

Chrissie showed him the same two bullets she'd shown to Ray Bailey. Willy identified his tag on the package and said they were the ones he had tested.

CF: Will you describe them for us, please.

WM: They are nine-millimeter bullets, considerably deformed.

CF: But not so deformed you couldn't determine the size, is that right?

WM: Yes, that's correct.

CF: What, if anything, did you conclude from the appearance of these bullets?

WM: The amount of deformation was consistent with having hit a fairly hard target. One of them was dug out of a half-grown silver maple—that's a pretty soft tree. The bullet was still in fairly good shape, and its size was consistent with the wound track through the victim's arm, so we concluded it was probably the bullet that struck her first. The second, you can see, is considerably more deformed, but its original size can still be seen on the base here. That size, nine-millimeter, conforms to the entry wound on the victim's forehead. This bullet would have passed through two layers of bone as well as brain tissue, and then burrowed into the dirt, and the flattened condition of this bullet is consistent with that scenario.

CF: Were all three wounds found on the body of the victim consistent with this kind of ammunition, Mr. Meeker?

WM: Yes. The doctor and I agree: the size of wounds on the victim could have been caused by these bullets.

Chrissie entered them into evidence, brought over the much-disputed handgun found under the Explorer on the day of Benny's arrest—the one he either had or hadn't thrown away—and asked Willy to describe it.

WM: That's a twenty-two caliber revolver, a Ruger.

CF: And did you examine it to see if it was the gun that killed Shelley Gleason?

WM: Well, I knew as soon as I saw it that it couldn't be.

CF: Why is that?

WM: The bullets found at the crime scene were too large to have been fired by this gun, for one thing. Also, with a twenty-two, that ammunition is so much less powerful, it could never have inflicted a through-and-through shot like the one found in the victim's head. A bullet from a gun like that revolver would've been still in her head someplace.

CF: Did you test the revolver to see if it worked?

WM: Yes, it was in good working order.

CF: Was the gun loaded when you got it?

WM: Yes, there were six shells in the cylinder, Remington twenty-two longs.

Chrissie took the twenty-two back without entering it, brought him another package and asked him to open it. After he had the Sig Sauer in his hands she asked, "Did you examine this gun at the request of the Rutherford Police Department?" and Willy said, "Yes, this is my mark."

CF: Describe the gun, please.

WM: This is a nine-millimeter Sig Sauer P 226 handgun, a Swiss design of German manufacture, semiautomatic.

CF: Will you describe how it operates, Mr. Meeker?

Willy described the capacity, firing and reload characteristics of the semiautomatic, showed how the auto-eject worked and demonstrated the safety lock. The Gun Men lapped it up; most of the others glazed over. Never mind, I thought, the good part is coming.

Chrissie brought back the two bullets that had been found at the scene.

CF: In your opinion, could these two bullets have been fired from this gun?

WM: Yes, this gun fires nine-millimeter bullets like these.

CF: And will you tell the court whether you were able to determine whether in fact these bullets were fired by this particular gun?

WM: Yes, I test-fired this gun and matched the bullets I fired to the bullets at the scene. The lands and grooves on these two bullets match the marks on the bullets I fired.

CF: Can you explain to the jury what you mean by lands and grooves?

Willy turned to the charts he had hanging from a nearby bulletin board and showed them how a bullet twists through the barrel of a gun after it's fired, and the marks the finish of the barrel leaves on the lead bullet as it passes through. He showed them a picture of himself test-firing a gun into water, another picture of how he compared the markings under a microscope.

CF: So, to repeat, in your expert opinion there is no doubt that the bullets that were found at the scene where Shelley Gleason's body was found, the bullets that match the wounds on her body, were fired by this gun?

WM: That is correct.

Chrissie said she had no further questions. Reese got up and strolled over, looking thoughtful.

Reese Newman: Could you tell whether this gun you've just been showing us, the Sig Sauer that was found in the sinkhole, had been recently fired?

Willy Meeker: No. I can say that it's been fired since it was cleaned last, because there's still some residue left inside the barrel.

RN: But you don't have any way of knowing how long ago that was?

WM: No. You see, within a few minutes of firing the barrel would still be warm, obviously that wasn't the case here. The smell of gunpowder, well, you could smell that for a couple of hours, maybe get a whiff for five or six. But there was no smell left on this gun, it had been in the sinkhole for a week.

RN: Or longer, right? It could have been there for a month, couldn't it?

WM: Possibly. Though it wasn't rusted, but—

RN: Yes or no, please.

WM: Yes.

RN: No more questions.

Chrissie looked at Milo, who nodded. She jumped to her feet and said, "Redirect, Your Honor?"

"Go ahead."

She walked up to Willy and said, "You've said there's no doubt this gun fired the bullets that killed Shelley Gleason, haven't you?

WM: Yes, I did.

CF: So if this gun killed Shelley Gleason and she'd only been missing a week when she was found, the gun could not have been in the hole any longer, could it?"

WM: That's right.

CF: No more questions.

Dotzenrod allowed himself a quick, curious glance at Reese Newman as Chrissie went back to her seat. I was curious myself. I thought he opened the time window to suggest this might have been the right size gun but not *the* gun. The rifling demo was meant to foreclose on that argument before he made it, but I thought he intended to claim the bullets were too deformed to make identification certain. But then, when Chrissie closed the window by reversing his argument, he let her get away with it. Maybe we all have bad days, I thought, watching Newman contentedly shuffling papers.

That ended Willy's testimony. He had been thorough and patient, and he convinced me beyond a doubt that the Sig Sauer killed Shelley Gleason and the Ruger was irrelevant to the case. Of course I was already convinced of that. Of the people who counted, the Gun Men were still listening to every word and taking notes; the Hostiles were staring at Willy as if he had horns; and several of the Neutrals had begun looking like they'd missed their nap or were beginning to take it. The two youngest females were examining their nails, and the shapely thirtysomething brunette in the back row had begun looking at Benny as if she thought just once it might be fun to get it on with a dangerous man.

Fred Welch took the stand like a man seizing the high ground. Big, loud and confident, he seems to be not just sharing information but handing down truth, possibly reading it directly off stone tablets. He rattled off his degrees in criminal justice and his years in the military as well as several state crime labs, and went on to the story of the fingerprints in the Gleason case.

Dale and Benny had left several usable latent fingerprints on the Ford Explorer, he said, in a distribution that suggested Dale had done most or all of the driving while Benny controlled the choice of radio stations. The backseat glass and plastic yielded several partial prints of two persons not in any database.

Chrissie Fallon: You compared them to all the records in Minnesota?

Fred Welch: Much more than that. We compared them to

MAFIN—that's the Midwest database that includes Minnesota and the Dakotas—and then to IAFIS, the FBI records for the whole USA.

CF: And what population does that include, Mr. Welch?

FW: That's everybody who's arrested. Of course there are some blank spots. The reporting isn't complete yet from all the states and it gets more and more spotty as you go back a few years, but we're getting good coverage now for current records and going forward.

CF: Meaning these two sets of fingerprints from the Ford Explorer belonged to persons who've never been arrested?

FW: Pretty close. Almost certainly not in the last couple of years.

CF: Thank you. Now, did you examine latent fingerprints found on any other objects besides the car?

FW: Yes, we did. We lifted two almost complete thumbprints from an ammunition box half full of twenty-two longs that was found in a backpack in the Ford Explorer. And from the smooth plastic liner of the backpack itself, we got portions of three prints, from the right forefinger and second and third fingers of the same individual. The two thumbprints match Benny Niemeyer. The other three match Dale Trogstad.

CF: Did you attempt to lift fingerprints from the Ruger revolver that was found under the Explorer?

FW: Yes. Both handguns were fumed in an airtight box with Superglue.

CF: What if anything did you find on the Ruger revolver?

FW: There were two partial prints on the cylinder. We found a couple of characteristics in each that matched Benny Niemeyer, but not enough for a reliable identification.

CF: And the Sig Sauer semiautomatic that was found at the crime scene, what if anything did you find on that?

FW: The semiauto had no latent fingerprints on either the gun or the magazine.

CF: Is that consistent with the possible use of the weapon to shoot Shelley Gleason?

FW: Oh, yes. Only three to five percent of guns yield usable fingerprints. And the grip of the Sig Sauer had been wrapped with athletic tape, which won't hold fingerprints.

CF: For what purpose would a grip be wrapped like that, Mr. Welch?

Reese Newman: Objection, calls for supposition.

CF: This witness is an expert, Your Honor.

RN: He doesn't have mystical powers, though, does he? Can't see around corners or tell what people are planning?

Judge Dotzenrod: (gesturing) Approach.

Reese and Chrissie did their courtship ritual at the bench for a scant minute before they broke clean and came back to their tables. Chrissie, trying not to look pleased, asked again, "For what purpose would a person wrap the handle of a handgun, Mr. Welch?

FW: So it wouldn't take prints. It's a common criminal practice.

RN: Objection, obviously derogatory, Your Honor!

Judge Dotzenrod: Objection is sustained. Jury will disregard everything after the word, "prints." Proceed, please, Ms. Fallon.

CF: So you found no fingerprints at all on the Sig Sauer handgun, Mr. Welch?

FW: No.

When Chrissie finished with Fred Welch, Reese Newman came up out of his chair in a rush, asking, "Isn't it also true, Mr. Welch, that many competitive shooters wrap the grips of their guns so they won't get slippery from sweat on a hot day?"

FW: I've heard of that practice, yes. I don't believe Benny Niemeyer is likely to have attended many sanctioned matches, though, Mr. Newman.

RN: Objection, Your Honor, derogatory remarks about my client—

Judge Dotzenrod: Sustained. Jury will disregard everything after "yes." Please confine your answers to the questions asked, Mr. Welch.

RN: And on the Ruger, once again now, will you confirm for the jury that the partial prints you found on the barrel were not sufficient to allow an identification?

FW: That's right.

That ended the fingerprint testimony and left Trudy in the toughest time slot, at the end of the day when the jury was already groping through a fog of technical information. To even up those odds a bit, my girl had worn her best linen suit and put her hair in a roll, so she looked like nine million dollars, plus change.

9

"Wow, babe," I said that morning when she came downstairs. "You sure do clean up nice."

She flashed the million-megawatt smile that makes me want to bite her neck. Then she turned around anxiously, asking, "You mean it, it's really okay?"

"It's perfect, all the way around." I knew she was nervous; she'd been using her lunch hours all week to review her testimony. She had testified at several trials as a photographer, and a couple of times as a fingerprints expert, but this was her first time giving evidence about DNA, and she was worried about the long, difficult explanations.

The male jurors were going to watch her with interest whatever she said, I saw as she stood taking the oath from Mary. But most of the women looked friendly, too, so I thought she had a chance to clear the hardest obstacle for a witness, being liked equally by both genders.

But she had charts, those terrible DNA charts with the jagged peaks that turn jurors' minds to mounds of jelly. Fewer charts than her boss had used at Trogstad's trial, because unfortunately Benny had left very little DNA around this crime. But even with the few she had, when you're talking about fragments of protein so tiny that thousands of them fit inside the human cell—which itself is so small it can only be studied after two hundred degrees of magnification—you're asking people to think hard about an abstraction inside an enigma. At three in the afternoon? Please.

In plain English, most of the DNA that had been scraped and swabbed off the steering wheel and door handles of the Ford Explorer matched Dale Trogstad. Usable DNA samples that matched Benny Niemeyer were found on the Ruger revolver, on the radio dial of the Ford Explorer and on the ammunition box in the backseat that contained shells for the Ruger. All of that placed him in the Explorer with a gun, but not the right gun, and not necessarily at the scene of either the kidnapping or the murder.

The gasoline credit card proved to be smeared with such hopelessly mixed DNA it was impossible to sort out a clear sample. Weather and predation had so degraded the victim's body that it yielded no usable DNA but its own.

I steadied the easel and moved charts for Trudy while she explained her charted peaks and valleys, showed the jury the places where two alleles indicated a characteristic from each parent, the other places where a single peak indicated the same DNA inheritance from both. It was closer scrutiny of his bloodlines than anybody, including his own parents, had ever given Benny Niemeyer before, and it placed him in Shelley Gleason's automobile, beyond any doubt. Trudy's evidence confirmed eyewitness testimony but did not advance it further.

Benny's DNA was on the gun that didn't kill the victim, and the ammunition box held bullets that fit that gun, illegal for Benny to have but no help to our case today.

Trudy and Chrissie worked hard and did the best they could with it, but the jury was nearly comatose by the time she finished the last of the charts. Watching them doze, it was hard to believe her testimony had only consumed half an hour.

The judge gave us a ten-minute break, so I walked out with the BCA crew.

"Tell me the truth," Trudy said. "Was that one old guy in the front row snoring?"

"No, come on now, you did great. And now you're headed home, right?"

"Yeah, I drove my own car down. Willy's gonna check me out at BCA, Jimmy okayed it. It comes out even—they pay me for the time I'm not there or they pay me for the mileage."

"Trudy, a whole hour's worth of graft," Willy said. "Have you decided which sin to wallow in?"

"I'm going to hoe potatoes, pull carrots and pick beans."

"You work this woman too hard," Fred said, draping a big arm over her shoulders. "Why don't you come along with me, sweetheart? I know how to treat a beautiful woman."

"You picked the wrong victim," Trudy said, grinning up at him as she slid out of his embrace. "I'm the slave driver at our house, especially in the summertime."

"Is that true, Jake? You're pussy-whipped in your own garden?"

"Yup. She keeps a cat-o'-nine-tails hidden in the okra." Fred had to assert his superiority over me somehow before he could leave, so it was best to get it over. I nudged Trudy's elbow, said I'd see her soon and hurried back inside, where Judge Dotzenrod was saying, "It's a little after four o'clock. How many more witnesses does the prosecution mean to call?" They consulted their list. Milo said, "Three, Your Honor."

"Are they here?"

"Yes, they are."

"In that case we'll proceed."

Outside courtroom 208, a small cluster of pale-skinned, surly young adults were waiting on the bench nearest the door. They were friends of Dale and Benny, all we had been able to find of a much larger group that had been around last year when the two were arrested. Kylee Mundt was not the only witness missing since Trogstad's trial ended.

Brandi Bernauer was first on the stand, a pale girl in her early twenties with a tongue stud and a hoop in her left eyebrow. She seemed to be having a little trouble staying awake.

She had not testified at Dale Trogstad's trial because Milo was wary of her flakiness and he had other, better witnesses then. But twice in pre-trial interviews, she had clearly stated that she had seen Dale and Benny riding together in the Ford Explorer on the street in Rutherford, and that Benny had called out to her, "How do you like our new car?"

As Milo questioned her, she began to tell the story again, with subtle changes. She remembered she had seen the two men riding together in a Ford Explorer, and yes, she guessed it might have been after Shelley Gleason disappeared.

"Did the defendant say anything to you that day?" Milo asked her.

Brandi looked at him dully for a moment and said, "Defendant?"

"Benny Niemeyer, the defendant sitting there with his lawyer. Did he speak to you that day?"

"Uh . . . I guess he said hello," Brandi said.

"Is that all he said? He didn't lean out the window and—"

"Objection! You Honor," Reese said, "prosecution is leading the witness!"

"Sustained."

"Do you remember if he said anything else to you that day?"

Her eyelids fluttered. "Hello is all I remember."

Milo started to go through the whole scene again, but Reese protested that he was badgering the witness, and the judge agreed.

"No further questions," Milo said, and came back to the table walking stiffly, as if his joints hurt.

Reese had only one question. "Who was driving the car?"

"Dale was."

"Thank you, nothing further."

Todd Lansing was a friend of Dale Trogstad. Like Dale he suffered from what psychiatrists call blunted affect; he was so detached he hardly seemed present in the room. He worked part-time in a music store downtown and his social life centered on hip-hop music, murderous lyrics shouted to a hypnotic beat. His friends came by his apartment after work to listen to his collection, he said. "After work" seemed to mean anytime between midnight and dawn. Dale Trogstad and Benny Niemeyer had visited, after midnight in late April, maybe about a week before Shelley disappeared.

"Did you often see Dale and Benny together?"

"They went around together some."

"They were close friends?"

Lansing shrugged. "Benny seemed to like Dale a lot, called him his bud. Seemed like he kind of got off on that."

"And on the night in question, did they have any news?"

"They said they had guns," he said. "They were gonna do something."

"What were they going to do?"

"I don't know exactly. Something for money. I thought—"

Milo said, "Did you see—" He stopped, realizing he had stepped on his witness's last words, and said, "Excuse me, go ahead."

"I thought they were just talking." Todd's pale, indifferent eyes wandered toward Benny for a moment and he shrugged again. "Benny talks a lot."

It was an odd, ambiguous little put-down, and caused a discernible shifting in the jury box. Todd Lansing's dismissive shrug reduced Bad Benny to an absurdity.

Milo said he had no more questions. Reese asked, "Did you see Dale and Benny after Ms. Gleason disappeared?"

"No."

"So you never had a chance to ask them if it was her car they took?"

"No."

"As far as you know it could have been just talk?"

"Yes."

Raven Crenshaw, Milo's third witness, had channeled her anger into vindictiveness. Her hard gray eyes darted from face to face, looking for somebody to wound.

Fifteen months ago, in an interview, she had recalled how Benny and Dale had come to her apartment in early April and said they were going to steal some guns and "jack a car."

"Gonna start a regular crime wave," Benny had boasted, according to Raven. "Get our names in the paper. You gonna be readin' about us, man."

"You didn't report the threat to anyone?"

"Report it?" She sneered. "If I reported every fool thing Benny Niemeyer ever said I wouldn't have time for much else."

Milo had hoped to use Raven's testimony at Trogstad's trial, but she was in detox then. Reviewing her information last month, Chrissie had asked her, "Let's see, you said Dale and Benny came to your apartment with two other men, is that still your story?"

"Why would I change it? You think I lied the first time?"

"No, no," Chrissie said, "I just thought we should review it together now."

Raven's everyday sneer changed to a leer. "You tryna tell me what to say?"

"Of course not." Chrissie let it go. Milo would not have used her at all today except that he had so little else. Kylee Mundt was still missing and so was the swamper from the bar on South Broadway who had proudly told us, the week after Shelley Gleason's body turned up in a sinkhole, that he knew all about this crime because his bud, Benny Niemeyer, had described to him in detail what they were going to do. His name was Souphong Li, or possibly the reverse. The IRS had no record of him after that month, and nobody else remembered him at all.

Raven gave her name and address and said she worked at Nails and Company.

"That's, uh, manicures?"

Raven settled her hair behind her ears. "Acrylic enhancements."

Milo Nilssen: Okay. Was there a day last year when Dale Trogstad and Benny Niemeyer came to your apartment?

Raven Crenshaw: Um, yeah. It was after work. Maybe five, six o'clock. Dale and Benny and two or three other guys.

MN: Did they say anything about their plans?

RC: Oh, they said they just got up, they were killing time till it was late enough to—(clears her throat)—they usually stayed up all night.

MN: Did they mention plans for later on?

RC: Oh, Dale was bragging about he had all these guns, he was ready now and he was going to start jacking cars.

MN: And did Benny say he was going to help him jack the cars?

RC: Um . . . Benny? (examining her long purple nails) I'm not sure if Benny was there that day.

MN: (trying not to swallow his tongue) Ms. Crenshaw, didn't you tell us earlier—"

Reese Newman: Objection! Your Honor, counsel is impugning his own witness! Does he want us to hear her testimony or not?

Judge: Sustained.

MN: Let's try it again. Would you tell us, please, as nearly as you can remember it, *word for word* what Dale said to you that day?

RC: Well . . . word for word, boy, after all this time? I don't know.

MN: Tell as nearly as you can recall.

RC: Well. I believe he said something like, "We got the guns now and we're gonna jack us some cars and make some real money."

MN: And by "we" he meant himself and Benny Niemeyer, is that correct?

"Objection, leading the witness," Reese Newman said.

"Sustained."

MN: I'll rephrase. What other person was Dale including when he said "we"?

RC: I can't say.

MN: Why can't you say, Ms. Crenshaw?

RC: He didn't say.

Milo looked at the wall for a few seconds, presumably saying *Om om om*, gave up on that visit and asked Raven, had she seen Benny and Dale together on any other occasions? She said yes, seemed like they were together a lot that spring, Benny would follow Dale anyplace, always calling him his bud. It was the best Milo could get from her and he quit on that note.

Reese lobbed Raven a softball. "Did you know Dale and Benny well, Ms. Crenshaw? See a lot of them?"

"No, not really," she said, pulling at the long tendrils that hung down from her bangs. "They were just guys from the neighborhood. Came in the shop sometimes, came to my place once or twice."

"So you really don't know what their relationship was?"

"Their relationship?" She seemed to be trying to decide if he had just said something dirty.

"Do you know if they spent much time together?"

She pursed her lips and looked at the ceiling. "Off and on, I guess."

Reese said he had no further questions.

Milo said, "The prosecution rests."

"It's almost five o'clock," the judge said. "Let's talk about tomorrow. Is the defense ready to proceed?"

Reese sprung his big surprise. "The defense will not present any witnesses, Your Honor."

Milo and Chrissie turned and stared at each other for two seconds, turned back to the judge and tried to look cool. Reese had given them a list of a dozen possible defense witnesses; they had pages of questions ready for them. Besides Benny's parole officer and a couple of social workers, they were mostly friends of Dale and Benny. It was not a very imposing list, but somebody on it might furnish an excuse to a juror who was inclined to acquit.

Reese's decision not to mount any defense at all meant either (a) his list had shrunk even worse than Milo's had, or (b) Reese had the prosecution's case pegged for a loser and wanted the jury to hurry up and consider it while its flaws were still fresh in their minds.

"In that case," Dotzenrod said, "closing statements can begin as soon as we reconvene in the morning. Let's move the time up to ten o'clock sharp, and if your closing statements can be fairly concise," his tone was dry, "I'm inclined to give the case to the jury tomorrow. I won't keep you sequestered over the weekend," he assured the pleading faces in the box, "but we'll decide on a time of adjournment after we see how we get along here."

I hustled back to the station. Most of the cubicles in my section were empty, with notes on the desks telling me where the detectives had gone. Bo, with his back to his office door, was talking on the phone in that quiet voice that never carries past the mouthpiece. Rosie stared raptly at her computer monitor with her hands tented; Kevin was punishing his keyboard with stiff one-finger pokes; Darrell Betts was charting something. In her cramped workspace in the hall the steno, LeeAnn Speer, typed steadily with a sound like soft bullets. I pulled up my e-mail, saw nothing critical and thought about what a long day tomorrow might be. Two minutes later, I was on the road home.

10

Trudy was in the garden, in cutoffs and clogs, picking lettuce. All her courtroom polish was gone; her hair was braided down her back. One big basket full of carrots and beans stood at the corner of the garden; two empty baskets waited. I got into the ragged jeans I keep for yard work, snagged two beers out of the cooler on the porch, went out and held them aloft at the end of her row. "Come out and cool your liver."

It's something my first boss used to say, I don't know why. He ran a paper delivery route and paid a half-dozen grade-school boys peanuts to jump off his pickup and run around the block tossing rolled-up newspapers onto front steps. When we got too noisy or started to fight over space on the truck, he'd lean out his open window and say, "Hey, kid, cool your liver." I said it now in the hope of coaxing a smile out of my girl, who was looking a little grim about green and leafy vegetables.

"Oh—" She pushed back a stray hair, leaving a trail of fine black Minnesota earth.

"Come on. Take a break, and then I'll help you with the rest."

"Okay, deal." She rinsed her hands at the hose by the shed and came over to the lawn chairs under the big oak. There were a lot of things we didn't have yet on our run-down country estate, but we had elegant old shade trees that demanded to be sat under. Trudy glugged a big swallow, leaned back and sighed. "I swear, that zucchini's gone nuts."

"You're just too good at this growing thing," I said. "You're going to have to learn to hold back a little."

"It's your compost that's doing it."

"Oh, sure, blame the fertilizer."

"Well, I have to find a culprit somewhere. I'm being victimized by vegetables—how smart does that look?"

I held up my long-neck bottle and sighted through the glass across the huge, beautifully tended garden. Viewed like that, it looked like a cool brown paradise—plainly, not how it looked to Trudy right now. She had planted extra pumpkin and zucchini vines amongst the corn stalks this year, because last year the Sullivans became so hopelessly seduced by her baking skills that they bartered a spare freezer they jointly owned for all the zucchini bread and pumpkin pies she would bring them. They were running a separate tab, recording the descending total of her indebtedness for the freezer on a brown grocery bag pinned to the wall in Dan Sullivan's kitchen. The day she planted that extra zucchini I begged her not to, reminding her how fast it puts out when it gets going. Not having been born yesterday, I did not mention that conversation now.

"Tell you what," I said. "Since I got home at a decent hour for once, why don't you show me what else has to get picked tonight and I'll do it?"

"Oh, Jake, I'm fine, I just—"

"Please don't be brave. You had to explain DNA to a bunch of woodenheads this afternoon. All I did was move the charts. You're beat; go take a shower. Then if you'll cook that steak that's in the refrigerator and maybe, pardon the expression, a few vegetables? There's a bottle of Shiraz in the cupboard and who knows, I might even blow in your ear before this wild night is over."

She did and I did and we both felt a lot better by morning. Then it was Trudy's turn to cheer me up after she asked me, at breakfast, "Will this be the last day of the trial, you think?"

"Good Christ, I hope so. The lawyers are scheduled for closing statements this morning; I think I can stand that if I don't inhale. Then I want to see Benny Niemeyer put away where he belongs and after that I'm hoping very sincerely—" I told her as I packed my August sandwich "—not to see Milo Nilssen again for a long time."

"He is kind of a fussbudget, isn't he?"

"He makes me feel like I'm getting hives on the inside of my brain."

"Hoo, man, hives on the inside. Here, you got me through last night. Let's see if I can get you through today." She put her arms around my neck and kissed me tenderly.

When she pulled her head back I said, "That's much better but I'm still a little tense. Better try one more."

So I went to work pretty cheery, briefed the chief on the trial and checked on my staff. Kevin and his Property Crimes boys were busy writing up reports of missing boat motors and coolers and cameras, all the stuff that's so easy to pick up out of yards and picnic sites in late summer. Ray and his crew had a fresh August crime-wave going, a nerve-jarring series of murderous brawls that seemed to be fueled by something stronger than testosterone and a twelve-pack. I left them all working hard on their less than perfect world and skulked off guiltily to my observer's seat at the courthouse.

Milo had withdrawn into himself like a turtle; he didn't look up from reviewing his closing statement. Chrissie took time to give me a tentative little smile. Benny was brought in and started his belt ritual with the deputy. He looked jumpy and ominous, like malice afore-thought with a fever. Watching the jury file in, he let his eyes linger on the female jurors, tensing his shoulder muscles so they strained against his shirtsleeves. A nerve twitched above his jaw. *Just keep being yourself, Benny,* I thought, *you're doing our job for us.* The woman in the back row recrossed her legs, letting her skirt ride up her thighs.

Closing arguments are more interesting than opening ones; the case has been presented so there's more red meat to chew on. Chrissie took the first round and was suitably indignant about the cruelty of the murder, the blameless young woman snatched off the streets of her hometown where she had every reason to feel safe, subjected to hours of terror and finally brutally murdered. She reviewed the DNA and fingerprint evidence that placed Benny in Shelley's car and his boasting in advance about this hateful crime. She said society must punish such wanton cruelty to the full extent of its laws, lest our streets be ruled by thugs. Pointing to Benny, she asked them directly: send him to prison for the rest of his life, make certain he can never again cause the sorrow you see in this courtroom today. Pointing to Shelley's family, clustered stern-faced in the second row, she said, "Give them the only thing we can give them that will help their grief, the satisfaction of knowing that Shelley's killer can never harm another person."

I thought it was kind of a barn-burner, and was happy to see a number of jurors looking at her with new respect when she finished.

Reese Newman stood up next, easily dominating the courtroom with his smooth good looks and supreme confidence. He extended his sympathy to the family and fiancé of the victim and agreed that the crime was horrifying. Then he leaned across the railing of the jury box and added, in a confidential hiss that carried to the far corners of the room, "But Benny Niemeyer didn't do it!"

He held up a list and began checking items off it with a big red pencil: Benny's DNA in the victim's car, did it place him at the scene of either the kidnapping or the murder? Of course it didn't. His fingerprints on the second gun: totally irrelevant. The question of whether he threw the second handgun or Dale Trogstad threw it: a distraction, really. The gun was in the car, who cares who threw it? It doesn't speak to the question you're being asked to judge here today.

"The question, ladies and gentlement of the jury, the only question that matters, is this: did Benny Niemeyer kill Shelley Gleason? And remember, the burden of proof is on the state. Benny Niemeyer doesn't have to show you he's innocent. They"—pointing to Milo and Chrissie—"have to prove he's guilty. And they haven't done that! The prosecution hasn't come within a country mile of proving that!

"His name on the signed receipts for the motel room in LaCrosse: so what? The statements he made to others about planning the crime: again, so what? Boys brag. It might not be an attractive thing to brag about, but we're not here to decide if Benny's a nice boy, are we? Not deciding if he should win a popularity contest, are we? No, no, we only have to decide one thing now: did he kill her?"

Reese cast doubts for half an hour, told them they had no choice but to find his client not guilty, and sat down.

Milo got up, stern and quiet, and paced in front of the jury box, reviewing the core facts they must not forget: extensive evidence that the two men were together, announcing their car-jacking intentions for weeks before the crime. They told people before the crime they were going to do it and afterward bragged that they had. They were seen in the victim's car the day after the murder, and arrested together in it three days after that.

Then he pounced on Reese's assertion that the state hadn't proved Benny did the killing. "Remember," he said, "it doesn't matter whether the defendant's fingerprints are on the murder weapon or not, because it doesn't matter if he pulled the trigger or only watched. The law says if he assisted in a murder, then he's guilty of that murder. And there's ample evidence that he did! Benny Niemeyer was in on this crime from the planning stage right through the execution of it, and he was found in Shelley's car, enjoying the rewards of his terrible crime, days after she died."

Then he came down hard on the egregious nature of the crime. "They took the car at gunpoint. There was nothing she could do to stop them; they had the car," he said. "They could have let Shelley go; they didn't need to kill her to get what they wanted. They killed her and hid her body," Milo said in a voice that shook with outrage, "because they thought it would give them a few more days to drive her car. They took what was rightfully hers and then killed her so they could have more time to play with it.

"I implore you, ladies and gentlement, don't let him go free to do it again to somebody else."

That was it. The judge gave the jury his instructions, the courthouse clerk swore in the bailiff and entrusted the jury to his care. Marty took them to their quiet room, and began carting in the boxes and stacks of records they would have to consult.

It was still a few minutes before noon. I looked at Milo and Chrissie. They looked back at me and we all shrugged. We had worked on this case for so long, there was nothing we had not already said about it. A wave of terrible depression washed over me; I had to force myself to move. As I headed out the door I heard Reese Newman, behind me, making nice with Milo, thanking him for a well-run trial and then congratulating him on his attractive new assistant. I glanced back. Reese's expensive haircut was inclined above Chrissie's hand; she looked up at him with her tentative smile, and I wondered again why a woman so confident about her work seemed so ill at ease socially.

My office felt good to me that afternoon. I plowed through e-mails, briefed the chief on the status of the trial and held a week's-end review of new cases with Kevin and Ray. At four-thirty the phone rang and Chrissie said, "The judge just sent the jury home for the weekend. They're due back at ten A.M. Monday."

"Well, he promised them the weekend off so they wouldn't hurry, so that's good," It was just something to say; I had no idea if it was good or bad. I was still clueless on Monday, anxious by Tuesday, and increasingly twitchy the rest of the week as they stayed sequestered in their quiet room. By the time Chrissie called Friday, I was so wired I hung up the phone while she was still saying, "The jury's coming back."

Broadway was jammed up again, so my shortcut worked well. The courthouse elevators had crowds in front; I went up the stairs like a bat out of hell and dodged through stragglers still heading into courtroom 208.

I made it to the prosecutors' table just in time to watch the foreman stand up and give the court the unanimous verdict of the jury: Benny Niemeyer was not guilty.

11

There was an interval of shocked silence after the verdict was read. Then the judge polled the jury, got a unanimous verdict of not guilty for the second time, thanked them for their hard work and excused them.

"There being no other charges against the prisoner," he said, "he is free to go." He looked at the sheriff's deputy, who was still standing uncertainly against the wall, and raised his eyebrows. The deputy reached Benny in two long strides, knelt and removed the chains that held his legs together.

Benny turned toward the prosecutors' table and smiled. Slowly, taking his time, he pursed his lips and blew Milo a kiss.

His own lawyer stood beside him, presumably waiting to be thanked. Benny didn't even glance at him. He swaggered away from the defense table, across the front of the courtroom from right to left. I heard a quick intake of breath behind me, as the gallery, used to the comfort of seeing Benny in chains, watched him go free.

As he passed Chrissie, who was standing in front of the table collecting papers, he leaned toward her with a wolfish grin and said softly into her ear, "Eat your heart out, bitch."

I turned to see if she needed help and saw Milo, who was closer, start toward them from the other side. But then some kind of understanding flashed between him and Chrissie. She met his eyes, raised her left hand in a forestalling gesture and shook her head, and for just a second I saw a strange, bright expression cross her face, something I couldn't read, but certainly not fright.

Then Reese was there saying, "Can I give you a lift somewhere, Benny?" He walked his client down the aisle with a hand under his elbow, murmuring in his ear.

Milo inclined his head toward the Gleasons and Dan Frye, who were standing in front of their seats looking as if a thousand explanations would not feed the hunger in their hearts. Chrissie nodded, put down her stack of papers and followed him toward the family, where they began to pat shoulders and murmur about other charges and a civil suit. They came back to the prosecution table after a few minutes, looking as if they were in need of consolation themselves.

"Buy you a drink?" I asked them.

"Nah," Milo said. "I don't like to drink in this neighborhood. How about walking us down to the parking garage, though? I'd like to talk about Plan B for a minute."

"Okay." Joining the outgoing stream of observers and court functionaries who had crowded in to hear the verdict, we pushed down the stairs and out through the packed front doors.

Crossing the busy plaza, avoiding the curious stares of people who were looking to see how we took the loss, I asked him, "Where do you want to start?"

"Any place that will get him back in jail. What have you got left over that we could use?" At the elevator doors to the parking garage, he pushed the button and asked me, "You down here too?"

"No. But I'll ride down with you." On the way down I asked him,

"How about felon in possession of a firearm? We've got his DNA on the Ruger and his fingerprints on the box of ammo. He's on parole; all we have to do is notify the feds and he's gone."

"Sure. Hell, if we wanted to work at it we might nail him for the original burglary of the guns at the Aldrich house. You've never charged anybody with that, have you?"

The door opened at Level A and Milo and I got out. Chrissie held the door open and said, "I'm down on B. You need me anymore tonight?"

"No. Go on home. Don't think about any of this until Monday. You did a helluva job, Chrissie." She smiled at him gratefully as the door closed. We walked together across the dead-air stench of the parking garage. At his car door, Milo turned and said, "Hell with it. It's Friday night and I'm not going to think about that fucking outlaw any more this week."

"Fine with me. Monday morning?"

"Yeah. Pencil me in for about nine o'clock. I'll be hung over, I promise you. Better make it your office. Your guys have all the earlier crime files."

"Fine." I was walking back toward the elevator doors when a shout came up from below. I turned and saw Milo, who had started to get into his car, climb back out and stand with his head cocked, listening.

There was more loud yelling, two voices now, and Milo roared, "That's Chrissie!" We ran down our separate aisles between cars, arrived at the ramp together and pounded down it toward Level B. I got the strap off my holster halfway down and drew my weapon as we rounded onto the lower level, looking everywhere. The yelling seemed to be coming from the middle of the big space, which was nearly filled with cars. I ran toward the noise and saw two figures rise up out of the surrounding cars and tumble into the aisle, fighting.

Then I watched, dumbfounded, the spectacle of Benny Niemeyer being kicked in the nose by a nearly naked man. Milo ran past me yelling at the top of his lungs. Benny looked up and saw him coming, ran back between two parked cars, vaulted a low metal barrier between two rows and ran at top speed toward the exit ramp. He was holding a torn scrap of dark cloth against his face, and scattered a trail of blood behind him as he ran. I braced and raised my gun, but Chrissie's voice, behind me, yelled, "Don't shoot him, Jake!"

I looked around; Milo shook his head at me across the intervening space and made a nullifying gesture with his hands, like an umpire calling a runner safe on first. "Let him go, Jake," he called.

What the hell was going on? It was too late to stop Benny, anyway; he was disappearing up the ramp. *But where was the naked man?* By the time I turned back, Milo was somewhere between the cars saying, "What can I do to help?"

Something silver flashed in the air and Chrissie's voice said, "Get my jogging suit out of the trunk, will you?" Milo caught the keys, turned and opened the trunk of Chrissie's little blue Escort. I stayed a row away from the naked person crouched behind a car as Milo walked past me carrying the cotton suit.

I heard him ask, "Are you hurt?" and Chrissie's answer, low and scornful, "No, but he is. I broke his fucking nose."

Milo chuckled, a soft, satisfied sound I'd never heard out of him before. After two minutes of rustling noises, Chrissie walked toward me in a pale blue jogging suit and serious running shoes, and got in her car. She didn't quite look at me, or maybe I didn't quite look at her. She backed out, gave us a little toot and drove up the ramp.

"Well now," Milo said, watching her go. "Maybe we ought to have that drink after all."

We went into the shiny, impersonal hotel bar around the corner, got vodka and tonics in tall frosty glasses at the bar and carried them to a tiny corner table where we had to sit sideways and talk across our shoulders in order to keep our knees from locking like Legos.

"So," I said, after a long pull on my drink, "your assistant's name is really Christopher?"

"Used to be," he said. He took a big, thirsty swallow himself and stared at the wall a few seconds.

I said, "If you'd rather not talk about it—"

"No, now that you've, uh, glimpsed the situation, I want you to understand what the deal is. It's kind of, um, inspiring, to tell you the truth." He pulled his nose and cracked his knuckles; he must have another whole set of body rituals that went with inspiring thoughts.

"I started searching Internet databases last spring," he said, "for upcoming law school graduates. My usual problem: I needed a smart kid who'd work for peanuts."

"It isn't going to get better, either."

"I know. But I found one—her grades were just spectacular, and she said salary was not her major concern. She wanted a smallish town where she'd get a chance to start trying cases right away. She had everything, dean's list, *Law Review*—from Columbia, imagine. I was curious, so I phoned her and she agreed to meet me off-campus.

"Naturally I was expecting to meet a real dog, you know? Why else would a star from the top of the class want to trade down like that? I thought maybe a harelip not fixed right, or some skin condition that wouldn't heal. I got to the restaurant on time, and there sat Chrissie, looking very—well, you know. So now I was curious as hell.

"She was completely straightforward, no beating around the bush. 'I'm not what I seem,' she said, 'but I propose to fix that.' We talked for three hours, she told me all her plans and we made a deal."

"So Christopher's a transvestite," I said. "What's to plan?"

"Plenty. Because Chrissie's not gay, Jake. She's a transsexual, a woman in a man's body. What she wants is corrective surgery to fix one of nature's mistakes."

"You don't say."

"I do say. Quit making provincial wisecracks, will you? You're more sophisticated than that."

"Well, excuse me all to hell."

"See, there you go. It's a habit we fall into, guys out here in the heartland. We think we have to act like bozos a certain amount of the time to fit in. The truth is Minnesota's changing along with the rest of the country; all we have to do is go with the flow."

"Christopher has raised your level of consciousness."

"Okay," Milo said, "be a smart-ass. It's nothing to me." He took another big drink and brooded at the wall.

I watched his grim profile a minute, thinking, *What the hell am I doing?* I knew he was right; I was being a jerk, but I felt very ill-used. I remembered trying to help Chrissie when she walked in with her heavy load of records, and I felt like they'd both been laughing at me.

Milo was starting a new round of tie-smoothing and hair-patting, though, and rather than run out of the place and leave a nice cool drink I said, "I feel kind of hoodwinked."

"Why, for Christ's sake? It's got nothing to do with you."

"Maybe not, but he really had me fooled."

"She. Get that through your head. Chrissie's a woman. She didn't fool you. She just presented herself in her true colors."

I sat back in my chair and stared at him. He looked like the same old Milo, but his head seemed to have filled up with insights I would never have guessed at. "You're really on board with this idea, aren't you?"

"A hundred percent. She's so courageous!" He shook his head in wonder. "She's been working with a clinic in New York for a couple of years, getting hormone shots and so on. I don't know all the de-tails, but she told me they recommend their patients live a year or two as the opposite sex they want to be, dressing the part and walk-ing the walk, before they have the surgery. That way they can see if it suits them as much as they thought it would."

"Well. So, does it?"

"Absolutely. I've never been around anybody before who was happy all day just to be who she is." He brooded into his drink. "I'm envious, if you want to know the truth."

"Be damned. So that's why Chrissie wasn't insulted when Benny called her a bitch, huh? I couldn't figure out the look on her face. She was just pleased she convinced him, wasn't she?"

"Delighted. Yes." He gave that low, satisfied chuckle again, such a surprising sound to come out of Milo. He rattled the ice in the bot-tom of his glass, took a last long swig and said, "Working with Chrissie puts a whole new spin on things."

"I bet." I stood up, "I'm going to owe you a drink, because I can't stay to have another, okay?"

"Absolutely, me too. I gotta go. I'll take a rain check and—" he stuck out his hand "—look forward to collecting." It was an awk-ward moment, almost a love fest for Milo and me, after years of barely avoiding hostilities. "Oh, say, listen." He turned back to me with his briefcase in his hand. "She's trying to keep it secret, for now. Do you think—?"

"Don't worry, I won't tell." I wasn't even tempted. That week in August, there was never time for a story that complicated.

12

Back at the station, most of my crew were cleaning up their desks, their minds already out the door. "Meet me in the small meeting room," I said, "for five minutes." I gave them the bad news about Benny quickly, so they could get their bitching done fast and forget it over the weekend.

We were just breaking up when the chief came hurrying down the hall and said, "Jake? Is it true? Aw, hell. What ails that jury anyway?"

"I don't know, Frank. I thought we had it nailed. But now that it's too late I realize we should have been ready to arrest him on another charge before he got out of the courtroom."

"Ah. Yeah. What else have you got?"

"Milo and I talked about it. Easiest would be just turn him over to the feds for possession of a firearm. Although Milo wants to hang the Aldrich burglary on him."

"Oh, clever thinking," Kevin said. "I like the image of Big Bad Benny negotiating with antiques dealers."

"Discussing étagères," Rosie said, and everybody laughed but Darrell who said, "What's an Etta Share?"

"We left off the firearms possession charge for the trial," I told Frank, "because we didn't want to confuse the jury. I guess we should have just accepted going in that all juries are confused, and piled it on."

"I can't believe—they actually just turned him loose? That's insane! Did Milo screw it up, you think?"

It was so tempting. If I'd said yes, he'd have believed me. Cops work so hard to make cases, when they don't get convictions they need to believe the lawyers blew it or the judge was a muffin. What else is there? It's always clear to us that we did our part.

"No, Milo and Chrissie both worked hard. And I thought it was going pretty well, witness by witness as we went along. I guess we didn't have quite enough after the judge ruled out the evidence that he knew where the body was. But—we all knew Benny was guilty so I guess I thought the jury'd see it too."

"There's no doubt about his guilt, is there?"

"Chief, he knew where the body was. He was riding around in her car the day after the murder. He bragged about it to everybody he knew in the North End."

"Damn. Well." He stood up and stretched and the space around the table seemed, for a few seconds, too small. Then he shook himself back down to size huge and we all took a deep breath. "Better hurry and come up with something. I've been watching that kid pick up bad habits since he was nine years old, so I know he won't stop at one murder. Benny never stopped at one of anything in his life."

"I'm on it." He went back to his office and I looked at my watch. "Damn, though, it's after five o'clock."

Ray said, "Can't solve 'em all in one day," his one-size-fits-all excuse.

"Too true," I told my crew. "Monday morning at eight sharp, be ready to prioritize what else we have to do next week besides start all over on Benny." There was a little round of groaning but it was ten past five. They were all past due at a happy hour or two. They got up and got out of there before I could think of anything else. All but Bo.

He was standing quietly at my office door when I got back to it, hugging his elbows. In ten years or so of working vice, he had evolved an appearance that fit in any place, from a biker bar to a school picnic. His clothes were an odd mix of shabby and elegant, usually jeans and a black T-shirt under an old tweed jacket that hung well on him. His hair curled around his head like one of those Greeks you see on coins, and he wore a diamond in one ear.

"Whatcha need?" I said.

"I've got my eye on two possibles. Motor homes. For the portable meth labs I was telling you about?"

"Oh. Yeah?"

"Neither one's in town this afternoon but I've got some spotters in the RV parks gonna call me if one of them turns up. Darrell's agreed to split the surveillance with me if you'll okay the overtime."

"Absolutely. Anything else you need?"

"If this is as small as I think it is we can cover it with backup from whoever's on duty in the squads. If it looks like it might get bigger, I'll let you know."

"Sounds fine. What about Nelly—you got that covered?" Bo's a single father since his wife walked out to follow her crack habit.

"Darrell says he doesn't mind taking nights. And Maxine said she'd take Nelly on a weekend day if it breaks that way."

"Okay. Good luck, keep me posted." As soon as he was out the door I phoned Trudy's cell. When she answered I said, "Where are you?"

"Still in the lab, for about twenty more minutes. I want to finish this one batch because—you don't want to hear." Now that she's analyzing DNA full time, her work days are pretty mysterious to me.

"Okay, listen. I've got one stop to make and I'll still beat you home. And hey? I think I'll pick four ears of corn for us to try, okay?"

"Um, yeah, some of it's ready. Be choosy. And then, will you start the grill? And put out the chicken? By the way, any word from the jury?"

All over the country, now that we have cell phones, people are having these backward conversations, in which we address the most mundane items first: pick up the boys at the game, I'm going to have the tires rotated, did you get the charcoal? And then, Oh, by the way, do you know we're at war, there's an earthquake, the polar cap is melting?

"Jury came back," I said. "I'll tell you when I see you."

My stop was at Maxine Daley's house. She was my foster mother for the best six years of my childhood. Now that I'm a cop and she's a day-care provider, we maintain an adult friendship that features a lot of interrupted sentences.

If you carried a chart of Maxine's day-care schedule, you could tell the day and time by the faces in her front window. Two small ones peered out as I drove up, but one disappeared while I parked. A few seconds later a tiny girl pushed open the front door, narrowly missed mashing herself as she tottered through it and crawled to the edge of the stoop. She sat up there, slid on her rump down the two front steps and then staggered along the sidewalk toward a beat-up Camaro crying, "Mommy!"

The second child appeared in the front door a minute later, holding Maxine's hand. Maxine waved to me and helped the toddler down the steps while her mother, who had just parked behind me, got out and began throwing things off the child seat in the back of a Dodge Dart painted five different colors.

"Hi, Honey," Maxine said, and put her face up.

"Brought you some veggies." I kissed her and carried the bag inside while she walked the babbling child to her mother.

"There," she said, coming back in. "Done for the day! Oh, that Brittany—the first kid that ran out by herself?—she knows no fear! She's two months younger than Brianna, the one I just helped down the steps, but she's already figured out how to open the screen door and get down those steps. I'm gonna have to rig up a kid-proof latch so I can have fresh air in here." She peered in the sack. "Oh, that wonderful lettuce. And peas, good, even my little kids like those. How about a cup of coffee?"

"I better not. I need to get home and start the grill. Where's Eddy?" Her foster son was beginning to occupy a slot in my life that seemed to have been saved for a kid brother.

"Here I am," he said, crawling out from behind the couch. He hid there sometimes when the little girls got too demanding. Eddy was eight and a half but looked younger because he stopped growing for a while, the year before last, after his father killed all the rest of his family. Lately he'd been eating and sleeping better, but sometimes he still kind of tuned out. Anyway he was with Maxine now, the best luck a bad-luck kid can have.

He came over and put his arms around my leg. "I can sit a minute," I told Maxine, "if you have time." I sat down and Eddy hopped in my lap without asking. He'd only started doing that a couple of months ago, and I wanted him to keep it up. I took his nose in my thumb and forefinger and wiggled it gently a couple of times, and he said softly, "Kin I see the cuffs?"

I've always liked being a cop, but when Eddy came into my life it got better because he thought it was terrific. He loved my handcuffs, my gun and my badge; they were the first things that roused him out of that awful frozen silence where he spent so many months. I didn't let him handle the gun yet but he could play with the cuffs and the shield all he liked. I unclipped the cuffs off the back of my pants and told him, "Okay, Mad Dog, I'm takin' you in."

He snickered a little, not quite a real giggle yet but getting there, and stuck out his puny little arms. I clipped the cuffs on and said, "There! That ought to hold you," which was ridiculous since they would fall off as soon as he let them. For some time he held his arms out carefully in front of himself, then slid them off and sat fingering the shiny metal.

Maxine sat down across from me and let out the footsore five o'clock sigh of the day-care provider. "You look extra tired," I said. "Rough day?"

"Oh, no, it's just—I talked to Patsy today and you know how it is. She always kind of gets me going." Patsy was her daughter. She was blind. She lived at the School for the Deaf and Blind in Faribault, where she worked. She made her own way just fine, but sometimes she couldn't resist playing on her mother's sympathies a little. "It's her birthday Sunday, and for some reason that always makes her depressed."

"You should go see her. Couldn't you? There's a bus in the morning, isn't there?" Maxine couldn't drive a car; she had holes in her peripheral vision.

"Yeah, but that long ride both ways is not so good for Eddy. And then there's nothing for him to do down there. I mean there's a playground, but strange kids, you know—" Eddy wasn't sociable yet.

"Leave him with me. Us. We're both going to be home the whole weekend, working on the place."

"Well, but you're so busy—"

"He can help pick beans and peas; he's good at that. You remember how to pick stuff in the garden, don't you?" He had the cuffs off, playing with them; he nodded absently and gave me his almost-smile. His face couldn't quite make the jump all the way into happiness yet, but his eyes had that wet, bright look that meant he was feeling pretty good.

"There, see, it's all set." I looked at Maxine. "What?"

"Oh, I hate to just dump on Trudy when she has so much to do."

"We won't dump on her. I'll ask her right now." I dialed my cell phone and she answered with traffic noise all around. "Can you hear me all right?" Another inane thing to say on cell phones.

"Just about. What's up?"

"I'd like to have Eddy come out and stay with us this weekend so Maxine could go see Patsy for her birthday. Is that all right with you?"

"Uhh . . . sure, I guess so. Eddy's good in the garden and that's where I'll be."

"There," I said when I hung up, "it's all settled. I'll come get you in the morning and take you to the bus, and then Eddy can come on home with me." I looked down into his pale, wincing little face that was just beginning to dare to live again and asked him, "You want to learn how to put up hay?"

"Okay," Eddy said. One-word answers from Eddy equal a speech from anybody else. Maxine and I smiled happily at each other. "I'm gonna let you out of jail now, pardner." I took back the cuffs and put him down. "Be ready in the morning, okay?"

Maxine said, "Oh, Jakey, thanks."

I smiled into her strange eyes, one green and one brown, and said, "We'll enjoy having him. See you in the morning." I drove home whistling. Maxine and I had lost each other after social services took me away from her when I was nine. I found her again by accident a couple of years ago. Since then we've stayed in close touch, because you can't expect to get that lucky twice.

I had chicken marinating and roasting ears ready for the grill by the time Trudy got home. "Welcome to my country estate," I said as she walked into our chaotic kitchen.

"Why, thank you," she said, putting her purse away. "What do you call it, Wrecks R Us?"

The walls were up, but not drywalled yet. Most of the floor had the first layer down, raw plywood. In the corner where the cellar door would soon go, anyone could plainly see that our plumbing and wiring were brand new. Every surface in the kitchen had been stripped of anything but the cutting boards, bowls, baskets and knives we were using to process a steady stream of garden produce.

I poured two glasses of white wine, admiring how incredibly elegant jug wine becomes in stemmed glasses on the drainboard, alongside the rubber gloves. I held them up to the light and said, "This is a modest little white wine, but I think you'll be amused by its chutzpah. Ms. Hanson, you are not to set foot in the garden area. We're going to sit in those chairs by the front of the house while I tell you the sad story of my day and you help me cool down and get over it."

"Wait," she said, "long drive." She went in the bathroom, came out and stood by the kitchen table and drank half her glass of wine. She set it down on the butcher block with a little click and said, "Friday afternoon traffic truly sucks. Fill 'er up. Now, you were saying?"

We went out and sat in the shade while I told her how a jury of his peers had turned Big Bad Benny loose. She was outraged. "What do you think? They just didn't pay attention? I was afraid while I was talking that they weren't exactly following my part."

"No, you did fine; the charts were wonderful." (She did and they were but nobody really gets DNA except scientists.) "We just didn't have enough, I guess. We could never quite put him at the scene of the killing. With Dale, we had his DNA on the right gun, and her credit card in his wallet. We had Benny all around those places, but we couldn't quite put him right there."

"I wonder how he did that?" She sipped, put her glass down, stretched and said irrelevantly, "God, it's nice here, isn't it? It's worth all the hassle, isn't it? To live here?"

"I'm glad to hear you say so. Sometimes lately—"

"Don't say it. I know what I've been like lately." She sipped some more wine. "I just get tired sometimes, you know? But I wouldn't trade this place for any place else I've ever seen on earth."

I said, "Amen," and we touched glasses.

Trudy kicked her shoes off, tucked her feet under herself and said, "What I started to say was, why do you think the second case was so hard to prove? Benny Niemeyer never seemed particularly clever to me—"

"To put it conservatively."

"So how do you think he managed to cover his tracks so well?"

"See, but that's what's so damn frustrating; it doesn't seem to me he covered them at all! He bragged about the crime to Kylee Mundt and Brandi Bernauer and oh, who else, those Schmitt boys who testified at Dale's trial and that Thai dishwasher who disappeared—he said watch our smoke, man, me and Dale we're gonna jack a car, get our names in the papers! He told Rosie where the body was, damn it. It's just a piss cutter we didn't get to use that—"

"Be careful, lover. You're not cooling down; you're heating up."

"You're right." I sipped my wine. "I'm not gonna talk about it anymore. Hell with it. If I let Benny Niemeyer spoil my nice Friday night, that's one more crime he gets away with." I drained my glass. "You mind making a salad? I'll cook the chicken."

The corn and chicken fit fine on the grill, which was wedged into a tight space on the porch between garden tools, buckets and boots on one side, and two big coolers full of fresh vegetables on the other. Aesthetically we were still a few cards short of a full deck in our dream home, but we had a new roof on the whole house, and good insulation. Compared to last summer, when we were living in a tent in the yard, or the winter before that when we nearly froze, we were becoming almost mainstream.

We ate outside, of course, at the picnic table under the biggest oak. "This corn is just right," Trudy said.

"Best I ever ate." I slathered butter on my second ear.

"I bet you say that every year, don't you?" Trudy took another one too.

"Sure, because it's always true." In Minnesota in August, there's fresh sweet corn and then there's everything else.

We were lingering over the last of the wine when the familiar *pock-eta-pock* of Ozzie Sullivan's ancient Chrysler Imperial sounded in the driveway. When he finally got the engine to turn off I yelled, "Back here, Oz," and he walked around our cars and came over to the table saying, "How'd you know it was me?" We all laughed. Ozzie and I have been talking about adjusting the timing chain on his Chrysler as long as we've known each other. We'll get to it one of these years.

"Well, say," he said, settling on the far end of my bench, "I got a proposition."

"Quick, get the calculator," I told Trudy.

"No, this one's easy. Dan got that great deal he's been telling you about on the drywall for your upstairs rooms."

"Ah. Good for Dan." We were supposed to furnish the materials on this house job, but what usually happened was, Dan Sullivan found the best deals and I paid for them. Ozzie's brother had an uncanny nose for a bargain.

"Well, so, we could put in your walls this weekend. But the trouble is, I just finished the second cutting on the hayfield across the road there. So my question is, you wanna run the baler tomorrow so I can help Dan finish off your bedrooms?" Our construction deal was pay as you go, and as usual, Ozzie was trying to work me a little harder on the barter end so he and Dan could get in some building hours, for which I paid cash.

"I could do that. I guess. If you tell me all the baler's secrets." Most of Ozzie's farm equipment dated back to the proud early days of the John Deere Company.

"No sweat," he said. "The baler's easy."

"I bet." I told him about my promised run to town in the morning.

"No problem. Hay won't be dry enough to bale till after nine o'clock."

After he left we sat listening to the soft calls of mourning doves while the sun went down behind the neighbors' windbreak. As the first stars came out I asked Trudy, "What's red and white and greasy all over?"

"What?"

"These paper plates, which I'm about to throw in the garbage."

"Aren't picnics great? I'll wash the salad bowl."

"Okay, and it will take me three minutes to clean the grill. And then if you'll meet me upstairs I'll show you how to play a new game I just invented."

"A game?" Three glasses of wine had allowed her to forget all about traffic; her eyes had a nice bright shine. "Am I supposed to ask what it's called?"

"It's a variation on farming called, 'Who's Got the Part that Fits Here?'"

"Oh, jeez." She giggled all the way into the house. On the porch she gave me a bump with her hip and said, "Actually, that grill could wait until morning, couldn't it?"

13

The phone rang while I was getting ready to go to town the next morning. "Oh, Jake, good, I caught you," Maxine said. "Listen, honey, I want to save you a trip to town because I'm not going to be able to go."

"What happened?"

"Well, Bo Dooley brought Nelly here about four o'clock this morning, said he was sorry to come so early but there's some drug surveillance thing he's been working on that's got, you know, stuff *happening*. He seemed kind of excited, and I didn't want to slow him down so I just took her and put her to bed. But I certainly don't expect you and Trudy—"

"Maxine. Hang on a minute. Just—hang on." I put the phone against my chest and walked to the bathroom, stood behind Trudy while she brushed her teeth and said, "Say no if you want to."

"To what?" It came out bubbly. I told her. She spit thoughtfully and said, "I don't know. I have a ton of work to do." She met my eyes in the mirror. "You want to do it for her, don't you?" She smiled suddenly, reached over, and took the phone out of my hand and said, "Maxine? You go ahead and go, hear me? No, I mean it. Eddy and Nelly play so well together. It's no more trouble to have them both. Don't even think about it. See you tomorrow night."

"You're a good person," I said, taking the phone back. "Thank you."

"You're welcome. I might need some help finishing up tomorrow though."

"You got it. I better hurry up and get her to the bus." Maxine was dithering by the front window when I got there, and the kids each had a duffel packed, so Maxine taped a note for Bo onto her front door and we made it to the bus depot with about a minute to spare.

Trudy was already in the garden, her hat bobbing in the corn rows, when we got back. The kids and I ate breakfast, found the hats they keep out here and the two smallest buckets on the porch and went out to the pole bean frame. Eddy liked to get inside it and pick beans from underneath. One result of the horror that wiped out his family was that he felt safer in small, enclosed spaces. I showed Nelly the right size beans to pick and set her up on the outside with an extra bucket to stand on if she wanted to reach the top. By ten o'clock I was across the road baling hay.

I was a second-year hay farmer now, and had pretty well conquered my fear and loathing of the job. Except that it's hot, dusty work, and the chaff gets down your neck and sticks to your sweat and itches, and the sharp ends of bales give you a rash and the pollen makes your nose swell shut and your eyes water, there is not that much to hate about haying, if you disregard the noise and the sunburn.

By lunchtime I had finished baling what Ozzie had cut, and walked across the road. The Sullivans came downstairs as I walked into my house, Dan saying, "Weatherman says rain late today." So after lunch they came back with the tractor and flatbed trailer, and the three of us loaded the hay bales into the barn while the kids played house on two bales at the foot of the jerky little conveyor belt.

Thunder was growling behind black clouds in the west by the time we loaded the last bales on the trailer, and the first gust drove rain hard against the roof as we drove into the barn. We left the load on the trailer because the Sullivans needed to get home and see to their stock. They were driving out of the yard and the kids and I were sprinting for the house when Bo drove in.

"Hi, Dad!" Nelly ran and jumped into his arms, wet and laughing, as he got out of his car.

"God, Jake, I'm sorry about this. Maxine should have told me; I'd have worked something else out. Trudy," he said, coming in carrying Nelly, "I owe you a big one."

"No, you don't. We all had a good day. Be careful; don't fall down the cellar." As soon as he'd admired our new wiring and plumbing she said, "But we're all tired now. We need to sit down and drink beer and Kool-Aid for a while and then eat something. Why don't you stay?"

He protested that they must get out of our way. I handed him a beer, moved a stack of towels off a chair and said, "Sit. How could you be in anybody's way in this kitchen?" As soon as we sat down, Nelly hopped on his lap and Eddy sat on mine. I met Trudy's eyes and said, "What should I do for dinner?"

"Oh . . . I've got lasagna in the oven. In half an hour you could make a salad."

"Okay. So is it all right if the kids play cards in here for a few minutes and Bo and I take a walk?"

"Sure." She cleared bowls off one corner of the table and found the cards. "Nelly, you remember how to play Crazy Eights?"

"Is that the one where you match the picture in the corner?"

"The numbers or the pictures, that's right."

"Okay. I always win, though."

She did, but Eddy didn't mind. He liked holding the cards, and doing what Nelly told him to do. He didn't expect to win anything.

Bo and I found slickers on the porch, took another beer apiece out of the cooler out there and squinched across the yard through blowing gusts of rain. In the barn, we sat on Dan Sullivan's flatbed while he told me his story.

"The call came shortly after midnight," he said, "from the night caretaker at Shady Rest. Said one of the rigs I'd asked him to watch for was backing into space forty-six. I called Darrell and he said he'd get right out there, so I went back to sleep.

"I figured it was a long shot. I spotted those two rigs the other day when I was nosing around. I hadn't had time to get anything solid. But they get a certain look, you know, kind of sloppy and maybe the awning tied on? Or a broken window." Like most good street cops, Bo usually knows more than he can quite explain.

"Darrell went out in his own car?" Darrell's usually pretty picky about where he takes his Probe.

"He's got a fishing car now. You haven't seen it?" His smile was like summer lightning, a flash and then gone. "His uncle gave him his 1972 Olds. It's okay if you're not staking out anything in a nice neighborhood. All the upholstery's shot so it's hell to sit in for long, but you know Darrell."

"Mmm. Old Iron Butt."

"Well, he just doesn't complain. So he watched this tacky old Bounder till about four o'clock in the morning and then he called me and said, 'Two visitors in the last ten minutes, better come out.' I took Nelly to Maxine's, and by the time I got to the trailer park, they were coming along every few minutes."

"Customers?"

"Dealers. Young ones, just kids. Fourteen, fifteen, most of 'em.

The best part, Jake, you know how they're dealing the stuff now? On bikes and skateboards."

"No shit? So that's what they wanted those things for."

"What?"

"Kevin's been complaining about a lot of stolen bikes and skateboards."

"Ah. It's really pretty clever, Jake. To look at them, they're just kids on playthings. They can make their deliveries in the daytime, get home in time for supper. Sit there and eat Mommy's tuna surprise as innocent as you please, I bet."

"They rode into the RV park on skateboards?"

"Mostly they ride the bike with the skateboard lashed across the handlebars. Probably get to a certain point, lock up the bike and do the rest of the route on the board."

"What about the rough stuff, I wonder? You think all these kids are packing?"

"Those two little shits we brought in had shivs in holsters under their jeans. And after we found both of those I thought the second one looked a little too contented so we stripped him and found a switchblade taped flat to his chest under his Hawaiian shirt."

"Easier than packing I guess. No ammunition to carry."

"And quieter and more accurate." He gulped the beer and swallowed, while thinking. "Right now we've only got the two that were there when we decided to go in after the operators, but I think by Monday they'll give up some more names."

"The dealers in the trailer, you know them?"

"No. I don't think they're from around here."

"What do they say?"

"Lotta bullshit, so far. I woulda liked to wait, you know, set something up, maybe a sting, but the setup looked so temporary—they didn't even have their levelers down."

"How many kids did you see?"

"Six, before the two we got, and Darrell said two before I got there. So ten? We didn't know if that might be the whole crew and they were getting ready to leave. So soon as we were sure what they were doing we called for a couple of squads and went in."

"Was it pretty Wild West?"

"Not really. We figured there couldn't be more than two or three people in that Bounder and we were right. Man and wife team, actually."

"Oh? You see their marriage license?"

"Never thought of that." His lightning smile flashed again. "Vince Greeley brought along that big hooligan tool they call the Key, and his body bunker. He gets his jollies on the night shift, doesn't he?"

"Vince does like action. The arrests go all right?"

"Smooth as silk. The back door on the RV looked like it was rigged for a quick exit, so Darrell and I waited back there and Greeley and Longworth went in the front. Sure enough, soon as Greeley hit the door with the hooligan and yelled, "Police!" the dealers jumped out the back. It was almost like we held out the handcuffs and they stuck their arms in."

"You got anything on 'em yet?"

"His name is Frankie LeFever, kind of a biker type. He's taken a couple previous falls for dealing. I asked him, 'You want to help yourself out?' and he said yes, but then I had the other three there, I couldn't really take him aside, you know, so his usefulness for a sting is pretty well blown."

"But he'll give you names?"

"Yeah. He started playing cute with me, trying to raise the offer a little, so I just booked him on possession and told him to think about it. He'll do the best for himself that he can. The woman's pretty beat up. Frankie has tattoos on both arms that say 'Iron Man,' looks like he's been using some of his iron on her. Casey showed up with the big van so we had a cage for the couple—that was handy. Darrell and I rode in with Greeley and Longworth, each of us in back with one of the little bike riders."

"So, you been in booking all day?"

"Well, and pulling up records on Frankie. One for dealing pot in Buffalo, one in Mankato for meth. I spent some time in interrogation with the kids before we released them to their parents. Once we found both of his knives, the kid I rode in with was all charm. He's been doing this for a while so he's pretty savvy—we might get some help out of him. You'll see what we got by close of business Monday." He flattened our beer cans and tossed them in the trash. "I think I kept you from your family long enough."

"Yeah, we better find out how the card game is going."

After dinner Bo washed and I dried and then he carried Nelly, asleep on his shoulder, out to his car.

"Eddy needs a shower," I told Trudy, "but what do you think?" He was blinking fast, and he kept sliding sideways in his chair.

"Let's just sponge him off." In five minutes, he was asleep on the parlor sofa, and ten minutes later we were upstairs snoring like Eddy.

We were up before sunrise Sunday morning, but we barely had our jeans on when the Sullivans drove into the yard and yelled up, "Okay to start?" Ozzie must have really needed that cash.

"Fine," I said, leaning out the window, "but I can't be your gofer today. I gotta help Trudy before she disappears into the cucumber patch."

"Do what you gotta do," Dan said. "We can't take any risks with the pie lady."

So for another long, sweaty morning, Eddy followed us around our humid, incredibly productive garden, mostly hunkering in patches of leafy shade humming to himself. Trudy and I weeded and trimmed and plucked, and by noon we had a clean garden and four bushel baskets full of produce ready to send home with the Sullivans.

"This is great," Trudy muttered, washing carrots and radishes at the hose. "Now we don't have to make deliveries." She caught them as they came out of our house door and loaded them up, then ran after them just as they were starting the car. "Wait, wait, you each get a bucket of sweet corn, too!" She got big smiles for those.

"Hot damn," she said, coming back to the garden, "do you realize what this means, my sweet lover?"

"What?" She looked so incandescent, I thought maybe she was thinking about blankets in the hayloft again.

"This very afternoon, Jake Hines, you and I are going to pick every zucchini in this garden and run it through the Cuisinart and into the freezer."

"Oh," I said. "That'll be great, won't it?"

We were mopping up our green-speckled kitchen at four in the afternoon when Maxine phoned from the bus depot. I offered to come get her for dinner in the country but she said, "Oh, Jakey, I'm tired and I bet you are, too. Why don't you just bring me my boy and we'll do it another time?"

So I made the trip to town while Trudy took a shower and heated the leftover lasagna. I was yawning so hard by the time I finished it, I just threw the paper plates in the trash and shut up about red and white and greasy.

14

Coming through the tall doors of the Government Center the next morning, I heard Rosie Doyle say, "Ah, here's the boss now." I looked up and saw her coming down the broad staircase beside Ray Bailey, who looked like a calamity in search of a place to happen.

I waited at the bottom. "What?"

Ray said, "Caretaker says there's a body in Aldrich Park."

"Just that, no details?"

"Didn't sound like he wanted to look real close."

"Ah. Well, listen, I have to get our meeting started right away. I've got an appointment at nine. Call me as soon as you know anything, will you?"

"Gotcha."

I found everybody else around the table, Kevin and his three Property Crimes detectives, Bo and Darrell from Ray's section and LeeAnn Speer, the steno for the whole section who comes to the Monday morning meeting so she'll have some idea of what's going on the rest of the week.

I gave them a heads-up on the call Ray and Rosie were out on, and Bo reviewed the arrest of the meth dealers and their delivery boys.

"Mom 'n' Pop Meth," Kevin said. "I love it."

Bo turned his ice-blue stare on Kevin, waited a couple of ticks and said, "The motorhome is not a lab. It was loaded with product but they make it someplace else." Bo thought Kevin fooled around too much and should grow up. Kevin joked more when Bo was around because he resented Bo's attitude, called Bo a WALT, his acronym for Wrapped A Little Tight.

They were two good detectives with different styles, so I was trying to stay out of the line of fire till they got over it.

Darrell said, "Also, these little turds on bikes are so young, you have to think these lab people are recruiting through school sports programs. Or Parks and Recreation."

"Or the juvenile court system," Bo said, interested. "Worth checking out, yeah." Darrell looked gratified. I had never thought to pair him with Bo before, but it seemed to be working for both of them.

"So all those skateboard heists last spring, that wasn't just for fun, huh?" Kevin said. "It was organized?"

"Maybe," I said. "Pull up the report forms from that streak, will you, Kevin? Make us a list of the makes and license numbers on the bikes, and markings on the boards. See if you can match any of the stuff we brought in with the kids. You'll have to charge the adults today, right?" I asked Bo.

"Darrell's working on it. The male in the RV is a parole violator. We can hold him on that while we take the woman to court."

"And the kids, what do you have in mind?"

"We released them to their parents Saturday with the proviso that they show up here this morning. If I can establish that it's the first time for both of them and they test clean and I get enough cooperation, I'm not inclined to charge them, just get a commitment for counseling and some follow-up with HHS. Okay with you?"

"If you're sure they're not using. How about a warning about a folder in your drawer and all hell breaking loose if you see 'em again, though, huh? Did you—" My cell phone rang. It was Ray. "The meeting you mentioned at nine, that's with Milo, right?"

"Yes."

"Better get him on the phone and tell him to meet you here instead."

When Ray finished talking I told the seven people around the table, "Okay, go ahead with what you've got to do right now and we'll finish this later today." I caught Milo just as he was leaving his building.

Pokey's ragtop Jeep and the department Crown Vic Ray was using were lined up at the curb by Aldrich Park. Milo and I pulled in behind them and walked over to where Ray and Rosie stood looking down into the abstract concrete hills and valleys of the skateboard pit.

Pokey was down there, bent over the body of a man sprawled on his back, with his head propped awkwardly on a skateboard.

"Benny Niemeyer went skating?"

"Some time after closing last night, I guess," Ray said. "And that's not the most amazing fact I have to tell you."

"Oh? What is?"

"Looks like Benny went up for an ollie all alone out here in the middle of the night with the lights off, and made a bad landing that broke his head."

"That Benny," Milo said. "He always was a thrill seeker, wasn't he?"

15

A ramp curved into the skate-park pit from the end of the iron railing. The four of us walked down together. I squatted next to the body and said, "Hey, Pokey."

"Oh ho, Jake Hines in person." He sat back on his heels and wiped sweat out of his eyes onto his shirtsleeve. "This fella ran outa luck last night I guess."

"Looks like it." The top of Benny's forehead sported a big, bloody goose-egg swelling. Both eyes were black and swollen nearly shut, and his poor nose, broken by Chrissie in the garage Friday night, looked as if it had been knocked even further off center in this fall. His clothes were soaked with the blood that was pooled around him on the cement floor of the pit.

"What time last night, do you think?" I can never resist asking, maybe because he never wants to say.

"Ah, well—" He screwed up his foxy little face and squinted thoughtfully up at the bright sky. "Never mind about when; what you oughta ask is why."

"Why what?"

"Ain't that what I said?" I stared at him till he said, "Big strong bozo like this, little head bump and he falls over dead. How come?"

His cell phone rang. He pulled it off his belt and held a brief conversation, mostly grunts on his end.

He replaced the phone looking pleased. "There now, ain't very often you get everything you ask for, hah? But that Stuart is very good, smart guy." Stuart is the head doc at Hampstead County Medical Clinic. "Told him this autopsy oughta be done right away on account of no acute trauma showing, and he cleared a room."

"You mean you're going to do it this afternoon?"

"Sooner! Soon as hearse gets here and carries body over there. Some action, hah?"

"Well, fantastic—but now, Ray's got to take pictures and we need to do a walk-around, take some measurements in case—"

"You can't mark spot, draw picture with chalk?"

"Sure, I'll do that," Rosie said. "I've got some chalk."

"Sure!" He beamed at her. "And we'll get fingerprints, blood samples, whatever you need over there at lab."

"But the photos—"

"Take 'em now! Listen, Jake—" he had to keep his gloves clean so he nudged me with his elbow and then held one bony finger aloft till he saw he had my full attention "—this fella's head ain't hurt that bad. You listening? Need to get inside, do some tests quick—" he looked down at Benny's ungainly body sprawled on the hot cement "—some funny business here I think."

"So you're saying—"

"Do sleuth stuff quick and let me take body. Coupla days, maybe I make your life a lot easier, yah?"

"With what? What are you looking for?"

He spread both hands in front of him and rocked them in unison. "Don't know till I see, hah?"

"Swell." The classic disclaimer. Everybody off the hook but the hapless detective. "Ray, you got a camera with you?"

"Sure, it's with the crime-scene kit. We're not gonna call BCA on this, huh?"

"It's a very screwy accident, but I don't see any way to call it a homicide yet, do you?"

"No. Okay, I'll get pictures, Rosie outlines the body, we'll do a walk-around and then what, string some crime-scene tape, I guess, huh?"

"Fine," I said. "And then, Ray, you'll follow Pokey to the lab for the autopsy, right?"

"Guess I'll have to. What's his hurry, I wonder? Hell's he thinking, Ebola or something?"

"I don't think so. Something about not thinking the head wound is very serious."

"The guy is dead. How serious do we need?"

"I don't know. There's really no way to close this park, is there?"

"Nope. No fence. I asked dispatch for one patrolman to help us keep the kids away till we're done," Ray said.

"That gonna be enough?"

"Well, with the tape, we can make it work," he said. August vacations had made us even more shorthanded than usual, so the chief had asked us to lay off asking the squads for any more than we had to.

"And you'll take a good look around the body, huh?"

"Oh, yeah."

"Doesn't look real promising, though, does it?" Rosie peered around at the smooth white cement valleys.

"A skateboard and a lot of blood," Ray said. "But we'll take a look."

"That skateboard," I said. "Let's be extra careful with that thing, huh?"

"Well, sure," Rosie said. "You're thinking it's—"

"The only weapon in sight," I said. "If this turns out not to be an accident."

"Hey, there's the TV truck," Milo said. "You want to talk to them, Jake?"

"Why don't you do that?"

"What's his name, do you remember? The photographer?"

"Doug Prentiss."

He wrote it down. "So, we're calling this an accident, or not?"

Ray and I looked at each other. Ray said, "Till after the autopsy let's call it an incident."

"Stick with me, then, will you, Jake?" Milo said. "It's Benny Niemeyer for sure, isn't it?" I walked up with him to where the white truck with KORN TV lettered on the side sat at the curb. "I couldn't hear—what did Pokey say about cause of death?"

"Said it looks like a fall," I said.

Milo looked at me to see if I was kidding and said, "Well, duh."

I shrugged. "That's all he said."

"Doug, how are you?" Milo said, giving the TV photographer a big smile. Milo was getting the hang of elective office.

"Hi. I'm handling this solo," Doug said. He chewed nervously on a pencil, all the interview equipment he had besides a piece of scratch paper folded in half. "So tell me in short words, what's going on?"

"We just started the investigation, but I'll give you what we've got and you can check with my office after three for an update." Milo waited while Doug checked the light and lined up his shot. When the red light came on he repeated the little I'd just told him in three different ways, naming Benny Niemeyer and adding all the boiler-plate about RPD working hard to determine the cause of death and the county attorney's office keeping an eye on developments.

"So, it's not an accident?"

"We don't know that yet."

"Why are you here, then?"

Milo glanced over at me, standing out of camera range. I raised my eyebrows. He turned back to the camera and said sternly, "Benny Niemeyer was recently acquitted of the murder of Shelley Gleason, so naturally my office is interested." He waited a couple of ticks and added, "It's an odd coincidence." It didn't make much sense but it satisfied Doug Prentiss, who was mainly concerned with making sure he got a good picture.

When it was over we walked back to our cars. "Well, so," Milo said, looking down into the pit where Pokey, Ray and Rosie were working, "adjustment time, huh?" Seeing Benny dead had wiped away his remorse over last week's verdict, and the TV interview had restored his usual neurotic intensity. "At least we can forget about looking for anything more to pin on Benny."

"To my way of thinking," I said, "we just traded a small job for a big one."

"You think putting Benny back in the slammer would have been a small job? It didn't seem like it last week."

"It could have been if we'd included the gun." Our fiercest arguments, all during the preparation for the trial, had been over my insistence that we include the .22 Ruger that Winnie found under the car. "A convicted felon in possession of a firearm—no way he coulda beat that."

"We didn't want to confuse the jury," Milo said, rubbing his knuckle against his forehead where apparently his promised hangover hurt worst.

"Right," I said. "We certainly didn't want to risk confusing the jury, did we?"

"Well, now," he said, going stiff, "what's this, a fit of twenty-twenty hindsight?"

"Maybe. If we'd put him in jail where he belonged he'd be alive now."

"I don't know what's eating you." He opened his car door, smoothed his hair in back and looked at his watch. "As far as I'm concerned, finding Benny Niemeyer dead just means one more nuisance is off the street."

"Except now we've got to figure out how he died, and then if Pokey's mojo is working we'll maybe have to find out who killed him."

"If by any chance you do that," he said across his car door as I walked away, "try to bring me some proof, will you?"

I guess he couldn't resist it, but he wiped out all the good feeling that had developed between us on Friday night, and made me feel like fool for ever opening up to him. I got in my pickup and slammed the door, started the motor fast and gunned past him, throwing gravel onto his car. It was a childish move and I damn near paid for it at the end of the block when two elderly women in a Buick Riviera pulled serenely across the intersection in front of me, talking to each other, oblivious. I slammed on the brakes, made a squealing noise and left rubber on the street. The women in the car never looked at me, but Milo, of course, watched contentedly.

Back at the station, the chief's door was standing open, so I walked past Lulu while she was busy at the copier, sat down in front of his desk and described the body in the pit. He rocked back in his big chair and fixed me with his pop-eyed stare. "You don't look like you think it's an accident."

"A longtime hood decides to take up recreational skateboarding in the middle of the night? What are the odds? Does PK do any boarding?"

"What? Oh, uh . . . he used to. Not so much anymore. My son is changing. He's gonna be a senior next year and lately I caught him once or twice reading a book." Frank had said more than once that parenting his only son through adolescence had made police work look easy. "Something you want to ask him?"

"All of a sudden we got skateboards up the yin-yang, Chief. For a month last spring they got stolen every day. Now they're apparently being used for drug deliveries, and this morning there's one down in the skateboard park with Benny Niemeyer. Like it or not I gotta learn more about skateboarding, seems like."

"What about this meth business—" he picked up a copy of a report "—that Bo found in the trailer park?"

"Well. We're just getting started on it, got four suspects to question and haven't found the lab yet. Benny Niemeyer picked a damn inconvenient day to die."

"Why should he change his modus operandi right at the end? You haven't asked BCA for help yet?"

"Waiting to hear what Pokey says after the autopsy."

"Did he agree it doesn't look like an accident?"

"Pokey was being an inscrutable Ukrainian wiseass this morning. But he sure hopped right on the autopsy. I expect I'll have something soon."

I went along the hall and stuck my head in Kevin Evjan's door. He was scrolling through records, stopping occasionally to print one, while he listened to an old Patsy Cline tune, drank coffee and ate a doughnut and cooled his stockinged feet in front of a tiny fan clipped to a corner of his desk. Kevin takes pleasure in multitasking.

"Your feet are hot?"

"It's August." He kept his eyes on the screen.

"Thanks for clearing that up. You're finding stolen skateboard records?"

"Indeed yes. Piles." He showed me.

"I have to interrupt you for another couple of jobs. Bring a notebook, and come into my office."

He gave an exaggerated sigh, put the back of his left hand against his forehead and said, "Oh, God, the pressure."

"Today," I said, walking away. Bo's right, I suppose, that Kevin fools around too much. But he's got every reason to be cheerful. He got all the best genes from his Norwegian father and Irish mother so he looks like a Minnesota poster boy, blond and handsome. He's always been teacher's pet and now every woman he meets wants to take him home. With luck like Kevin's I might try a little clowning myself.

"Whazzup?" He brought his coffee, crossed his legs comfortably.

"The two guns that surfaced in the Gleason killing, the Sig Sauer that killed Shelley Gleason and the little twenty-two Ruger revolver we found under the Ford, they were part of a larger heist, weren't they?"

"Sure. At the Aldrich house."

"Okay. Do I remember right, that it was kind of a strange conglomeration of stuff?"

"For sure. There was the Sig Sauer and a Glock twenty-one, both well-made practical handguns for somebody who really wants to knock something down. Then, lessee, a set of dueling pistols, no use in a fight but elegant antiques with plenty of value to a collector. And then the Ruger. We couldn't figure out the choices."

"Maybe because that's what there was?"

"No, oh shit, you should see the roomful of guns they came out of—that Aldrich is a real collector. So Andy and I kept asking, with everything to choose from, why would anybody pick that Ruger? Not valuable like the dueling pistols, quite a bit less powerful than the Sig Sauer and the Glock."

"Andy Pitman answered the complaint?"

"Yes."

"Okay, and the other things, the antiques?"

"Four pieces of antique silver, a teapot and three trays. They showed me some pieces they said matched the ones that were stolen—decoration all over, very elaborate."

"And?"

"Well, obviously I don't know as much about silver as I do about guns, but again, out of a mansion that's loaded with treasures, those items seemed like odd choices."

"You've never retrieved any of the stuff, right?"

"Till those two guns surfaced in the Gleason case."

"Okay. I want to see copies of all your records on that burglary, including your interviews with—who'd you talk to, Nelson Aldrich himself?"

"Some. His daughter handled most of it. She said he got tired easy so she found the insurance records and all."

"She lives there too?"

"Uh-huh. And her husband. Peabody, his name is, James Peabody. Man, you ever want to meet somebody truly cool and upper-crusty, Jake, there's your guy. Got one of those Eastern seaboard accents—kinda George Plimpton? Right off the top shelf."

"I'll save him for a special treat. Lemme see the records ASAP."

"No problem. Where are you going with this?"

"Fishing. Benny's death doesn't exactly look like an accident so I thought I'd take another—"

"Wait, wait! Benny Niemeyer is dead?"

"Nobody told you?"

"No! Goddamn, what's the use working at the cop shop if nobody tells you the news? Is that the call Ray and Rosie went out on?"

He was making so much noise that Andy Pitman, walking by, stuck his head in the door and said, "What's happening?"

"You know what, guys," I said, aware of time passing, "I need to bring everybody up to speed and assign some jobs, so let's not waste time going over this more than once. Kevin, get those records and meet me at Ray's table in fifteen minutes. You too, Andy, I'll see you there." I walked out to LeeAnn Spears's desk and said, "Who's here right now?"

She looked up at her board. "Clint Maddox, Andy Pitman, Kevin Evjan. Let's see. Rosie and Ray are still at the park, huh? And Bo and Darrell are over at the jail talking to those four suspects they brought in over the weekend."

"Call Maddox and the two in the jail and tell them I need them at the big table in fifteen minutes."

When we were all together I told them about finding Benny's body in the park.

"Another skateboard," Bo said. "Goddamn."

"Yes. How are you doing with your suspects down there?"

"I'm mostly concentrating on the woman's deal right now because she's gotta go to court this afternoon."

"Right. What are you asking for?"

"Well, the names of their other delivery boys, of course, and the location of the lab or labs, names of any other dealers. Bulk suppliers for their acetone, rock salt, all that shit."

"And you're offering what?"

"Reduction to fourth-degree selling."

"She going for it?"

"She's pretty vague. I'm not sure her brain's exactly tuned in."

"The delivery boys want to help," Darrell Betts said. "But they don't seem to know much beyond this one dealer and their customer lists."

"But I'm talking to LeFever about helping himself," Bo said. "I sent word to Milo to come over and parley."

"He get back to you?"

"He was busy in Aldrich Park—well, you know. But he sent word ten minutes ago that he'll be over here soon." Bo looked at his watch. "I think if I stay on this—"

"Okay. While you're at it find out about these damn boards, okay? How'd the boys get them, were they furnished or did they swipe their own? Why did Benny have one? Was he delivering? Okay," I said, as Bo looked at his watch again, "go. Keep in touch." Darrell followed Bo out of the room in lockstep, pleased to be working with the big kahuna.

"Pokey's doing the autopsy right now," I told the others. "Ray's observing. Before we go on, Kevin, we should notify, uh, somebody, about Benny's death. Can you spare one person to look for his next of kin?"

"Somebody who'll admit to being related, you mean? I guess— uh, Clint, can you?" These days Clint Maddox gets most of the jobs requiring what Kevin calls "sensi-fucking-tivity." He moved up to detective division just before Lou French retired, and took over his chores as Uncle Kleenex, the guy who takes most of the calls from weeping women.

"Sure," Maddox said. "Must be somebody. He grew up here, didn't he?"

"Yup," I said, "and he's been getting arrested since he was about eight, so there's plenty of documentation. I'll give you everything I got on him for the trial."

"Anything else?" Kevin said. "Remember we don't do windows."

"We'll see about that. Now, back to the guns. Who investigated the Aldrich burglary?"

"I did," Andy Pitman said. He's the other recent recruit in my team, famous in the department for the big difference he made in a very tough neighborhood while he was in the People Oriented Policing program.

"If Andy handled the call how come you know so much about the Aldrich family, Kevin?"

"Because Andy came back to the station after the first interview and said, 'Man, if I was an insurance agent I'd sure be taking a close look at this burglary. It's a very odd bunch of stuff, and there's really no telling how long it's been gone.' So we went back and talked to them together."

"And?"

"By then the claims guy was there and everybody was smiling. Everybody but Nelson Aldrich; he still wanted his guns back. But it was obvious the Aldrich family was such a good account the agent wasn't going to question anything, and I could see that Helen—that's the daughter—was mainly concerned about having her father so upset, she wanted everything over as quietly as possible. And I mean, obviously the Aldriches don't have to pull any nickel-and-dime swindles on their insurance company, so we got out of there and filed the sucker and forgot about it, till two of the guns turned up in the Gleason case."

"Did you re-interview the Aldriches at that time?"

"No. We were going to but Milo kept saying the stolen guns were small potatoes compared to the other stuff you had on Dale and Benny, remember? So we put it off and in the end you didn't use the gun charge at all."

"Uh-huh." I didn't want to go over that again. "This the file?"

"Yup."

"Good. Keep after that match on the skateboard records, will you?"

I went back to my office and read through the record of the Aldrich burglary. Besides the feeling of mismatch in the stolen guns, the other thing that jumped out at me was the fact that the time of the theft wasn't known. Nelson Aldrich, the report said, had taken a guest into his trophy room to show him the dueling pistols, and discovered them missing from the case where they were always kept. Looking around for them, he began to notice other empty spots in other cases. With each gun he found missing, he became more upset, and soon he had enlisted the help of the housekeeper and his daughter in an inventory of the whole house. The two women agreed that three trays and a teapot were missing from the dining room sideboard. They were formal items, heavy silverplate, seldom used, and like the guns they might have been missing for some time.

My phone rang. Ray said, "Jake? I think you ought to come over here and let Pokey show you a couple of things."

16

Ray is not given to frivolous impulses, so I didn't argue. It was no big deal anyway; Rutherford is growing fast, but most of the core facilities are still within a few blocks of each other, so I was parking my pickup in front of the Hampstead County clinic in ten minutes. Lab number three, Ray had said, straight down the hall from the front doors.

Pokey and Dr. Stuart were in their weird OR drag, salmon-colored plastic shrouds with matching booties and shower caps. Ray stood half a step back from the tall steel table in his usual nondescript clothing, filling his little spiral notebook with tiny neat script.

Benny was naked on the cold steel table with his body cavity wide open, most of his important organs in containers on a wheeled wagon nearby. The skin of his scalp had been peeled and pulled down over his face, and they had cut out the crescent of bone that allowed them to lift out his brain. X-rays of his head and shoulders were clipped to the lighted view box on the wall.

"Here comes head gumshoe," Pokey crowed as I walked in. "Gonna deduce right away what to think about dead guy, I betcha."

He learned his English, along with several other languages, in the course of a long impromptu walk he took across Europe to flee a work camp in the USSR. He was still short on articles but adding inventive combinations of old and new American slang almost daily.

"Doctors." I nodded to Stuart, who stood, gray-haired, slender and dignified, across the table from Pokey. "What's up?"

"Well, as you can see in these X-rays," Dr. Stuart said, moving to the view box, "the skull and upper parts of the axial skeleton have sustained no significant damage." He pointed. "See, there's a hairline fracture here on the frontal bone, right under the site of that swelling you saw. In other words, a good bump on the head. The parietal bone is completely intact. There's no dislocation of the sphenoid or temporal bones, as you might expect from great downward force at the top of the head. And the top cervical vertebrae are completely undisturbed. The nasal bone is broken; that's what caused all the bleeding."

I thought about explaining to them that Benny's nose had been broken before, but I couldn't think of a way to do it without getting into Chrissie's story, so I let it go.

"Now step back here and we'll show you—"

They showed me the crescent of the frontal bone they'd removed first. "Here's hairline crack," Pokey said, "good enough for headache maybe, but not gonna kill anybody."

"And the brain," Dr. Stuart said, "see here—" He showed me there were no bruises and no hemorrhaging. "We thought we might find a cranium full of blood, but there was none. All the blood was out front, a little from the abrasion on the forehead but most of it from the broken nose."

"Is no evidence of concussion," Pokey said.

"No cerebral edema," Stuart said.

"Okay," I said. "Tell me what you think did happen." Their plastic wrappings made crinkly noises as they turned to look at each other and back at us.

"No use speculating any further till we're done," Stuart said. "We haven't got the results of the blood work or the tox scan yet."

"Okay. Thanks for your time," I said, and the two plastic action figures nodded benignly and went back to their happy muttering.

"I just wanted you to see what they're showing me, Jake," Ray said, walking out with me, "so we're on the same page later when we get the autopsy report."

"Good idea." We stood a minute on the front step together, enjoying the bright sunshine and the fact that all our organs were inside where they belonged. Autopsies are even better than funerals for getting your priorities back in order. "One thing, Ray, I think you better bring that skateboard back with you when you come."

"Yeah, that's just what I was thinking, the accident theory is looking iffier all the time, isn't it?"

"Damn straight. And even if the skateboard didn't kill him it's the only weapon we've got."

"So you think maybe BCA—"

"I think I'm going to hand it over to Trudy and beg her to find some DNA on it that didn't come from Benny Niemeyer. Better bring back his clothes, too, you never know."

"Right. Lots of blood on the clothes, so maybe—and there's a lot of blood and tissue on the board where it hit his head. I suppose it was Benny's head, but—"

"Or where his head hit the board. We haven't completely eliminated the possibility of a fall yet, have we?"

"Haven't eliminated the goddamn tooth fairy, so far." He went back inside.

———

Darrell Betts walked in the door of the Government Center with me, smiling. He said, "Man, have I got some glossy shit to lay on you."

"My man! Come with me."

"Well!" He sat down in front of my desk and did his muscle-man settling moves, rotating his outsize neck inside his shirt collar, flexing his jaw. "Remember I told you those delivery boys were pretty interested in making a deal? Well now, this one guy, Sean Lynch, is practically begging to cooperate because otherwise his dad's gonna kill him."

"Oh? Who's his dad?"

"Guy that owns the High Times Bar."

"You've got Denny Lynch's boy down there? Aw, shit."

"He said he knew you. You like him?"

"He's a good-natured guy who works hard, is really all I know."

"Yeah, well, Denny's no saint. But he's never been into drugs so he's pissed off at Sean big-time. He told the kid, 'If you don't tell these people everything you know I'm gonna have your balls in a vise grip.' "

"So you think you might get—"

"So I brought you this list." He unfolded it, beaming.

"His customers? Darrell, didn't Bo tell you we don't go after the customers?"

"Of course. But Sean wrote this out on his own before I could stop him, and when I saw the third name on the list I asked Bo if I could show it to you." He passed it over.

I looked down the list. "Kylee Mundt?"

"Isn't she the girl that saw Benny in the Ford with Dale, that you drove us all crazy for weeks tryna find for the trial, but we never?"

"Yes. And this is the right address, Sixth Avenue Northeast."

"Oh, you really know her, huh?"

"I hardly know her at all, I just know her address very well from sending people there to try to find her. She hasn't been home or at work for over two months. Her mother claims she's out of town and she doesn't know where. But Sean delivers meth there?"

"Every week, he says."

"Okay. Let's go down and talk to Sean some more. He's been Mirandized?"

"Yup. And Denny says his lawyer's on the way, but Denny wants him to talk anyway."

"What does Sean want?"

"To get his old man off his back, mostly."

"Good. Okay if I talk to him for a few minutes?"

Darrell rolled his eyes around, surprised I asked. "Sure."

"It won't interfere with anything you've got going with him?"

"I've hardly said a word to him yet. Denny's been there."

"I understand. How old is he?"

"Sean? Fifteen."

"First offense, right?"

"Right."

I put my card in the electronic lock, we pulled the heavy steel door open and walked into the sally port, then were buzzed through the second door as the first one locked. Bo sat in the first rank of interview cubicles, leaning forward to question a gray-faced woman in a prison jumpsuit. Beyond him in the next cubicle, Denny and Sean Lynch faced each other, their family resemblance as plain as their mutual anger.

Bo said something to the woman on the other side of the glass, and got up. She looked up at him dully and withdrew into herself as he came out to where we stood. He said, "This one's about ready to go to court."

"She give you anything?"

He shrugged. "She's too scared. Keeps saying she doesn't know anything, just does as she's told."

"Might be true."

He shrugged. "Truth is pretty flexible for meth addicts."

"She's hooked?"

"Sure. Look at her face." It was gray and flaccid-looking; her checks were sunken and several teeth were missing. "I finally got her to tell me her real name, so now I've got her first arrest records, in Sioux Falls. Want to see how she looked eight years ago?" Even in the awful jail photo she was beautiful, with glossy black hair and great eyes. The woman in the cubicle looked as if she had lived thirty hard years since then. "I offered to try to get her into treatment, but she's not attracted to that; she wants more meth. What do you think about Kylee Mundt?"

"Very interesting. I know you don't like to mess with the buyers but I'd like to find out if he's been delivering to Kylee for the last two months. Will it screw up what you're doing if I talk to him?"

"No. I'm pretty well convinced the boys don't know any other dealers but these two. They were recruited by the woman—at the skate park, by the way. They both seem to have concerned parents, so I'm inclined to offer release to home supervision with no records if I get promises of counseling and follow-through."

"Good. You think LeFever's going to help you run a sting?"

"I doubt if he'll be much use for that. If I could have taken him aside at the beginning—but there were too many other people around. I figure the word is out by now on this arrest. He won't be able to make a buy for a while. Best I can do is try to get some names."

"Okay. You know," I told Darrell, "I hate interviewing in those cramped little cubicles. Why don't you bring Denny and Sean up to my office and I'll meet you there?"

"Okay. The trouble with having Denny here," Darrell said, "is he wants to do all the talking."

"I know. We'll fix that too when we get them upstairs."

I went back upstairs and placed three chairs in front of my desk. Then I closed the door so my nameplate showed, CAPTAIN JAKE HINES, CHIEF OF DETECTIVES. "Use everything you've got when you need to," the chief always says, "and remember you've got plenty."

Denny Lynch's handsome, flushed face was conflicted as he came in, wanting and not wanting to ask for favors for this son who looked so much like him. A fast-talking, funny man, a good bartender and great storyteller, he had built his bar trade around his charm and a core group of three or four dozen hard-drinking buddies whose roistering exploits were legendary.

"Denny," I said, and then, "Sean, is it? I'm Captain Hines." Sean looked defiant, hot and quick-tempered like his father but at least, I thought, not turned off.

"Jake," Denny said, "whaddya think of this crap-for-brains I got here?"

Families are the hardest. Denny wanted me to tell him his boy was going to be fine as soon as we got him over this little speed bump. At the same time, he wanted me to help him scare the kid shitless without inflicting any lasting damage. Apart from the impossibility of doing all those things at once, RPD had its own urgent needs. For starts, to find how deep Sean had crawled into this sewer, was he using, hooked on the money, getting high off the risk? This help he was so willing to give now, was it bogus or real?

"Denny and Sean," I said, "listen hard to me now, because we don't have much time. Decision time's coming up, and if we don't make this deal Sean has to go to court. You both understand the deal, right? He cooperates fully and tells us all he knows, we consider that this is his first offense and we don't even file an arrest record. You and his mother agree to total supervision and family counseling and we make this first time go away. You clear on all that?" I looked at Sean, who tried to look tough.

"Goddamn right," Denny said, "and after that he has me to deal with—"

"Okay, but first you both have me to deal with," I said. "So here's what we're gonna do. You're going down the hall with Darrell, Denny, and answer some questions he's got for you, and I'm going to talk to Sean alone for a few minutes."

"Oh, well, now," Denny said, sitting back, getting redder, "I don't know if I—I think I ought to—"

I got up and walked to the front of my desk. "Denny." I put my hand on his shoulder and squeezed a little and then a lot, enough to get through the two shots of Jack Daniel's I figured he'd awarded himself to get ready to come down here and bail out his son. "We don't have much time at all and we're dealing with some heavy shit here today, you know what I'm saying?"

He stood up with sweat on his face and nodded and walked away with Darrell, not happy but not wanting to cross me just then. Darrell would pump him for family stuff, names of siblings and his wife's first name and daytime phone, Sean's friends and hangouts and grade averages and any recent trouble in school. We didn't need any of it right now but it would come in handy later if today's deals didn't hold. One thing about police work, you get to know there's no end of useful questions.

I checked the tape in my recorder, turned it on and asked my first useful question. "Sean, you waived your right to silence, did you?"

He tried surly. "I guess."

"No. Don't guess. Decide, right now, or you go back in a cell and the deal's off."

"Jeez, come on, we already said yes."

"There isn't any 'we,' Sean. You're the only one in here with me; your daddy can't help you now. This is a grown-up game you bought into. We have very severe laws against dealing drugs in this country, and if you don't play this exactly right you could get sent away to a reformatory for a long time. Do you have any idea what that's like?"

He was watching me now, spooked and silent. I waited a couple of ticks and struck the surface of my desk hard with my fist. "Well, do you?"

He jumped and said, "No, I guess not."

"That's right, you don't. So I'm gonna tell you. You'll be sharing living space and mealtimes and an exercise yard with guys who are bigger and meaner and a lot more experienced than you are, gang members from the Twin Cities who've been on the streets for years, and they're going to look at you like so much fresh meat. Whenever they feel like it they're going to use your body for whatever gives them pleasure, and you're going to let them do it because they're going to keep you scared so shitless every minute of the day, you'll do anything to keep from getting hurt again. All I have to do is stand up and call Darrell, and you go back to jail with no deal at all. He'll book you down there and then the rest of your life is just a pile of shit."

Sean Lynch's eyes grew bright with unshed tears. He hated that. He swallowed hard and whispered, "Whaddya want?" His lips trembled and he hated that worse.

"I want you to decide for yourself and tell me, *Do you waive your right to silence?*"

"Yes. Yes!" He watched me a few seconds, and said, "I already gave the other guy a list of customers."

"Sergeant Betts. Remember his name. He's going to be important to your future."

"Okay, Sergeant Betts." He was really trying to please me now.

"The list you gave him was a good start. Now tell me about Kylee Mundt."

"What about her?" He saw me start to stand up and cried, "Wait! I don't know her very well but—" I settled back and he asked me "—what do you want to know about her?"

"How long has she been a customer?"

"Long as I been on the route."

"How long is that?"

"Little over a year."

"Have you always delivered to her at this same address?"

"Yes."

"She's never skipped any deliveries?"

"Kylee? No."

"You deliver every week?"

"Yes."

"And there hasn't been any interruption in the service to Kylee in the last couple of months? She got her usual order every week?"

"Just like always."

"You deliver to her in person? You see her every time?

"Hardly ever. I just put the envelope through the mail slot."

"How does she pay then?"

"Nobody pays on my route. I don't handle any money at all."

"Ah. You have only low-risk clients, huh?"

"I guess. They pay direct, some way. They told me I don't need to know."

"The couple in the RV told you that?"

"Yes."

"How do you get your cut, then?

"They pay us when we pick up the stuff."

"They do? How much?"

He squirmed. "Five bucks apiece. I know they're probably cheating us, but—"

"Big time. Yes."

"But then twenty or so deliveries every weekend? Hundred bucks for a couple hours' work, you can't make that bagging groceries, y'know?"

"You don't end up in prison from bagging groceries either." I heard a little commotion in the hall, and then a man in a blue suit went past my door talking to Denny. "I see your attorney's here. Sergeant Betts and I are going to tell him about the deal you made with us, Sean, and what we agreed to do for you. And for the rest of the time until you get out of this mess, which will be a lot longer than you imagine today, he's going to urge you to follow his advice and do everything he tells you, because he'll be on your side."

"What about you?"

"Sergeant Betts and I are not on your side, but a deal's a deal. We may have occasion to come and see you again from time to time. We'll expect you to tell us anything you know, and in return we're going to see to it that this terrible mistake you made doesn't stay on your record. Because it would wreck your chances of getting into the good schools you want, you know that, don't you?" I sat and watched him a minute. "Tell me, are you using?"

"No!" He was just a shade too emphatic. I watched him another full minute, till he began to squirm. "A little pot once in a while. None of the hard stuff."

"Do you need help getting clean?"

"No!" Very indignant. "It's just for fun. I don't need it." I heard the echo of all his father's best customers saying, "I could quit any time."

"You'll get tested before you leave. It's painless, you pee in a cup.

You'll get tested again every time you go to counseling for a year. There's just a bare chance in hell you'll eventually get your life back to the way it was before Saturday. Are you grateful to hear that, Sean?"

"Yes. I am. Thank you, Jake." He stood up when I stood up.

"Captain Hines," I said. "Sit. The sergeant will come and take you back. Watch your back till you get out of here, Sean. Even a county jail has some very bad guys in it, sometimes. Like your recent boss, for instance. That thug you've been peddling drugs for, he's done time for assault, did you know that? He almost killed a man with his bare hands."

I left him chewing over that dismal news and beginning to feel, I hoped, somewhat anxious. Just as I opened the door I turned and asked him, "You gave us the complete list, right? Everybody you've been delivering to?"

"Yes, sir." He answered promptly and sounded sincere. I saw his tell, though, a little twitch in his left cheek. Sean was extremely cool for fifteen, but not quite cool enough.

Darrell was waiting in the hall by his workstation. Denny and the lawyer were inside.

"He left somebody off the list," I said.

"Aw, shit," Darrell said, "I thought I made the sale."

"You did. And I did some more convincing myself. He wants to deal but—" I shrugged "—there's something—"

"Some*body*," Darrell said, "is my guess. Somebody he's more scared of than you and his dad put together. Probably Iron Man Frankie. I'll tell Bo."

"Yes. Tell him Sean's using, too. He claims nothing stronger than pot but you better test for everything. Here's something else to think about. How could Kylee Mundt, who works as an office temp, afford to pay three months' advance rent on an apartment and then go live somewhere else?"

Darrell frowned as if he was considering the question but I could see he was too busy to think about Kylee Mundt.

"And why would she do that anyway," I said, talking to myself now but unable to stop, "when it's nothing special, a top-floor walkup with bath in the hall, right on the edge of the North End; she could find another one like it any day of the week."

"You could ask her mom, maybe," Darrell said, edging toward the door of his cubicle.

"I could do that," I said, "but I bet she won't know the answer to my other question, which is how did Kylee get herself on the elite list of meth customers who are such good risks they don't have to pay the delivery boy?"

"What? There isn't any such a thing. Is there?"

"Sean Lynch says he never collected from anybody on his route."

"He's lying."

"Why would he?"

"I don't know. But I don't believe him."

"Okay. But tell Bo that's what he says; he better ask Iron Man about it. Has Bo decided how big a book to throw at LeFever?"

"Well, obviously third time dealing plus parole violation. He was thinking about a contributing charge for each one of the kids, but that gets a little awkward if we want to cut them loose."

"Well, we can decide that on a case-by-case basis after you find the rest of the delivery boys, huh? Maybe you'll find one or two that aren't as fresh and clean as these two. Let's get LeFever to tell you about his elite customer list. And find out who Sean left off it. Well, and what Kylee Mundt had to do to get on."

"Uh-huh, uh-huh." Darrell scribbled fast. When he finally stopped he raised his head and said, "This lawyer's advising Denny not to let Sean talk any more."

"That's his job. You know what I think you should do? See if you can get Sean's mother in here. I've met her, she's very straight. When Sean tests positive for pot I bet she'll have all kinds of home remedies to suggest."

17

Ray was in his glass-walled office, scowling at his desk. I stuck my head in, saw he was transcribing notes from his tiny pocket notebook and said, "LeeAnn will do that."

"She has trouble with my writing. I like to do it myself anyway; it helps me remember."

"Okay. Did the docs decide anything?"

"They want to wait for the blood work. Be a couple of days." He sat back and rubbed his eyes. "They asked me to get his medical records from Stillwater."

"Oh? Why?"

"Didn't say. They keep trading puzzled frowns. Pokey said there's no use talking about it till they see if they're onto something."

"Okay. We've got enough to do with Bo's drug busts right now anyway." I sat down in front of his desk. "You talked to Kylee Mundt's mother last week, right?"

"Uh." He blinked a couple of times, switching focus. "Yeah."

"She still wouldn't say where Kylee was?"

"Claimed she didn't know. What do you want Kylee for now?"

"She turned up on the customer list of one of those meth delivery boys Bo brought in over the weekend."

"Hell you say?" He sat back, looking shocked. "You *sure?*"

"Number three on Sean Lynch's list." I watched while he swiveled away in his chair, scratched his head thoughtfully a minute, swiveled back. "Hard to believe?"

"I would have never guessed Kylee was using. I know she still sees that crowd she went to school with, and some of them will do anything to get high—especially her mope of a brother. But Kylee's always held on to a job, helped her mother."

"Did you ever actually get a look at her apartment?"

"No. She was never home when I went there."

"Why don't you see if you can get a warrant? Get the landlord to let you in, talk to him while you're at it."

"Her."

"Okay, her, find out what kind of a tenant Kylee was, was she home every night or not, alone or with boyfriends, what did she do for fun?"

"Jeez, you really got it in for her all of a sudden, huh?"

"Ray, a data-processing temp in an office pool, she pays three months' rent in advance and leaves town? Plus now it turns out she's getting a meth delivery every week, and she's on a list so special she pays direct some way, doesn't even have to pay the delivery boy? Do the math."

Ray puffed out his cheeks, raised his eyebrows. "The math on the meth, huh? Jeez, I'll tell you, Jake, for me this just doesn't compute."

"Gotta go with the information we got, Ray."

"I know. But I'm telling you, Kylee isn't the party type. Her mother's always said she didn't know what she'd do without Kylee, how in the world she'd manage with Roger is how she said it, if it wasn't for Kylee."

"Thought you said her mother wouldn't talk to you."

"Oh, she got paranoid after Roger went to St. Cloud. Before that—I left messages with her several times before Trogstad's trial when we needed to find Kylee, and back then she was always helpful and nice."

"Talk to her again, will you? Tell her it would be in Kylee's best interest to show up soon."

"Okay. I'll get at it this afternoon."

"And you know, for the apartment, and the mother? Maybe you ought to take somebody along. See if Buzz could go with you."

"Or I could go," Rosie said, behind me. "I'm right here."

"Ah, Rosie, you're back. You bring back anything more from the park?"

"Not a thing. Pokey took the skateboard—"

"We know. Ray brought it back."

"Oh? Anyway, he took swabs of the blood on the cement and that's really all that was there. I went over the whole area a couple of times but I didn't find anything else. The caretakers have some blood to clean up but otherwise it's a nice clean crime, if it is a crime. Did we decide that yet?"

"Not yet. By the way, Ray? Give Kevin the serial number on the board, maybe he can match it up to his theft records, find out where it was stolen. So now, Rosie's your partner again, okay? What?" Kevin was standing in Ray's doorway.

"I got matches on the two boards Bo brought in with those kids." He waved the records. "They were lifted out of Aldrich Park on the same day in April."

"Call Bo, he's over in the jail, tell him. Talk to the owners who lost them and find out as much as you can about where they lost them and how."

"Okay. Also, the guns came back from the CA's office. I guess there's no reason why I can't give them back to Nelson Aldrich, huh? Make the old guy happy."

"Um . . . I guess. We don't need them anymore."

"Would you like to ride along when I deliver them? Chance to meet the town royalty, see the fabled mansion."

"Another time, maybe. Oh, have you got the number for Roger Mundt's warden? Save me some time."

"Sure. You want to talk about Roger? Talk to me, I can bad-mouth him with the best."

"Bring the warden's number to my office and you can trash Roger good."

"Here you go," Kevin said, five minutes later. "Joshua Reems, you won't have any trouble with him, he's a straight-arrow guy."

"Hang on while I get him on the phone."

Kevin was right, Warden Reems didn't mess around. In five minutes I had an okay for a three P.M. prison interview. My watch said 11:20. I told Kevin, "I've got about ten minutes. Tell me all you can about Roger in that much time." I sat hunched over paper towels on my desk, gnawing away at my vitamin sandwich, while Kevin reminded me how hard it is sometimes to catch a thief.

"Six fucking months we chased that little bastard. He had to have somebody on the inside; he knew the layout of every house he hit, the easiest way in, even a fallback way out."

"How do you know that?"

"Twice the owners woke up and chased him, and he went out the quickest way, not the way he'd come in. The other thing, he had some good place for a stash and we never found it. He got everything out of sight fast and when we finally caught him he would never admit to any of the earlier thefts; we only got to charge him with just what he had on him that night."

"But you're sure he did the other jobs too?"

"Sure, they were all the same modus, quick in and out, small high-end loot like stamp collections, painted miniatures, jade carvings. Once an inlaid chess set worth fifty thou—we've never recovered that either. And none of it ever reappeared in the Minnesota market. I got a lot of help from insurance agents and the legit dealers who'd sold the stuff—we got the information out. We never found one piece."

"I forget, how'd you finally get him?"

"By accident."

"His or yours?"

"One of each. He forgot a second alarm on a wall safe—did I tell you he seemed to have the numbers for all the best damn combination locks in town? And when it went off and he ran for it, he ran down the alley behind Pine View Drive where yours truly was just climbing hurriedly into his car after, ahem, falling asleep in the course of a, shall we say an assignation?"

"I'm in a hurry, let's just say you got laid and press on, okay? What time was this?"

"Three-thirty in the morning. Roger had a couple of nice pearl necklaces on him. He tried to ditch them in the dark but he had the homeowner right behind and me in front, so—it was a happy ending if you leave out the fact that I spent the rest of the night booking that filthy little sneak and had to work all the next day in the same clothes."

"Police work is hell sometimes, isn't it?" I looked at my watch. "Any remarks about Roger's personality? I really gotta go."

"I'll walk you out, I'm going to see Bo in the jail anyway. Roger is just a mope," he said as we walked downstairs. "He's had his hand out, grabbing for more than his share, all his life. His mother trained him to expect her to do everything for him and she brought up his sister to do the same. Crying shame how those two women feed him, do his laundry, keep a roof over his head. Poor Roger, his mom says, can't seem to find himself."

"You don't think he's lost?"

"No, he knows where he is, he's in Sloth City where he intends to stay. Dropped out of school when he was fifteen or so, now he's, let's see, twenty-three and he's had maybe three jobs, each lasting weeks not months. Gets girlfriends, uses them as long as they support him, cuffs them around a little and runs back to Mama when they start to complain. Why are you going to see him?"

"Thought he might know how his sister earns her meth money."

"He probably knows, he might have set it up himself. But he's been inside for a while now so he probably won't tell you anything for nothing. What have you got to trade?"

"Not sure. What's he like most?"

"Pussy and meth."

"Not much I can do about those."

"Well, but you know he got a pretty flexible sentence. First time and no violence, and he caught a break and got Judge Alice."

"Ah." Alice Heffron, some cops call her Judge Muffin. She's inclined to give young first offenders a window of opportunity.

"I think it was two-and-a-half to ten. You should talk to Warden Reems. If Roger's been a good boy he'll be eligible for a first parole hearing sometime next year. You offer to help with that, he might lay some news on you."

I was on my way by 11:40, hit the ring road around Minneapolis during lunchtime hell, by some miracle emerged onto I-94 thirty minutes later still sitting upright in a red pickup with all four fenders. I was actually ten minutes early for my date with Roger when I parked in front of the red-brown granite walls of the St. Cloud Reformatory, so I took a few minutes to chat with Warden Reems, who confirmed that so far, Roger had done nothing to compromise his chances of early parole.

"But he shows no sign of remorse either, and I have Kevin Evjan's statement that he did nothing to help retrieve the items he stole, so yeah, it could go either way. Go ahead—get whatever you can. I'll go along."

I realized when they brought him in that I'd never seen Roger Mundt before. I'd seen his picture and the stories in the *Rutherford Times-Courier*, so he seemed familiar to me, but in fact he had come and gone through the Rutherford criminal justice system without any assistance from me. He looked a little healthier than his pictures, cleaned up and clear-eyed. I'm assured you can get anything on the inside you can get on the outside, but it looked like Roger was staying sober in prison.

We all speak easily of "vibes," but Roger Mundt did actually seem to give off waves of resentment and self-pity. Accustomed to manipulating women for a living, Roger Mundt hated this male world where nobody gave a crap about him. Reems told me he had quickly been spotted by a large, mean long-timer who was trading him protection for sexual service, so he wasn't getting beaten up, but there were still a lot of goodies to miss.

I went right to work, reviewed the parole options coming up for him in less than a year and suggested we do some business.

He had a deviated septum with a postnasal drip. He sniffed. "I gotta trust you, huh? I can't get anything in writing?"

"No. I have to trust you too, which most people would say was a tougher call."

He did some private muttering and finally said, "Whaddya lookin' for?"

"Does Kylee keep in touch?" I asked him. "You hear from her lately?"

"Kylee?" He wiped his nose on his finger. I passed him a tissue from the box on the table and he wiped his finger thoughtfully. "My sister?"

"Your sister, yes. Do you know some other Kylee?"

"No." He pondered. "Why do you want to find her?"

"I have her meth dealer in jail and I'd like to ask her some questions about him."

"Kylee ain't got no meth dealer, man. You're way off base there. Whadjoo say your name was?"

"Jake Hines." I showed him my shield again.

"Well." He recrossed his legs. "Kylee don't do no drugs. You talk to my mom about this?"

"Not yet."

"Well, you should talk to her. That's who Kylee stays in touch with, not me."

"So you haven't talked to her?"

"Haven't talked in a while, that's right. Whadjoo say you could do for me when my hearing comes up?"

"I can tell them you've been cooperating with us. That'll make a difference." I watched his tiny, private sneer. "How long is a while?"

"Huh?"

"Since you've talked to Kylee?"

"Oh . . . maybe a couple months." It could have meant two months or a year.

"You know Benny Niemeyer's dead?"

His eyes flickered; he hadn't known. But all he said was, "So?"

"Was he your sister's boyfriend?"

"Benny?" Big sneer, almost a laugh. "Kinda fucking stupid question is that, man?"

"Was he?"

"Fucking kiss-ass Benny was in love with *Dale*, man, whereya been?" He enjoyed a little snorting laugh all by himself, muttering, "My *sister*, Jee-sus."

"So . . . Dale and Benny were a couple, huh? Not just partners in the car-jacking?"

Another big sneer formed on Roger's face. He opened his mouth to spit out another contemptuous denial, and then in a jittery second, like Wile E. Coyote coming back up over the edge of the cliff, he thought better of it and clamped his jaw shut. His little rat's eyes darted around while he thought. What he finally said was, "I don't know nothing about no car-jacking."

"You don't?" I watched him a few seconds, wondering, *Why would he lie about that?* He wasn't in prison yet when Shelley Gleason was kidnapped; he must have known about it. In fact the quote came back to me as I sat there—Kylee Mundt's testimony at Dale Trogstad's trial: "They stopped at my apartment. My brother was there; he saw them too."

I had wasted many an hour trying to find Kylee, to get her to repeat those words at Benny's trial. But only near the end did I realize that Kylee Mundt, the desired witness, was the sister of Roger Mundt, the notorious thief of chess sets and ivory birds. As he sat before me telling what seemed like still another senseless lie, my mind scrolled through preferred Quantico interrogation techniques. About the time I came to, "Try sympathy," my eyes wandered to his ropy right arm, where a garish jailhouse tattoo, a heart with the name "Izzy" inside it, looked new and a little sore. I asked him, "That your boyfriend?"

"My *boyfriend?*" He looked disgusted. "Where you gettin' your information, man? I ain't no queer."

"The warden said you had a friend in here—"

"Listen, asshole, you oughta try jailhouse livin' for a while, maybe you'd learn somethin'."

"So, you're saying Izzy's your girl?"

"One of 'em." When he flexed the muscle, the name expanded and contracted.

"You know, you could be out and seeing her in a less than a year, if you had the right people on your side when your hearing comes up."

He shrugged. "This fuck-up warden's got it in for me. I wouldn't be surprised he makes me execute the full sentence."

"I might be able to help you with that."

He muttered something under his breath that I thought was, *"Sure, hoss."*

"Tell you what, if you know how to reach Kylee you should get word to her, tell her she'd be doing herself a favor if she came home and helped us with these meth dealers. If you'd get word to her I'd put in a good word with the warden and the parole board." I waited. "Think about it, Roger. Is Izzy nice to you?"

A mean little shrug. "When she's awake."

"Must do something you like, to put her name on your arm."

More shrugs, and the curled lip. "She's got a nice big house and she likes to stay in bed all day, I like both of those."

"Nice big house, huh? How'd you meet her?"

He watched me, realized he knew a little nugget of truth that would shock me, and decided to use it. "We was in the same detox group at Fountain Lake Treatment Center in Albert Lea," he said. "With Diane. Know who I mean, Diane?"

I shook my head.

"Wife of that vice cop you got there, that Bo Dooley. Some vice cop, huh?" A vicious little chuckle. "Puts other guys in the slammer for doin' drugs but he keeps his wife supplied with all the rock she needs, no trouble about that."

It figured that losers like Roger would sit in jail cells telling each other stories like that about Bo, who had spent years trying to help Diane kick her cocaine habit. The last time she disappeared, it almost killed him but he gave up and filed for divorce for Nelly's sake. I knew he would never discuss Diane with Roger, so I wouldn't either.

"So you met a rich girl in detox, huh?"

"Fact." Roger looked pleased. "Just hit it off."

"So when you got out you helped each other stay sober, huh?"

"Shit no." He still had all the put-down looks kids learn in junior high; he rolled his eyes up to the ceiling and gave a tiny headshake that made him look younger. "We wasn't neither one of us voluntary. My mother called my juvie case officer after I wrecked her stupid car. And Izzy, she'd already been to all the big-bucks places, Shadel and Betty Ford and so on, so that time her rich-bitch mother said let's see how you like it the hard way."

"So how did she like it?"

The shrug again. "She said pukin' is pukin', so who cares what carpet's on the floor?"

"Good point. Was this just last year or—"

"Nah. While ago—three, four years maybe."

"And you've been seeing her ever since? Steady?"

He shook his head emphatically. "Off and on. I don't see nobody steady. I don't like to be tied down." He considered, his head on one side. "One good thing about Izzy, whenever I do show up I can count on gettin' laid."

"What does she want in return? Plenty of meth?"

"Sometimes. She likes to smoke crack too, sometimes mix a little roofie in her gin. Whatever's blowin' her skirt up at the moment, and almost everything does, man." Roger was looking mellower with every minute he talked about Izzy.

"Well then, Roger, if you've got all that fun out there waiting for you, why don't you make a little trade with me right now, and I'll do what I can to get you out of here pretty soon?" Something about the way I said it turned Roger off, or maybe he'd just been playing with me all along. He leaned across the gray table with his mean little smile and said, "Who the fuck you think you are, asshole? Come in here and feed me lame shit like that and think I'm gonna let you fuck me up the ass and say oh thank you sir? Stupid asshole cop." He got up and hit the bell and yelled "Guard!" and stood cold and gray-looking, so still he didn't even seem to breathe, till the guard took him back to his cell.

Another guard let me out on my side and walked me to the front entrance asking, "Did you have a nice visit with Mister Overdue's pussy?"

"That's what you call him?"

"Oooh, yes," the guard said with a hateful smile. "His boyfriend is overdue for some attitude adjustment."

"He's a bad-tempered boy?"

"He is indeed. And when Mr. Overdue gets his attitude adjusted, I wouldn't be surprised if Roger Pussy got so he didn't like this place much for a while."

I had to wait fifteen minutes to talk to the warden again. I asked for the transfer of records I needed and gave him a heads-up on the guard's remark. He was polite; he didn't quite yawn in my face. I hit 494 just in time for a refresher in stoplight hell. Once I was south of Eagan, though, it was just a breeze to Mirium, and when I drove in the yard Trudy was there, unloading groceries out of her car. I went over and patted her adorable butt and said, "I don't give you enough respect."

"You don't? Here, take these." She shoved bags into my arms. "Why are you sucking up to me?" she asked as we walked in the house. "What have you done?"

"What a question. I drove to St. Cloud and back at top speed, went through Minneapolis at lunchtime, came back at quitting time and got the finger three times today. For a treat in between I got to interview a sociopath."

"My poor lover, you want a hug? Now tell me," she said, purring against my neck, "why I deserve more respect."

"I forget when you do that. Okay, don't go away, I remember. You make that drive every day and come home with your lipstick on straight."

"Oh, well, but I start from south St. Paul and I don't look at anybody's fingers. What do I care which way they're pointing? Let's have a glass of wine and sit a minute." We carried lawn chairs around the construction litter in the front yard and found a spot in the shade. "Why did you go to St. Cloud to talk to a sociopath? Don't you see enough of those in Rutherford?"

"This one's special." I told her about Roger's sister and about his DNA records that I wanted her to compare with the records from the trial. "While I'm thinking about it, I've got a skateboard in the truck—wait, you haven't heard about Benny yet, have you?" I told her about Benny Niemeyer in the skateboard pit.

"Ah, shee. I guess that was predictable, huh?"

"Yeah. He was on that greasy slope."

"All his life practically, right? Sure, go ahead and fill out the paperwork, I'll take 'em in with me in the morning. They might wait quite a while in the queue, though. We're kind of jammed up right now." She held her arms up toward the tree above her and said, "Ah, how did I ever manage without this yard?"

"How did I? Remember when we first got this place, how Ozzie Sullivan laughed at us for buying a pig in a poke?"

"What a dumb guy." She stretched luxuriously in front of our incredibly messy old house. "How could anybody fail to see that this is the best place in southeast Minnesota?"

18

When we shoehorned a bigger detective division into the department, Ray Bailey got a new glass-walled office facing the conference area and the cubicles of his People Crimes detectives. Each workspace had just room for a desk, phone and two chairs, so the detectives took to schmoozing around the big conference table in the middle. Bo, the loner of the section, usually avoided these gatherings, and since he had drafted Darrell Betts for a partner on this drug bust, Darrell was usually missing too.

I heard the rest of them talking down there when I opened the door of my office Tuesday morning, so I dumped my briefcase, got a cup of coffee and joined them. The sun was streaming through the skylight onto the usual clutter of cups and notebooks, cell phones and pocket recorders and Palm Pilots. Rosie had a purse the size of a small gunnysack open on the table with all its contents out in a heap; she was repacking it while she finished an argument with Buzz Cooper.

"Sure, Rosemary Sheila Veronica Doyle. Don't you have four names?"

"Of course not. Why would I? Why would anybody?"

"Well, because my mother named me after her two sisters and then I took Veronica for my saint's name when I was confirmed. Weren't you ever confirmed?"

"Confirmed as what?" Buzz looked at me. "You got four names, Jake?"

"Damn lucky to have two," I said. "I don't even know how I got those, come to think of it." I asked Ray, "Did you make any of those calls yesterday?"

"Made all of them." His eyebrows expressed irony. "We're both right about Kylee Mundt, how d'you like that?" He opened his little notebook. "The landlady—Mrs. Burke?—says she's an ideal tenant, wishes they were all like her. Clean, quiet, pays her rent on time. Says she's been gone since June first, rent paid till first of September, hasn't heard from her but not worried. Kylee said she'd be back by then and if Kylee said it she'll do it."

"So, a Girl Scout," I said. "What was *I* right about?"

"She gets her mail and packages delivered to a little wooden box with a padlock and slot that sits right inside the storm door on the glassed-in porch on the front of the house. She hasn't had any mail deliveries since she left but she gets a package delivered every Monday morning by a boy on a skateboard. When Kylee's in town she takes everything out of the box, but since she's been gone the package is picked up Monday afternoon by a thin girl driving a dark green convertible."

"Is the landlady curious about the package?"

"Nope. Kylee explained that her friend has an illness and needs a drug that's much cheaper in Mexico. The friend has her own key to the box but not to the house so it's no trouble. Mrs. Burke isn't clear on why Kylee's sick friend can't have the drugs delivered to her own place but if Kylee says it's okay, it's okay."

"Jeez," Clint Maddox said. "Why doesn't anybody ever trust me like that?"

"You're probably not as reliable as Kylee Mundt," Rosie said, stacking her wallet, makeup kit and address book neatly beside her purse.

"And apparently Rosie and I aren't either," Ray said. "Mrs. Burke let us look at Kylee's room after we flashed our badges and let her read the warrant all the way through, but she stayed right with us the whole time."

"There wasn't anything to see, anyway," Rosie said. "Kylee Mundt has very few possessions. An old radio and a few worn-out clothes in the closet. A kitchen, believe me, the utensils would make you cry. *Spartan.*" She sorted pens, pencils, notebooks, extra combs and lipsticks into piles which she began rubber-banding together, *snap, snap.*

"So whatever she's making out of the drug deal, she isn't spending it on herself," Ray said.

"You still think she's not using?"

"Not a sign of any paraphernalia."

"Okay, and she has a bare-bones apartment and old clothes," I said, "and we still don't know where she's gone, do we?"

"No, because Mrs. Burke doesn't know and neither does her mother," Rosie said. "So they say. I believe the landlady but I'm not so sure about Mama, are you, Ray?"

"Mama's into motherhood," Ray said, "so I expect she'd lie to protect Kylee, sure."

"She loves to brag about how smart Kylee is, doesn't she? She said, 'She's not just some little dumb bunny, you know,'" Rosie laughed. "*Twice,* she said that, while she was telling me how Kylee got that extra job setting up records at the Aldrich house." She put her cell phone and tape recorder in her purse and began stowing the other possessions alongside them. We had all begun to watch, fascinated, how she loaded herself up like a pack mule.

"Kylee's been working at the Aldrich house? Doing what?"

"According to her mother," Rosie said, "Kylee's setting up a very complex system to keep track of all the family accounts, piles of money."

Ray consulted his notes. "She didn't have to lose her job at the temp office, by the way. Her boss likes her almost as much as her mother and the landlady. He said sure, this summer's slow and he did have to lay off five or six girls, but Kylee's one of his top people. He would have laid off almost anybody else before her, but she volunteered."

"He say why?"

"She said she had a little money put by and she could use a break. She said why didn't he let her go, give the work to somebody else and she'd come back in the fall."

"Which doesn't make any sense at all when you see that apartment, Jake." Rosie shuddered, and said under her breath, "*Weird.*" The thought of living without many purses' worth of feminine clutter seemed to give her the creeps.

"Okay. Write it all up and get back to whatever you were working on before Benny," I said, and went back along the hall to my office. Kevin followed me in, asking, "How's old sneaky Roger?"

"Not ready to deal, is the short answer. The trip wasn't entirely wasted, though. I found out Roger's DNA records are on file now at BCA—they're doing all felons now, remember?—so I filled out a request to get them compared to one of the samples in the trial records. You know, Roger hadn't been arrested yet when they ran those comparisons before the trial."

"Compare Roger's DNA? With what?"

"There was one little blood smear in Shelley's car that we never matched to anybody, remember?"

"Jesus, you want to hang Shelley Gleason's murder on Roger, now? You really get vindictive when guys won't deal, don't you? Remind me not to get on your bad side."

"You know what sneaky Roger said to me? He said, 'I don't know nothing about no car-jacking.' "

Kevin stared at me blankly and finally asked, "So?"

"Remember what Kylee Mundt said at Dale Trogstad's trial? 'My brother was there—he saw them too.' "

"Oh, yeah, she did say that, didn't she? Maybe she lied though."

"Why would she lie about him seeing Dale and Benny in the car?"

"If he was someplace else? Maybe stealing the silver service out of the mayor's mansion or the chalice off the altar at the Catholic church?"

"Or if he was actually in the car along with Dale and Benny?"

"Oh. I see. Well. Really, I wouldn't be shocked to find out he was in on that caper, Jake. We've never caught him at anything violent, but Roger's—well, you saw him, what do you think?"

"I think he's a very bad boy. Is the chalice really gone from the church?"

"I just made those things up. But plenty of other stuff is still missing. First chance you get, give me the date when Kylee said she saw Benny in the car, will you? I'll see if I can match it up with any of the complaints we failed to hang on Roger."

"Okay. How'd you get along with Nelson Aldrich?"

"Oh, the old guy wasn't feeling so hot yesterday, and Mrs. Peabody was having the Theater Guild to tea or something, so she asked me to come today."

"Mrs. Peabody is Aldrich's daughter?"

"Yes."

"Is it still okay with you if I come along?"

"Oh, you changed your mind about that, huh? Sure, fine. She said about ten o'clock. Can you be ready by then?"

"Yup."

"I couldn't find anything to put the guns in but this envelope box out of the supply room," he said, fussing with a parcel on his desk. "You think this'll be all right?" He must have brought the tissue paper from home. He was trying hard to do right by Nelson Aldrich's guns and he was nervous about it.

"You really like these people, don't you?"

"I'm *impressed* by these people, Jake. I *admire* them. Nelson Aldrich has enough money to live anyplace in the world, and he chose to stay here and give back some of the wealth he made here. How unusual is that? You know how much Aldrich Park cost?"

"No idea."

"Well, I don't have exact figures but it's several millions and every year he adds something new and wonderful to it, a beautiful golf course just coming on line this week. And now his daughter's bringing in an architect to plan a whole new theater complex. Every town should have an Aldrich family."

"Okay, I'll make sure my fingernails are clean. About half an hour?"

Kevin met me at the front door with a Crown Vic already cooled off. We rolled along leafy streets, the squirrels running fat the way they get in August, dogs lying in the shade with their tongues out. Two old guys in baseball caps stood talking across a fence on Sixteenth Street while their lawn mowers idled nearby. Kevin turned east at Seventeenth and then south at Jefferson and began climbing Millionaire's Hill, the view getting better as the houses grew larger and the yards more beautiful. The Aldrich house was at the top of

Cherry Hills Drive, on a cul-de-sac with a double gate that stood open.

We drove along a gravel driveway lined with poplars. There were glimpses between the trees of broad lawns on both sides, a gazebo near the front corner on the right and a rose garden near the hedge on the left. A man was mowing grass, another one running an edger. There was a pool behind woven fencing farther back on the left of the house.

"Nice place," I said, as Kevin parked on crunchy gravel at the left side of the entrance, beside a black MG with a bag full of Titleist clubs in the boot.

"Beautiful, inside and out. I want it *all*." We walked to the beamed front door and he rang the bell, which chimed gently inside. I watched robins grazing on the lawn until a slender chic woman of no particular age opened the door and said, "Good morning."

"Mrs. Peabody? I'm Kevin Evjan." He gave her his card.

"Of course, you're the one who came up last year, aren't you? When we had our burglary." She smiled at him. "Come in."

That's how sweet life is if you're Kevin Evjan. Andy Pitman was up here too—twice, in fact—but Kevin's the one she remembers, and when she sees him again, she smiles.

She led us through a slate-floored foyer with high-backed chairs against the walls, tall porcelain urns with Chinese paintings on them and a grouping of black-framed ink sketches. We went down two steps into a deep-carpeted living room with several clusters of seating and a whole wall of windows looking out on a flower garden.

"Mrs. Peabody, this is my boss," Kevin said, when we stopped by some chairs. "Captain Jake Hines."

"How nice of you to come." She took my hand. Her eyes were very blue. Something about the way she moved and stood lent uncommon elegance to her simple clothing.

"My husband was hoping to be here to say hello to you," she said, "but he's playing in the kickoff tournament at the new golf course and he got one of the earliest tee times this morning." "That's right," Kevin said, "that's today, isn't it? Mr. Peabody does a lot of work for the foundation, doesn't he? I saw him at the dedication of the park addition, encouraging kids to try out the skateboard pit."

"Well, yes, James has been trying to lend a hand now that my father is getting kind of fragile. He's particularly interested in the new things at the park. He's been pushing the foundation to emphasize leisure time amenities for working people and their families. Oh, James," she said as a man came down the staircase and along the hall, "you are home, I didn't hear you come in."

"Whose car's in front of the house? You have other men with black MGs living here?" He smiled at her, coming down the steps. "Hmmm? Come clean, now."

"Silly," she put her arm through his as he came up to her, "I came in the back way; I didn't see it. Darling, you remember Lieutenant Evjan? And this is Captain Hines."

"Pleasure," he said. "Heinz, is it? Like the ketchup?" He had a crinkly smile and a firm, freckled handshake that suggested frequent use of the golf clubs we had seen outside. He wore a white knit shirt under a madras jacket, and I thought that the people in India who wove that cloth would be proud if they could see how he looked in it.

Mrs. Peabody asked us, "Won't you sit down?" She sat across from me with her legs crossed at the ankle. "I told Father you were bringing two of his guns back," she told Kevin, smiling again, "and he was very pleased. He's in the library—we'll go in there in just a minute. He isn't always as strong as we'd like these days but he particularly wanted to thank you himself."

"Before we do that," I said, "I wonder if I could ask you about Kylee Mundt?"

"Who?"

"Kylee Mundt. What kind of work does she do for you, exactly?"

She looked at me blankly. Kevin was looking at me too, his face saying *What the hell is this?* Then her husband said, "Darling, I think he's asking about the girl who's helping Elizabeth set up her Mac."

"Ah," Helen Peabody said, "is that her name?"

"We're both of us hopelessly computer-phobic, I'm afraid," James said. His smile was self-deprecating, but of course he knew the room he sat in excused him from irksome chores like hooking up a printer. "And our daughter seems to have inherited our lack of mechanical skills. So when she began to want a PC for school our attorney found a girl at the bank who said she could help."

I said, "Your daughter lives here with you, does she? Elizabeth?"

"Well, yes," Mrs. Peabody said, "she does. Since she's still in high school." It was a simple question that only needed a simple answer, but for some reason her blue eyes were not quite as cordial as they had been before.

"We haven't seen Kylee for a while, come to think of it," James said. "What is it you wanted to know about her?"

"She has some information I need, I think, but I can't seem to find her," I said. "Do you think your daughter might know where she is?"

"I don't know why she would," Mrs. Peabody said. "She's just doing that one job for us, isn't she, James?" She looked at her husband, who said, "Right, just the Mac."

"They do seem to be taking forever with it," Helen Peabody said. "I don't see why a few little programs for school have to be so complicated."

"Well, but there you go," James Peabody said. "If we knew that, we could help her ourselves, couldn't we?" They chuckled together and then their glances came back to me, inviting me to share the joke.

I went on looking from one to the other of them until Mrs. Peabody said, "I suppose it's possible Elizabeth knows where she lives. I just got back from a meeting. I don't know . . . James, do you happen to know if Elizabeth's home right now?"

"I haven't a clue, I'm afraid," he said. "I just walked in the door myself." He got up and walked toward a cupboard in the corner. "And I'm thirsty. That was a fast nine holes we played. Can I get either of you fellows something cool to drink?"

"No thanks," Kevin said, and Mrs. Peabody said, "Kevin agrees with me that it's still a little early, James."

"Early for what? I'm just getting a soda." He stood with his back to us, though, so his wife couldn't see what he poured in his glass.

"You know I just remembered," Mrs. Peabody said. "Elizabeth's taking a tennis lesson this morning. Why don't I have her call you if she knows anything about this computer person, Lieutenant Hines?"

"Captain," I said. "Would you do that? Here's my card." She took it from me without meeting my eyes, and set it on the table beside her without looking at it. She turned to Kevin and said, "Well, shall we give Father his guns?" I followed them into the library, mostly because I was curious about why she didn't want me there.

I understand, of course, that I am not the police detective of a Minnesota matron's hopes and dreams. I'm rising as fast as I can above a hardscrabble upbringing in foster homes; meantime my demeanor is Law Enforcement Standard, courteous but straightforward. I wouldn't argue that I fit naturally into a mansion on Cherry Hills Drive, but I thought Kevin was right; Mrs. Peabody was the real deal, so I didn't suspect her of either racism or snobbery. It seemed to me she objected to my questions, not to my person, and I wanted to follow her around all day till she showed me why. I knew I couldn't do that, but I could go along and see how she behaved with the great Nelson Aldrich in his retreat, so I did.

The library had tall mullioned windows, a couple of them rolled open sideways to admit light and air from the shady north side of the house. All the walls that weren't windows were lined with books, on floor-to-ceiling shelves with a ladder that ran along on a track. There was a long table with two green-shaded lights, a Persian rug on the polished wood floor. The room was saved from too much perfection by a clutter of architect's drawings and pens on the table, and a couple of books lying open on the arms of chairs.

The man sitting in a leather wing chair near one of the windows had a book in his hands, too, but he wasn't reading. He seemed to be musing. He looked up as his daughter approached and I saw his eyes were just like hers.

"Father?" She bent over him and picked up one of his hands. "Remember I told you the policeman was bringing your guns back this morning? Well, here he is." She straightened and turned toward Kevin with a sweet smile. Kevin stepped forward, set the cardboard box on Nelson Aldrich's gray flannel lap and lifted off the lid.

"Ah. Well, now, look here." His thin hands trembled a little as he pulled the Sig Sauer out of the box and held it up to the light. "Isn't this nice, Helen? Thank you, young man." His bright blue eyes searched Kevin's face as if memorizing it and he smiled, and Kevin smiled back at him, gratified.

He hefted the gun in his palm and said, "It's so nicely machined, isn't it?" He thumbed the finish thoughtfully, slid the magazine out and worked the action. "Holds fifteen rounds, see? Yet it's so light." He replaced the magazine and sighed happily. "Nothing like a good design well executed."

Sitting back, he began to reminisce. "You know, I've been to the Sauer plant in Germany. It's up near the Danish border. They told me the story there, how these great Swiss designers from a company called SIG came to them with the design—"

We stood in front of him like obedient schoolboys while he told us a great deal that we already knew about the most attractive features of this handgun. The chief considered one of the Sig Sauers for the department once; Kevin and I sat on the committee that helped him decide instead to buy the Glock. We had our reasons, mostly money and the high-tech plastic Glock's ability to stand up to almost anything, even Minnesota weather. Reasonable people might disagree with our decision, but we were both well past needing a training course in handguns. But Nelson Aldrich was enjoying his discourse, so we stood still and listened.

When he paused for breath, Mrs. Peabody said quickly, "Well, Father, that's very interesting but perhaps we should thank these two fine officers now and let them get back to work, don't you think?"

He grew a tiny frown between his eyes and told us, "My daughter means this subject doesn't interest her." He stuck out his hand to me. I shook it while Kevin stood helplessly by. Nelson Aldrich said stiffly, "Thank you for coming."

"You're welcome," I said, and stepped back as Mrs. Peabody said, "Well, and here's Lieutenant Evjan who I think actually, uh, wrapped the guns and all—"

Kevin stepped forward and stuck out his hand, and Nelson Aldrich shook it without looking up. After a couple of shakes, though, he seemed to perk up. Looking up into Kevin's handsome, eager face, he smiled a little and said, "You know, I've been to the Sauer plant in Germany. It's up near the Danish border. They told me the story there, how these great Swiss designers from a company called SIG came to them with the design—"

There was a moment of disorientation, as if we had stumbled into a pucker in time and must run a piece of it over. Then we both realized we were looking at a man who had no idea he had just said these words before. Kevin understood it at the same second I did; I felt him stiffen beside me. We stood again like good boys in front of Nelson Aldrich, keeping our faces as attentive as we could, but this time Mrs. Peabody cut in just as he began to dismantle the gun.

"Yes, well it's wonderful of you both to take the time to come by like this and we're ever so grateful for the return of the guns, aren't we, Father?" She put a hand firmly around Kevin's upper arm and walked him out into the hall and along to the slate-floored foyer with me following. As we passed the living room entrance I caught a glimpse of James Peabody standing by the glass doors, looking out at the flowers with his cool drink in his hand.

We both shook hands with Mrs. Peabody, who smiled and thanked us once again. Then we were outside on the crunchy gravel in the bright sunshine, and we didn't speak again till we were outside the gates and headed downhill.

"I had no idea," Kevin said. "I hadn't heard. God, it's awful, isn't it? Alzheimer's."

"Worse for the bystanders, I guess."

"But this was a brilliant man, Jake. A couple of his inventions have made important differences in how medicine's done. Jesus, wasn't she wonderful, though? Fantastic timing."

"Looks like she's had some practice."

"You should have told me you were going to ask about Kylee Mundt," Kevin said. "Why did you, anyway?"

"Kylee's on the client list of one of the drug delivery boys Bo brought in over the weekend. Denny Lynch's boy?"

"Are you serious? You don't mean Sean Lynch?" He stared at me open-mouthed.

"Watch the fucking road!" I clung to my seat belt as a UPS truck barely managed to stay out of my lap.

"Shit!" He overcorrected and almost ran off the other side into thin air. "I'm sorry," he said, when he was back in his lane, "but Jesus, Sean Lynch delivering drugs on a stolen skateboard? Some days I think being a cop in my own hometown is a mistake."

"You know the kid, huh?"

"He was in my first Scout troop. I taught him the Pledge of Allegiance."

"Maybe you better do a refresher."

"I'd need one myself first. But I still don't get it—what's that got to do with Kylee doing a job for the Peabody kid?"

"Maybe nothing. It just came up and it seemed like an odd coincidence, so as long as you were going anyway I thought I'd ask. Did it seem like Mrs. Peabody didn't want to talk about it?"

"No, it seemed like she really didn't remember she'd ever seen the girl. Do you realize how many people she probably meets in a week? Now that I see how bad off her father is, I realize she has to manage everything."

"What's to manage? I mean, he sold the business years ago, didn't he? The lab or whatever?"

"Aldrich Manufacturing. His dad started it. They made lab supplies, beakers and tubes and so on. Then he invented the Aldrich shunt, and the world began to rain prizes and money on him."

"What's the Aldrich shunt?"

"A bypass thingamajig. For clogged arteries or some such. His is, what, cheaper? No, longer lasting I think. Anyway, Nelson Aldrich is that rare thing, a guy who was born rich and then made good."

"Okay, but what's left for Mrs. Peabody to do? If the business is sold and the money's in the bank?"

"In the bank, God, that's so last century. There's the foundation,

Jake, the Aldrich Fund, eight hundred million, soon to be a billion and they're putting every penny it produces right here in dear old Rutherford. This year the new golf course, next year the theater and pretty soon a new wing for the art museum. The Aldrich Fund is Rutherford's angel."

I watched the fine houses along the street as we looped down Millionaire's Hill. "Too bad the guy who made the money won't get to enjoy watching it build stuff."

"Damn shame, yes. But think of the foresight that went into what's happening now, Jake; he was smart enough to set up the foundation and appoint the board of directors while he was still compos mentis, so now the good works can keep rolling along without him."

"Are the Peabodys on the board?"

"Oh, I'm sure. Well I mean, I don't know of course, I'm not a member of the—why do you ask?"

"Just curious. You'd think a couple with so much important business going on would need to have it all on a computer."

"Oh, well, I'm sure they do, in several places, but—come on, Jake, you can't expect the people with the money to punch in the numbers themselves."

"I suppose not," I said. "After all, they have to worry about making the amenities accessible to the working class and all."

"Oho, now we see that our hero is really just eaten up with envy and indulging in a fit of reverse snobbery."

"That's right. I want his car and house and jacket, so I'm building a conspiracy theory around him."

"Are you? What's he supposed to be conspiring about?"

"I don't know yet, but there's a helluva difference between what Peabody just said Kylee Mundt was doing up here and what Kylee's mama said."

"Oh? I forget, what did Kylee's mama say?"

"That Kylee was setting up a lot of important accounts for the Aldrich household."

"Oh, well, come on, that's probably just Mama exaggerating. What mama doesn't?"

"Does yours?"

"She would, Jake, but it's never been necessary."

"Oh, Jesus." We laughed a little harder than the joke deserved, because it felt so good to be out in the bright sunshine, putting distance between us and the old man in the library, who had just reminded us that time alone could rob you of everything you'd earned.

19

"Pokey just called," Ray said on the phone Wednesday morning. "Said he's on his way over with the autopsy report."

"Be right there."

Hanging up the phone, I heard the chief say, "Well, good morning, Pokey."

"Hey, big chief in person." Something about McCafferty's good-cop persona brings out the worst in the coroner, who can't resist ragging on him. "What you need so many lazy lummoxes sitting around this place for?" He sounded like Krushchev at the UN. "Better get 'em out onto street, not gonna catch bad guys in here, hah?"

"Good suggestion," Frank said, "surprised I didn't think of it myself. Who you looking for, Pokey? Can I—" and then Ray's voice came from the end of the hall, "We're down here, Pokey."

I got up to follow him and ran into Frank in my doorway, pointing silently to my desk. I went back and sat down, and he came in and closed my door. Easing his bulk into my extra chair, he tortured its legs while he fiddled with my paper clip jar. "I just got a call from Reese Newman."

"Oh, yeah? He heard about Benny, huh?"

"About Benny?" Frank looked puzzled a minute, blinked his eyes and said, "Oh, that's right, he did defend Benny, didn't he?"

I watched him line up my tape dispenser with the edge of the desk. "He wasn't calling about Benny?"

"No, he wanted to—" He arranged my stapler precisely next to the tape dispenser, sat back and rubbed his cheeks a couple of times. Finally he blurted out, "Tell you the truth he called to complain."

"About what?"

"Says you and Kevin called on his clients yesterday and got them all upset."

"His clients? Which—" A weird little lightbulb began to glow in my brain. "Does Reese Newman represent the Aldrich family?"

"You didn't know that?"

"No, why would I know that? We just went out there to take their guns back, Frank. The guns from the trial, they were stolen from the Aldrich house, remember? Why were they upset about that?"

"He says you asked a lot of questions about their daughter that they thought were quite . . . 'intrusive,' I think was the word he used."

I put the heels of my hands against my eyes and pushed until I saw stars and lightning, took them away and said into the twilight they left behind, "You know, I had a feeling Mrs. Peabody got uneasy, talking about her daughter, but I couldn't figure out why."

"The girl's had a little trouble, I think, did some drugs and dropped out of school a couple of times."

"All that money," I said. "You'd think they'd send her to private schools."

"Well, they've always said Rutherford is their home and they wanted their daughter to know people here. But maybe Mrs. Peabody is sensitive about that decision, now that the girl isn't doing so well."

He thunked his big hands onto his knees and sighed. "Parents are a pretty sorry lot, Jake. You'll see, one of these days."

"Hope so. So help me, Frank, I didn't say anything offensive. I just asked if the daughter still lived at home."

"Well, there you go, the mother's probably sensitive because the girl should be in college by now. Anyway," he got up, obviously relieved to get the conversation over, "just give the place a wide berth for a while, huh? Let Kevin take their stuff back; he seems to get along with them all right."

The suggestion that I was too crude to deal with Mrs. Peabody hung in the air between us like a hissing snake. "Fine," I said. "Anything else? I need to hear what Pokey has to say."

"No, that's all, go ahead." He went out with his back humped up a little. I know him too well, I thought, I can tell when his blood pressure's high. He was my field training officer when I joined up, a handsome über-cop and superior marksman when I was a skinny recruit who couldn't even drive a squad to suit him, much less shoot to his satisfaction. He'd always been my role model, except when I wanted to throw a chair at his head, like now. Somebody had criticized the department and even though he suspected it was a bullshit claim his highest priority had been the good name of the department, as it always would be.

I went down the hall toward Pokey's voice wondering, *But why did they complain?* and then, *Why would the attorney for the Aldrich estate make time in his busy schedule for the pro bono defense of Benny Niemeyer?*

Then I was at the conference table, where Pokey's voice filled the room.

"—Like we showed you at clinic. No subdural hemorrhaging, no cerebral edema, no blood in cranium. Had that big goose egg on forehead, two black eyes and broken nose. Seen prizefighters get hurt worse and keep title, yah? So we send blood to lab.

"You know how I always do, Jake," he said as I sat down, "draw plenty of blood all at once so is no question of different evidence, divide in three parts. Send one-third to BCA, they do wonderful job but don't send results for two months. Send another third to lab here, get results back by next night."

"Why do you send some to BCA then?" Rosie asked him.

"So if case goes to trial, BCA testifies. Juries believe testimony from big-cheese scientists at state crime lab."

"Ah. What happens to the final third?"

"Gets frozen in lab with plenty paperwork so chain of evidence is intact when smart-ass defense attorneys want to prove our analysis is wrong," he said. "We say, 'You don't like? Run your own tests.' "

"Okay," Ray said, "so, he didn't die from anything we could see. What was it then?"

"Whoever beaned him with skateboard coulda waited few minutes, saved himself lotta effort. Was already dying, very close to dead from respiratory depression."

"Benny? A big strong guy like that? How come?"

"Remember we had you send to prison for medical records? At Stillwater, was decided part of Benny's problem was he was hyper, borderline hyper-thyroid and also hyper-stressed all his life from beatings and neglect. Couldn't sleep more than two or three hours at once so they gave him Valium to calm him down."

"I remember that—it was in his parole papers," Ray said.

"Uh-huh. Benny got prison docs to give him prescription to go out with. Night he was killed, Benny had good big dose of Valium in him. Then somebody gave him couple stiff drinks of Scotch with double helping of Rohypnol. You know this drug? Is date-rape drug. Roofies, kids call 'em."

"The sneaky prick pill," Rosie said.

"Sure. You havin' trouble gettin' your girl to put out? Give her roofie, time she wakes up good times all over—she don't remember nothing and you didn't even have to argue. Roofies mean never having to say you're sorry, one kid tells me."

"Isn't that romantic?" Rosie said.

"I suppose whoever spiked his drink," Ray said, "didn't know about the Valium."

"Probably not. Didn't care either. Put coupla Scotches and double dose of roofies on top, plenty to cause respiratory depression. Similar drugs used for anaesthesia, procedures like colonoscopy, you know about that one? No, you're all too young. Anyway, drugs like that, maybe Versed—what's generic name? Midazolan—are given in very small increments, slow, careful, and no more than five milligrams total. This fella had more than twice that much, two or three tablets probably mixed in drinks. So." He turned the autopsy form around in front of Ray and Rosie, and pointed with his pen.

Rosie read aloud, "Cause of death: Valium, alcohol and Rohypnol in combination. Mechanism of death: respiratory depression leading to heart failure. Means of death: homicide." She asked Pokey, "How do we prove he didn't administer all three substances to himself?"

Pokey gave her a foxy smile and asked, "And waited till he was almost dead before he hit himself on head with skateboard?"

"Ah. And we're sure it was a blow *from* the skateboard? It can't be a fall *off* the skateboard?"

Pokey looked happy. "Asks good questions, this lady."

"Wait, I know the answer to that one," Ray said. "I've got it in my notes. The skateboard had little bits of skin and tissue in the bloody spot where it hit him. The cement didn't have any, only blood. Pretty sure my pictures will show it. Does it say that here in the report, Pokey?" Pokey showed him where it did. The two of them beamed at each other.

"How about a suspect while we're at it?" I said. "You find any DNA that didn't belong to the deceased?"

Pokey sighed. "Wants old Ukrainian workhorse to solve whole case for him," he said. "How about fingerprint boys, can't they do something?"

"That mean you didn't?"

"Correcto. All samples perfect match for records from Stillwater. What about body? Anybody want it?"

"Maddox found an uncle out in Elgin," Rosie said. "He's coming in tomorrow."

Ray's phone rang. "Jake's right here," he said, and then, "Okay." He hung up and told me, "LeeAnn's holding a call for you from the warden in St. Cloud."

"Okay. Thanks, Pokey." I hurried along the hall, telling LeeAnn, "Switch it to my office, will you?"

Joshua Reems said, "Say, your boy got roughed up pretty good last night."

"I told you I thought they were planning something."

"Uh-huh. In the laundry, right at the change of guards—looks like it was pretty well organized. Roger's boyfriend bought the farm. Roger wants to talk to you, you interested?"

"You bet. Is he up to it today?"

"Yeah, he can talk. Some. But he's got some damage to his right lung. The doc says the wound looks a little septic and there's a chance of pneumonia. If you want to hear what he has to say, my advice is maybe you oughta get up here ASAP."

The trip felt shorter the second time, because I had Kevin to talk to, and he had something interesting to say. "Mrs. Peabody called me this morning."

"She wants your body, huh?"

"I wish. No, it's very strange. She thinks someone's taken another gun."

"Hell you say. What now?"

"It doesn't make any sense, but . . . she says there's a Beretta missing."

"That little weeny—?"

"That's the one. Beretta 950B, a sweet little thing about the size of my palm. Shoots twenty-two caliber shorts. Ever fire one?"

"I don't think so."

"I did once. One of my uncles was visiting, he got it for his wife and he let me try it out. I took it out and shot it at an old road sign from about twenty feet. It barely made a dent."

"And now Mrs. Peabody thinks this cannon is missing? What does she want us to do, order up the bloodhounds?"

"Ooh, testy, testy. No, that's the goofy side of the call, she didn't want to make an official complaint because she doesn't want her father upset again. She just wanted to ask me to watch out for it, she said."

I laughed. It felt good. "Did you assure her we'd put the whole staff on it?"

"Well, not right away because she thinks maybe her father moved it someplace and forgot to put it back. But I told her we'd watch all the reports in the five-state area."

"Good for you."

"I thought so. And she said she'll call me right away if it turns up."

"See, it's just as I said, she's after your body."

"Sure." He liked the idea, though.

"Let's talk about this visit. I'm going to give you first crack at him, to try to find out where he sold the stuff he stole and who helped him set up the jobs. But in case he's worse off than we expect, be prepared for me to cut you off so I can ask my questions."

We got through Minneapolis easily in midmorning, ate our brown-bag lunches in the parking lot of a gas station on the edge of St. Cloud and followed a guard into the prison infirmary a little before one.

Roger was chained to a narrow infirmary cot by one ankle. The restraint had rubbed him raw in a couple of spots and someone had put some ointment on it and padded the cuff. Roger looked feverish. All his contempt was gone; self-pity was his sum and substance now.

"Sumbitch sneaking bastards jumped us in the laundry, never give Roy no chance at all," he said. "Stuck a shank right here in my chest, see?"

"I believe you, Roger. I don't need to see it." He showed us anyway.

"You think you can get me outa this hell-hole next year? Is that what you said?"

"The warden said you hadn't done anything to delay your release," I said, "and he told me if you'd show remorse, tell us where all the items went and answer my questions, he'd tell the parole board you cooperated."

"Okay," he said. "I'm hopin' to stay in this infirmary a good long time, give everybody a chance to cool off and then maybe I can survive till spring."

"Good," I said. "Let's start with the antiques and collectibles."

Roger laid it out quickly, prompted here and there by Kevin's questions: Izzy made him maps for all the houses he burglarized, she had played in them since childhood and knew convenient things like servants' entrances, balconies and outside cellar stairs. Kevin read from his records, nodding, as Roger described some of the items, the chess set, some framed miniatures and the dueling pistols.

His good escape routes kept him from getting caught, he said, till that last time when he ran into Kevin by an unlucky chance. They had a kick-ass place for a stash too, he said, above the ceiling in Izzy's back closet. They had sold several items—he called it "movin' the merch"—on eBay and fenced the rest in Sioux Falls. He muttered an obscure name for the fence and claimed not to remember how it was spelled.

"Did Izzy get a cut of the money?"

"We spent it together, sure."

"For what?"

He shrugged as if the question answered itself. "Booze and dope."

"Okay," I said, "that about it, then, Kevin?" Roger was starting to fade and I still had a lot to ask.

Kevin said quickly, "We'll need Izzy's full name and address."

"Yeah, well, I gotta think about that one."

"Okay," I said. "While you're thinking, tell us, where's your sister?"

"Ah, shit, she's right out there in Kasson with my uncle, my mom's brother." He spelled the name and address while Kevin wrote. "She went to Cancún in June but she got sick of that in a hurry. She called Mom and said she was lonesome, so Mom called Uncle Harold, and he said she could stay out there. She just had to stay out of Rutherford till Benny's trial was over—no reason she can't go home now. Except—" He breathed a while, raggedly, and thought. "Maybe you better go fetch 'er, huh? Because this happening to me, now I don't know—" He seemed to run out of ideas then, staring at the ceiling, looking tired.

"Why didn't she want to testify at Benny's trial?"

"They thought—" his breathing had bubbles in it now and his voice was very faint "—people might start thinking about her and me being brother and sister and figure out how the drugs and antiques all sort of—" He closed his eyes; he was turning an awful gray-green color, and the sweat stood out on his forehead.

I said, "You want some water or something?" He nodded and I handed the glass to Kevin, who stepped outside the curtain to look for a faucet.

"Roger," I said. "You mean Kylee thought we'd find out she was taking deliveries?"

"And that the deliveries was—" he breathed raggedly a while "—too big for one person." He had been clearing his throat for some time and now he began to cough.

I heard Kevin asking, just outside the curtain, where he could get some water, and an attendant asking him sharply, "Who's that for?" I leaned over Roger, whose eyes were closed, and asked urgently, "Did Elizabeth ever get any roofies in her package?"

"Not that I saw." His eyes opened partway, lazily, like a sleepy child's. His voice was high and thin; I had to lean over him to hear him say, "She took them sometimes though. So she wouldn't mind when he—you know."

"Roger, what are you saying?" His eyes wouldn't stay open anymore.

The attendant drew back the curtain sharply, came over to the bed and said, "Roger? Can you hear me? How long's he been like this?"

"He just got sleepy," I said, "a minute ago." She made a sharp sound and went out onto the floor, asking someone, "Where's the doctor?"

"Roger," I spoke into his ear. "What's Izzy's last name?"

His eyes fluttered. A little foam came out of his mouth. I could hear quick footsteps coming our way. The doctor came in with the nurse then, said "You'll have to leave" to us and began fussing with the tubes on an IV that the nurse wheeled in. I stood up, picked my tape recorder off the bed and was turning it off, getting ready to go when Roger's hand reached out and tugged at my sleeve.

Pretending not to notice the doctor's impatient glare, I leaned down and put my ear in front of Roger's lips. His whisper had barely enough breath behind it to carry any words at all. "I ain't the one that knocked her up," he said. "I didn't have nothing to do with the abortion."

20

Kevin and I talked as fast as we could between St. Cloud and the north side of Minneapolis. When we'd covered what we both knew he asked me, "Did Roger ever tell you Izzy's last name?"

"No. But he said she took roofies sometimes, so she wouldn't, I'm not sure, mind about something, I think he said. And then he said the damnedest thing—" I told him about that last thin whisper about an abortion.

"Jesus. Heavy stuff. Still—"

"I know. Not illegal, and none of our business."

"Exactly. Hurray for things that are none of our business. You ever think there oughta be a few more?"

"Whichever substances you want to deregulate, I just went deaf. Anyway there's the second Brooklyn Center exit. So call Ray now, and then don't say another word to me till we get to Eagan, okay?" Kevin snickered; he thinks my aversion to big city traffic is hilarious. He did as I asked, though. As soon as I cleared exit 70 I said, "So, you got him? Are we set?"

"Good to go," he said. At Pine Island I turned off the highway and we took county roads down to Kasson, where Ray was waiting for us in front of Diggers Bar & Grill. I parked the pickup there and we climbed in the department car with Ray.

"You'll have to drive, Ray," Kevin said, "Jake's been through Minneapolis twice today and his nerves are completely shot." They had a nice chuckle over that.

"Just hold on a minute here, smart-asses," I said, "while I go in the bar and ask somebody how to find this address."

Ray said, "It's a pretty small town. Don't you think we could just poke around till we find Front Street?"

"I don't want to poke around." We'd been looking for Kylee Mundt all summer, and now that we had her address I had a distinct inner vision of her disappearing into a cornfield as we approached her uncle's house. I went into the bar with the address Roger had dictated to Kevin, got directions from the bartender, and endured the amusement of my colleagues as we drove west past substantial brick and wooden-sided houses and found Harold Friedlander's house in five minutes flat.

Even so she almost got away. Her uncle answered the door and talked to us while her aunt quietly went out through the screen door in the kitchen. If Ray had not been alert enough to wonder why a woman would still be wearing her apron as she backed her Chevy out of the garage, he might not have stepped quickly into the driveway with his badge held high. He was able to pluck Kylee Mundt off the backseat floor of the car because, luckily, her aunt's protective impulses did not quite extend to running over a cop.

We didn't want to put cuffs on anybody with all the neighbors watching. They didn't bother with peeking through the curtains. They came out on their front steps, stared and made comments like, "What's the big idea?" and "Where'd these yo-yos come from, anyway?"

The three of us stood close around the two women while I said, "We just came from Roger, Kylee. He gave us your address. He wants you to talk to us now because he's been attacked in prison, and he's worried that you might not be safe out here much longer."

Kylee watched me out of pale blue-gray eyes. She had stringy dishwater-blond hair to her shoulders and very pale skin; if she had been to Cancún she had not enjoyed the sun much. Her cheap shorts and T-shirt were like herself, shabby and tired-looking, and the flip-flops on her feet were the cheapest C-store kind. Whatever this girl was doing, it wasn't getting her a better life.

"Roger got hurt?" She seemed to be conditioned to think of him first.

"Yes. I'm sorry to bring you bad news." I looked around at the curious faces of her neighbors. "Could we go inside and talk?"

She looked at her aunt.

"Lemme see your badges again, will you?" Aunt Peg stood on her hot sidewalk, wearing a green printed housedress with a rose-flowered apron over it, and examined them carefully. Her hair was brown with a good deal of gray in it, and her perm was partly grown out, the top three inches straight and the rest frizzed out. She was a solid, confident woman, and she took her time. When she was satisfied she looked up at her husband, who was standing on the top step in front of his open door, and said, "They look okay to me, Harold."

"Okay, honey, why don't you come on in, then?" he said.

We stayed close to the women, going up the steps. It felt like herding wild rabbits. They looked peaceable, but I had no idea what they might do next. It probably depended on what they did last, I thought, and who knew what that was? In the living room the aunt and uncle offered us what were obviously their usual seats, two easy chairs with afghans on them, facing the TV set.

I said, "Any chance we could sit in the kitchen?" I wanted Kylee to sit where we could all see her face. Her motivation was completely mysterious to me, and I wanted to be able to check my impressions later with Ray and Kevin. We had looked for her for so long, I really felt as if I ought to check her into the evidence room and not bring her out till the whole crew was assembled to inspect her.

The four of us sat down around the small table, taking up all the chairs. Her aunt and uncle came and leaned against the kitchen counters, not exactly hostile but watching every move we made. It was a funny arrangement for an interview but I thought their protectiveness was a positive sign in an otherwise very confusing family picture, so I decided not to argue about it. I could arrest her if I had to—I had the drug charge and possible complicity in Roger's thefts. But we needed what she knew and I was hoping if we could get her to trust us so she would talk.

I put a fresh tape in the recorder and started it, said the day and date and time.

"Maybe it will save some time if we tell you what we know," I said. "We picked up your drug dealer and two of his delivery boys, so we know about the drugs."

"Oh." Her pale eyes made a circuit of each of our faces, lingering longest on Kevin's but finally coming back to me. She seemed to be waiting for me to tell her the rest. Her face was pale and somewhat worn for a girl in her mid-twenties but she didn't have the beaten look of an addict; she bore no resemblance to Bo's prisoner in the jail.

"Your landlady told us you get a package in your mailbox every Monday," I said, "and your delivery boy told us you don't have to pay him, you pay the dealer direct. Tell us about the delivery first. Is it all meth?"

"I don't know what's in the package. I don't have to know. He leaves it and I pass it along. I'm not involved in—I don't use anything."

"How do you pay?"

"I don't."

"And you don't know who does?"

"Um, yes, I know." Her eyes made that tour of our faces again. She looked like a cat making up its mind which way to jump. "How did Roger get hurt?"

"He had a protector in the prison who made the guards angry. I think they arranged to turn their backs while a gang took revenge. The protector's dead; Roger just got in the way."

"Is he going to be all right?"

"I'm not sure. He was badly hurt." She made a small sound, put the fingers of one pale hand against her lips and withdrew into herself. I let her sit quietly for a long thirty seconds. She didn't seem to be going to cry so I said, "Kylee, there's nothing more you can do for Roger. Don't you want to help yourself out of this jam he left you in?"

Unexpectedly, Uncle Harold cleared his throat and said, "Honey, I think you ought to listen to the officer. I've told your ma before; it ain't right the way she always expects you to fix everything that crazy Roger does. It's time you had some life of your own." Kylee looked at him and then at her aunt, who was nodding from her corner of the kitchen, turned back to me and said, "Okay."

"If you don't use the drugs," I asked her, "who does?"

Kylee blinked her pale eyes two or three times and squared her shoulders. "Elizabeth and Roger used all the meth."

"Elizabeth? Is that the girl he calls Izzy?"

"Yes."

"What's her last name?"

"Aldrich. Isn't it? Well, no, I guess it's the same as her father's. Peabody."

"Peabody? Are you saying your brother was sleeping with Elizabeth Peabody?"

She made a little *ump* noise, embarrassed to be talking about *that* in front of her elders, and finally said, "Yes."

"And Elizabeth Peabody's the one who helped him plan all those burglaries?"

"I didn't know they were doing that."

"But you did know it was Elizabeth paying for the meth?"

"Well, yes. He made it sound okay, though. Like it was just for recreation until she could get over wanting crack."

"Who's he?"

"Mr. Newman, the one that sent me over there in the first place. And maybe it was just for fun at first but after a while she wanted more and he said no—"

"Mr. Newman?"

"No, her father. That's what Roger told me. Her dad said she shouldn't use any more than that, so then she and Roger figured out how to get the money for more. I always delivered the package to her, so her dad didn't know she'd increased the order."

"Roger said there were some roofies for Elizabeth, too, you know anything about that?"

"Roofies? You mean that thing they call the—" her eyes slid around toward her uncle and back again "—date-rape pill? No. I don't see why—" she looked at her hands "—anybody would need to give one of those to Elizabeth."

The phone rang. Harold Friedlander answered it. A woman's voice, high and hysterical, spilled out into the kitchen, making us all sit up and watch him. Kylee, at the sound of the wailing voice, whirled in her chair and stretched her right arm toward the phone. Harold Friedlander said repeatedly, "Louise. Louise. Listen, Louise—" After a while he gave up and handed the phone to Kylee.

Kylee said, "Oh, Mama, what—" and listened in silence as the shrieking voice poured disaster into her ear. Gradually she began curling up around the phone until her knees hid her lowered face, and her bare left arm lay across the top of her head like a shield. From inside the curled bundle she made of herself, little sniffing sounds came out, and tears began to run unheeded down the sides of her thin white legs.

21

After a long time, the voice on the phone slowed enough so Kylee began muttering, "Mmm," and, "Uh-huh," and, "No," at intervals. Then there was a longish burst of barked demands on the other end. At the end of that she said, "Yeah. Okay," and handed the phone back to Harold Friedlander. "I have to go home," she said. "Mama needs me."

"We'll take you to town, Kylee," I said, "but you'll have to stop at the station before you go home, we've still got a lot of questions to ask you."

"No no no." She shook her head hard. "Roger's dead and I gotta get home and help Mama."

"I'll pack some clothes for you," her aunt said. "You can get the rest of your stuff later."

"Kylee," I said, "listen to me. I know this is a bad time for you but unless you pull yourself together now and help us, we have to arrest you for dealing drugs, don't you understand that?"

"Dealing? I didn't make any money off of—" She stopped and thought. "I mean it was just part of my job."

"Exactly. You got paid for delivering the dope," I said. "I'm sure Elizabeth Peabody will testify to that, and she'll probably also say you helped your brother with the burglaries."

"I did not," Kylee said. "She did that. I didn't even know about them till just before Roger got caught."

"Oh, but that won't matter to Elizabeth," I said. "She'll say anything that gets her off the hook now and her parents will back her up. Do you know how much clout the Aldrich family has in Rutherford?"

"They have a lot of money, I know that."

"Tons of it. And Elizabeth's been using you as a mule to ferry drugs for her and Roger. And now that we know about it they'll throw you to the wolves without another thought, don't you see that?"

"Jake—" Kevin began, shocked to hear me bashing his heroes. At the same time Harold Friedlander said, "Now see here, I'm not gonna let you bully my niece."

"I'm not bullying her. I'm trying to persuade her to help herself out of a jam."

"You're threatening her. Who do you think you are, anyway, coming out here and pushing us all around? I want you to know I've got some friends in this town and if I have to I can raise a stink you'll be able to smell all the way to Canada."

"Here's who I think I am," I said, and put my card on the table, "and what I'm doing is the job they pay me to do. You want stink, I'll show you some people in jail right now in Rutherford who would gag a maggot, and Kylee's been mixed up in their business, the *drug* business. Can you get that through your head? This is no kids' game; we're not playing beanbag here."

"It wasn't her," he said, but backing off a little, "it was her no-good brother."

"No. It was her. She took the money and delivered the goods, and now she has to tell us everything she knows about it and try to help herself out of this hole she dug, understand?"

"Baby?" He put his hand on the top of Kylee's head and tilted it so their eyes met. "What do you say about this?"

A few more tears leaked out of the corners of her eyes but she didn't turn away from him. "I guess he's got a point. I did take them their stupid drugs and if you come right down to it I did it to keep that extra job. So I suppose you could say I got paid for it."

"So whaddya think you oughta do?"

She closed her eyes for a minute, wiped the tears off her face, sniffed, opened her eyes and searched his face. "Talk, I guess."

"Okay, good. Hey, a little talk can't hurt anything." He leaned toward her till they were touching foreheads. "Right, sis? Just tell 'em everything you know and get rid of this mess. Will you?"

"Okay." They seemed to have a true bond of affection. I had a feeling Uncle Harold was the one reliable person in a world that kept collapsing around Kylee Mundt.

"There you go." He carried her green bag out to the car, asking me as we walked along, "You'll look after her, now, will you? You're not gonna be too tough on her?"

"No harm is going to come to her in the Rutherford Police Station," I said, which was true as far as it went but not entirely an honest answer.

When Kylee was belted into the front seat Harold Friedlander walked to her side of the car, leaned in and said, "Call me soon as you can, will you?"

"I will. Thanks, Uncle Harold."

Kevin and I climbed in back and Ray drove me to my pickup. As soon as we were out on the highway I called the station, got Rosie on the phone and told her, "This is a rush job. Call the superintendent of schools and tell him you need Elizabeth Peabody's school records faxed to you ASAP."

"You want high school, middle school?"

"Get a full set if you can, everything since first grade. Look through as many as you can before we get there."

"Which will be—?"

"We're just leaving Kasson. We'll be there in half an hour."

We were four miles north of the station in fifteen minutes, but then we hit construction, so my estimate held. We were upstairs in the small meeting room thirty-five minutes after we left Uncle Harold.

LeeAnn found Bo and Rosie for me and brought us a pitcher of water. "We'll go around the table clockwise," I said. "Everybody ask her what you need to know. Wait, where's Ray, though?"

"He's on the phone. He'll be here in a minute."

"Okay. Why don't you start, Bo?"

Bo wanted to know about the drop. "How long have you been getting the delivery?"

"About a year and a half."

"Always at that same address? You haven't moved?"

"No."

"Has it always been Sean making the deliveries?"

"I never saw who delivered it. It came while I was at work."

Bo had two little notebooks and was checking her answers against statements he had taken earlier from LeFever and Sean Lynch. He nodded, satisfied by her first answers, and asked her, "So you picked up the delivery when you got home Monday night and took it to work with you Tuesday, is that it?

"Uh, no. See, till this summer I was working days at my regular job, so I fit in the work at the Aldrich house evenings and weekends.

I didn't work every night, but I always worked Monday night," her voice took on a little edge, "and I had to try to get there by seven. Elizabeth would be waiting for me."

"But since you left town in June she what? Picked up the package herself?"

"I guess so. That's the way I was told to leave it."

"What about this week? Have you heard from her since the delivery was intercepted?"

"No. She doesn't know my—we're not in touch."

"Haven't been trading e-mails? No? No phone calls? How come?"

"We're not friends," she said, in that flat way she had, stating the truth baldly and letting it lie.

Bo looked at me. "That's it till we talk."

"Okay. Kevin?"

"Did Mrs. Peabody know Elizabeth was getting meth every week?" His big worry.

"I have no idea. I never saw Mrs. Peabody."

"You didn't? She never answered the door when you came?"

"Elizabeth's wing has its own entrance. I used that."

"Mom never came up to see how the two of you were getting along with the Mac?"

"The what?"

"Weren't you helping Elizabeth set up her computer for school?"

"Oh." She searched his face. Looking for clues, I thought, though it could have been just the usual female reaction to Kevin Evjan's pheremones. "Yes. But Mrs. Peabody wasn't—she was busy. And it didn't seem like the two of them were very . . . close."

"But Elizabeth's father knew about the drugs?"

"Roger said so."

"You never heard it from James Peabody himself?"

"Oh, no. I never—he hardly ever spoke to me at all."

"He didn't? You mean Elizabeth just told you what she wanted done and you did it?"

"Elizabeth?" For the first time since we found her, Kylee Mundt looked amused. The moment passed quickly and her pale face went morose again. "No, the lawyer told me what to do."

"Reese Newman? How would he know what Elizabeth needed on her computer for school?"

She watched him for about five seconds before she said, "He seems to look after everybody in the family."

"I see." Kevin looked at me and said, "All for now."

Rosie, still thumbing through a pile of school records, looked up and asked, "Were you working for the Peabodys four years ago, when Elizabeth was in ninth grade?"

"No. I've only worked for them for two years."

"Did she ever tell you what went wrong that year? What made her go from a straight-A student to failing, in the space of three months?"

"She never told me anything about herself."

"Did Roger tell you anything about it?"

"Uh . . . no. Except I think it was about a year later when he met her in detox, and I remember he said she'd already been to a couple other places. So I suppose she started flunking in school when she started drinking and using drugs."

"But you don't know what got her started?"

Kylee shrugged. "What gets anybody started? They try it and it feels good, I guess."

"Okay," Rosie said. "I'd like to show you these records later, Jake, but for now I guess that's it for me."

"Fine. I wonder what's holding Ray? Well, I'll go ahead," I said. "Why were you working for the Peabodys anyway? Didn't you have a full-time job at the secretarial service?"

"Yes. But I needed more money."

"For what? I don't mean to be rude but . . . your clothes and apartment look pretty cheap. Why did you need two jobs?"

She twitched in her chair making little outrage noises, *hmmp, hmmp*. Police interviews aim toward this place, where we've finally touched the sore spot. It's surprising how often it involves money. Ask them about their sex lives or their drinking habits or the times they beat up on Granny and they may dodge around a little but eventually they'll tell you all about it—they're dying to tell. Get to the money question, though, and they start acting like you just tore off all their clothes in public. In some way, money is the cover we use for the most intimate parts of ourselves.

Finally she said, "It was for Mama. The insurance company wouldn't pay when he wrecked her car because Roger was drunk and his license wasn't valid. Then after his next arrest she took a second mortgage on her house to get bail money and he skipped, they had to go find him. She was gonna lose the house so Mr. Newman helped me borrow—" She pushed her stringy hair off her face and started to leak tears again. "Every time we started to get out of the woods, Roger messed up again."

Ray and Kevin and I had already watched her cry once, so we knew how hopeless she could look. Bo and Rosie were new to her swamp of despair but they got enough of it fast. I was just getting up to pass her the box of tissues, about to suggest we could take her to her mother's house now, when Ray walked in.

"We're just about done," I said, "but I got it on tape."

"Good. I just have a coupla things myself."

Kylee's face was out of sight behind a handful of tissues. I watched her heaving shoulders and said, "Uh . . . maybe we better give her a minute."

"Oh? All right." He put his notes on the table, folded his hands on top of them and waited. A minute passed and then two. Rosie was checking her cuticles with her mouth pursed sideways and the rest of the detectives were inspecting their shoes by the time Kylee quit sobbing. Ray cleared his throat and said, "When was Roger in Shelley Gleason's car?"

Her hands with the wads of tissues in them came down onto the table, *thunk,* and her swollen eyes blazed at him out of her poor ravaged face. *"What?"*

Ray sat and looked at her, tapping his pencil softly on the table. After a few seconds he asked her mildly, "Didn't you understand the question?"

"My poor brother hasn't even been dead one whole day and you're already trying to hang a murder on him?"

"I haven't decided that yet," Ray said, "till I find out when he left that smear of blood in the Ford Explorer."

"You're making that up," she said. "He couldn't have. He was never in that car."

"I think he was. Trudy called just now," he said, turning to me. "I offered to come and get you but she said it didn't matter, said she could give the information to me. She had a few minutes while she was waiting for a batch to run, she said, so she compared that unmatched blood smear in the Explorer with Roger's DNA records and bingo, there's Roger in the Ford Explorer." He turned back to Kylee. "When you testified at Dale's trial about seeing Dale and Benny in the car, you said Roger was in your apartment with you. But he wasn't, was he? He was in the car with the other two, right?"

"Of course not. He never—" She glared at Ray Bailey for a few seconds longer and then her eyes seemed to lose focus. Her cheeks went slack and she slumped forward and buried her head in her arms on the table. For another dreadful period which was certainly not as long as it seemed, we sat around on folding chairs and watched Kylee Mundt weep.

I was getting ready to suggest Rosie take her to the bathroom and help her calm down when she sat up abruptly, flinging stray teardrops over the nearest law officers, and hit the table with both fists. "Oh, the hell with it!" she yelled, at the top of her lungs so that the sound bounced around the walls of the room and carried into the hall. LeeAnn's busy clatter outside our door went silent for a minute, and a sort of ringing silence held us all frozen till a cooler motor kicked on in a vending machine somewhere nearby, and gradually the rest of the building's noises resumed.

Kylee Mundt met Ray's eyes and whispered, "He's really dead, isn't he?"

"Yes."

"I don't—" she paused and took a deep breath, "—have to cover for him anymore."

"No."

The thought seemed to need a lot of getting used to. Ray let her take her time. Finally she said, in that flat voice she kept for the worst parts of her life, "Dale and Roger jacked the car and killed Shelley Gleason."

We all inhaled at once. Nobody moved, though.

"Why did Benny take the fall?"

She gave a sad little pitying headshake and said, "You have to understand, Benny *loved* Dale Trogstad. He was always trying to get Dale to say they were best buds, friends to the end. The three of them ran around together. Dale usually hung with Roger, but sometimes when Roger got in bed with Elizabeth or one of his other girlfriends, if they had plenty of booze and dope he might not even want to *move* for a few days, so then Dale would put up with Benny.

Benny was dumb but he could be plenty tough and mean and he had some connections from growing up his whole life with thieves and prostitutes, so sometimes he was useful when they were planning a caper. That's what they called that thieving and cheating they all did instead of ever doing any work." She was going good now, getting it all off her chest at last. We sat still while she took a deep breath, wiped off her face and pushed her hair back.

"The three of them planned the car-jacking together. Benny knew just how to do it, he said, from talking to guys in prison, and he had the connections at the chop-shop for selling the car after they got it. And Roger had access to the guns in Elizabeth's house."

Kevin said, "Did they take everything in that burglary at once?"

"They took all the guns at once. Elizabeth helped. They'd already been stealing things out of the house, silver and rare stamps, stuff that wouldn't be missed right away, and selling it for cash for more dope. So when Roger wanted guns to jack a car, it wasn't that big a deal; they just went ahead and took them."

"What about the extra guns, though? The revolver and the dueling pistols?"

"I don't know everything they did. Roger told me all this at the end while he was waiting for his trial after he got caught with the jewelry. I know they sold the antique pistols. And they took one revolver because Benny wanted it, that Ruger. Somebody in the slam told him that was the kind of gun assassins used, and that's the job he always wanted. He told Roger, 'Stick that in somebody's ear and pull the trigger and the bullet goes round and round, man.' I can still hear that crazy laugh of his after he said something like that.

"Anyway, they had the guns. They were bragging to their friends that they were going to make this big score, and then one night Benny got hired as a bouncer at the topless bar up on the highway and Dale told Roger, 'Let's do it while he's gone. He's so crazy I'm afraid he'll screw it up,' so they did. But then they got carried away and, you know, killed that poor girl, and by morning they were tired so they put the car in the garage at Dale's place and went to sleep. Benny came back and found them. He was way high on some dope he got on the job and when he found out they jacked the car without him he was so mad he started yelling and breaking up furniture. So to shut him up they said, 'Come on, Benny, we'll all take a ride.' "

"Is that when they came by your place?"

"Yeah."

"So Roger wasn't there with you?"

"He was in the car. But we agreed later I should always say he was at my place, had been there two days helping me move some furniture. What a joke, Roger helping."

"Why didn't Roger go with them to LaCrosse?"

"He did. But first they went and got Elizabeth and said, 'You wanna take a ride?' They had the money from Shelley Gleason's credit card and Elizabeth had some, too, so they rented a couple of rooms in LaCrosse and Roger and Elizabeth bought vodka and scored some meth. But Benny, you know, he never could sleep more than a couple of hours at a time and pretty soon he wanted to go on, but Roger and Elizabeth wouldn't budge. So Dale and Benny said they'd go sell this car and jack another one that night or the next night and come back for Roger."

"Why didn't Benny tell us where he was the night of the murder?"

"His pride," Kylee said. "He had told all their buds what they were going to do. He thought they'd laugh at him if word got around that Dale and Roger did it without him."

22

LeeAnn took Kylee to the break room for a snack while we held a short, not very amiable meeting.

I said, "Bo, I want to tell her if she keeps helping us like this we'll bury the drug charge."

"Fine with me," he said. "She doesn't know anything I can use, so why am I even here?"

"Because I was hoping you were going to uncover something to tie Benny into all this drug business. I figured that's what got him killed, but it's just like at the trial—we never seem to quite put him there."

"Hell, when she comes back let's just ask her if she knows whether Benny ever did any dealing."

"Okay. You asked LeFever, right, if Benny was working for him?"

"Never thought of it. Wasn't he in jail until after we picked up LeFever?"

"I think there was a day or two in there when he was out. You could check. And there's one other thing." I watched him while I

---

said it. "I've been thinking that right now would be a perfect time to set up a sting to catch Elizabeth Peabody."

"Catch her doing what? Oh, you mean picking up her delivery?"

"Yeah. Before she finds some other source, I thought we could have Kylee call her—"

"Jake." He gave me his ice-cold look. "If you got time for circlejerks with users you go right ahead and try that, but you're not going to talk me into throwing my career down that rathole."

"I'm curious about what's behind her drug use and I think if we could get her out of that house—"

"What's behind drug use is more drug use. When did you turn into Doctor Do Good?"

"Would it kill you to just trust me once?" He looked at his shoes. "Any reason you can't do it?"

He glared at the water pitcher a while and finally said, "Yes. The same reason you can't. Because when that little head case up on the hill screams foul and gets her high-powered attorney to sue the department, it's going to be our asses on the line, don't you know that much by now, for chrissake?"

I opened my mouth to argue—it was such a perfect plan, I had already envisioned the way she would step up on that porch and open the box, take out the package and turn—but then I remembered Frank saying, "Let Kevin take their stuff back. He seems to get along with them all right," and I sat back and said, "You're right. Forget it."

"Jake—"

"It was a dumb idea. Can we go on? Any other big issues before we get Kylee back?"

"Well, wait a minute," Ray said. "What about Kylee's perjury at the trial? Are you just going to forget that too?"

"Let's not bring it up unless she does," I said. "We might need one or two more bargaining chips before we're done."

"Well, *now that's* really rotten," Rosie said. "You tell her she's off the hook but then you keep something back to threaten her with later?"

"She's been holding out on us, hasn't she?" Rosie made a dissatisfied noise and began restacking her school records, *smack, smack,* on the table in front of her. "What else?"

"Jake," Kevin said, "are you going where I think with these school records? I thought you agreed it was her own business."

"What's her own business?" Rosie quit punishing transcripts and turned her nose toward me like a beagle. "The two of you know something you're not telling the rest of us?" She couldn't stand the thought.

"We don't know anything," I said, "and it's almost five o'clock. Let's get her back in here and wrap this up."

"We'll have to see you again," I told her when she got back. "There's more to go over. But we'll try to leave you alone now till after the funeral. There's a squad waiting downtairs to take you to your mother's house."

Ray looked disapproving as he watched her walk away. "We should at least charge her with obstruction of justice. She's known about the thefts and the murder since before we put Roger away."

"I know," I said, "but why show our whole hand at once? If we can keep her working for us like this, you have to admit she's quite an asset."

"If she stays around."

"Her mother's here and they're planning a funeral. Where's she going to go?"

"Where'd she go all summer? You still don't really know."

"I don't think she's likely to take off right now, and I'd like to keep her thinking we're on her side."

"Not that you probably have to," Rosie said. "She's such a doormat.

God, putting her neck in the noose like that for her pondscum brother. What was she thinking?"

Kevin said, "What, you wouldn't cut a corner for any of the Doyle boys, Rosie?"

Rosie turned on him with a sharp retort ready, but it froze in her mouth. She segued into a surprised look, blinked three times and said, "I guess I would have to think about it."

"See?" Kevin said happily, "like I always say, we all have our price, but it isn't always money."

"Oh, that's deep," Rosie said. "Anyway, don't worry, the Doyle boys ride herd on *me*."

"You know what I wonder," Ray said, "is how many lives we saved when we stopped Shelley Gleason's Ford Explorer that day."

"Good question," I said. "Sounds like they had their hearts set on at least one more, didn't they?"

"And if that one worked, why would they have stopped at two?"

"Come in," Maxine called, when I walked up to her open door. "How are you, Jakey-dum-diddle?" Eddy kicked his chair and made squeaky noises, his new way to show pleasure—he likes Maxine's nicknames. They were sitting at the kitchen table, playing cards. "You want some coffee?"

"No, thanks. Brought you some corn." I put the bag on the counter.

"I'm gonna win," Eddy said. His eyes looked wet and excited.

"Oh-ho, the game isn't over yet, remember I'm pretty smart," Maxine said. She slapped down a card and drew the last one from the stack, got up and looked in the bag. "Oh, good, we'll have that for supper."

"There, I did another one," Eddy said, matching the top card. He was watching the stack the way a kestrel watches a sparrow; I had never seen him so turned on.

"I don't have any more matching cards," Maxine said. She had two. "I'll have to skip this turn." Eddy matched the card he'd just put down, held up his empty hands and said, "All my cards are gone."

"Heck, I've still got five cards," Maxine said. "You won again, Eddy." He kicked his chair unmercifully and squeaked some more.

"Hey," I said. "Eddy, you're turning into a regular shark."

"More of a dolphin, I think," Maxine said.

Eddy's face had seemed frozen solid for a long time after he came to Maxine's house. Lately it had been thawing out gradually, and today he wore a look that almost qualified as a by-god smile. The cheeks were still stiff and the lifter muscles around his mouth needed practice, but the eyes took up the slack. When he got done punishing the chair he said, "I bet I beat Nelly tomorrow."

"You might at that. Say, I forgot to check the mailbox today," Maxine said. "Would you do that for me, Eddy?"

When he was out the door I said, "Nelly's not going to throw games to him like you do."

"I just did that today to keep him trying," she said. "I watched him playing cards with Nelly this morning and I realized he was only matching numbers. He didn't get the part about matching suits, so of course he couldn't win."

"You gave him a lesson later?"

"No, right then. Nelly loves to teach people, did you know that? She's already a big help with the two little girls. She helped me take the deck apart and we showed him about hearts and spades and so on."

"Wasn't he almost six when he came to you? You'd think he'd have known that."

222 | ELIZABETH GUNN

"I think Eddy's family was troubled for a long time before the big explosion."

He came running back, slammed the screen door and held up the mail, a few envelopes addressed to "Resident," and a catalogue. He watched Maxine glance through it. "Okay," she said, putting it down, "you can open it."

He moved it carefully to his place at the table, brought a table knife and began to slit open envelopes, one at a time, and lay out their contents with solemn attention. I remember doing that in Maxine's house when I was small. When you're a kid nobody ever writes to, junk mail is like a smile from a stranger, hard to figure out sometimes but better than nothing.

"I gotta go," I said. "You want to come out Sunday, tell us about your trip?"

"Fine." She hugged me. "Thank Trudy for the corn. Is she getting along all right with that big garden?"

"She hates zucchini in a deeply personal way, but otherwise we seem to be holding steady."

It was a perfect afternoon, so I left the radio and air conditioner off, rolled down the window and enjoyed the drive home the old-fashioned way—I even left the cruise control off. I called Trudy, agreed on burgers and beans for a quick supper so we could weed the peas and pick cucumbers. Good, an easy night. And I had a breezy half hour in my pickup first, to enjoy driving and forget about work.

But my mind wouldn't leave the day alone; I kept going back over the tantalizingly incomplete conversation at the prison with Roger Mundt in the morning, and the grotesque revelations from his sister in the afternoon. What a pair of bookends, I thought, like paradigms for the two extremes of family dysfunction. Roger felt entitled to take anything without asking; Kylee was obliged to give whatever was asked.

Family's such a roll of the dice, I thought. It's amazing people keep starting them. The harvest smells coming in my window kept cheering me up, though, and I made up my mind to think about good stuff the rest of the way home. The look on Eddy's face, for instance—thrilled to find out that even he can win. The win/lose component of that memory spun me back to the earlier scene in my office with Frank, though. *"Let Kevin take their stuff back. He seems to get along with them all right."*

I pushed the memory out of my mind, determined not to waste energy on anger and resentment. But there was plenty there to get mad about, my brain decided furtively on its own, creeping back for another lick at the grievance, like a tongue determined to play with a sore place in the mouth. "Intrusive"—that was the label the Peabodys stuck on me, and Frank repeated it like he'd never heard there was any difference between police work and interior decorating. The rich royals had phoned down from their hilltop to protest an intrusive inquiry by a member of the department, suggesting I didn't know how to behave in their fine house. Did Mrs. Peabody read my name off my card, I wondered, or did she just say *the dark-skinned one?*

But no, what was I thinking? Mrs. Peabody didn't call. Elegant rich women don't call; they have their attorneys call. What was that Kevin said? *You can't expect the people with the money to punch in the numbers themselves.* She had told Reese Newman to call, and that condescending bastard had sat in his posh office, wearing his perfect suit, while he said—

Why did he, though? Years of rigorous investigative training finally wedged a small notch in my rage, allowing a rational thought to bubble up. It was the one I'd been trying to get a handle on this morning, when Pokey's bravura recital of his autopsy report blew it away. I'd been asking myself why a class act like Helen Aldrich Peabody would call her smooth-as-glass attorney and say something as silly as, "A detective annoyed me yesterday, and I want you to call the chief of police and complain"?

And even if the elegant heiress somehow lost her cut-crystal poise and did that, I reasoned, why wouldn't her highly paid, worldly attorney say, "My dear, you have a rich foundation to run and your beloved father's breaking down. Do you really have time to be bothered by common trash like Jake Hines?" I could almost hear him saying it.

While we're at it, I decided, why don't we ask again why that able attorney in the hand-stitched suit took on the pro bono defense of Benny Niemeyer? In several days of observing Reese Newman in court, I had never once caught a glimpse of the kindly fellow quoted in the newspaper as wanting his lawn-trimmer to get a fair shake. "Bullshit," Milo had said, and he was right; the Reese Newman we watched in court was no do-gooder.

My thoughts were so absorbing, it was some time before I noticed that everybody on the road was giving me curious looks as they passed me. I glanced at my speedometer, saw my speed was down to forty-five miles an hour, and put my foot on the gas just as my phone rang.

I was out in open country near a farm driveway, and since I was already slowed down I pulled into it, punched TALK and said, "Hines."

"Say, I hope I'm not bothering you when you're busy," a man's voice said.

"No. Uh—" It didn't sound like a telemarketer, but I couldn't place the voice.

"Well, I got to worrying and then I remembered you left your card. So I told the Missus, I'm just gonna call him and see what he thinks."

"Is this Mr. Friedlander?"

"Oh shucks, I should have said that—how was you supposed to know?" I sat still and let him enjoy the joke. The more you interrupt a rambler, the longer it takes. "Well see, the thing is a fella came out here a few minutes ago. He had a note from Kylee saying it was okay for him to pick up her computer. It was a typed note but the signature was her handwriting all right—I'd know it anyplace. I asked him about the rest of her stuff, clothes and books and so on, but he said no, she'd get those later. She just wanted him to be sure to get all the discs that went with the laptop, he said, and he took the whole shootin' match."

"Huh. Why wouldn't she call?"

"See, that's what I got to worrying about, but not till—at the time, I guess I let him get me a little flustered. He kept saying he was in such a hurry, and she needed it right away."

"Did you call her mother?"

"After he was gone. But she made me really uncertain—I mean, Louise said she got a phone message for Kylee, just before she got home, to call Reese Newman's office. Kylee didn't want to do it, Louise said, but then she did. And Mr. Newman said could she come to the bank there for a few minutes and help him out with a problem? So Kylee said this will only take a few minutes, but now Louise is worried because that was over an hour ago and when she called the office was closed."

"Mr. Friedlander, you did right to call me."

"Does that mean you're gonna look into it?"

"Right away."

"Oh, good. Good! And listen, could you—if it wouldn't be too much trouble, could you call me back after you find out anything?" "I'll do it. I've got your phone number," I said, and hung up quickly because he was starting to talk again.

I backed out of the driveway, crossed the two northbound lanes and bounced across the median illegally. As soon as I was headed back south to Rutherford with the cruise control set on eighty-three, I called Ray's cell phone and caught him on his way home. He answered on the first ring and I talked very fast for several minutes.

I've never been more pleased with Ray's instincts. After the first few seconds he didn't talk at all except to say, "Uh-huh. Okay. Gotcha." Ideas were bumping into each other in my head and I needed to pour them out like that, quick and dirty. Because I didn't have it all sorted out yet, but I was pretty sure that, like Eddy, I had only been looking at half the possibilities.

While I waited for Ray to call me back I called Trudy and told her I had no idea when I'd get home. "Be careful, lover," she said, and got off the phone like the experienced cop's mate she is.

Two minutes later Ray called, already back in his office. "Records came up with all the license numbers and the watch captain put out an Attempt to Locate. Darrell's on his way back and so's Rosie. Hold on, call coming in." The sun sank low in my rearview mirror as I watched the road rush by and listened to the silence, gritting my teeth.

"Hanenberger's spotted one of the license plates on a Honda Odyssey," Ray said on the next call. "Hold on a minute." The last rays of sunset blazed against the metal storage sheds at the north edge of town as Ray came back and said, "We're gonna have Putratz meet 'em at the next light and have a look. Hold on." Two minutes later he said happily, "Bingo. Both of them. We got three squads taking turns on the tail but Rosie's already on her way in a Crown Vic to replace Hanenberger."

"Good man," I said. "You and Darrell good to go?"

"Darrell's bringing the old Dodge van up. I'm on my way. Call you back from there." Two minutes later my phone rang again and he said, very fast, "Go to radio now, channel nine," and the phone line went dead. I tuned to the tactical channel and heard Ray ask, "Jake, you getting close?"

"Just passing the car wash."

"Rosie, where are you?"

"Headed north on Broadway, crossing the railroad tracks now. Honda's two blocks ahead, still moving north."

"Okay, we see you now," Ray said a few seconds later. "Turn right at the next corner. Let us take the tail a while and you follow on First Avenue." I didn't want to blunder into the procession in my red pickup, so I pulled into the parking lot in front of a strip mall and waited.

Before long Ray said, "Honda's turning right at Tenth Street. Watch for it, Rosie." When he came back he said, "Honda just pulled into the park, heading into the parking lot by the picnic shelter."

I pulled back onto the street and drove south on Broadway to Tenth Street. As soon as I turned left I saw the old brown van pulled up tight to the curb, at the end of the block nearest the park. Beyond it, a Honda minivan was pulling into the paved lot. I drove a block toward the park, turned south, parked as soon as I could and trotted back to the corner in the gathering dusk.

Keeping a big messy box elder between me and the Honda, I peered through its lower branches, watching the Dodge and the Honda beyond it. Rosie pulled past me in the Crown Vic with no lights on, turned into Tenth Street, stopped two car lengths behind the Dodge and killed the motor.

Lights were coming on in the houses across the lake. I hugged the hedge along the sidewalk from the corner to the Dodge. When I walked up beside it the door slid open on the right side and I climbed in beside Darrell. Ray was in front, hunkered down with the radio mike in his hand.

The Honda had parked at the farthest end of the lot, as near the lake as it could get. Two men got out, in working clothes I thought at first but then saw they were the sportsman's version, hiking boots and name-brand jeans. One of them went to the side door of the van and took something out. The other man walked to the far end of the parking lot onto the grass, turned right along the grassy slope above the lake and kept walking till he disappeared. I couldn't see their features well in the dim light, but watching them move, I recognized them both: James Peabody and Reese Newman.

It was Newman who had taken a parcel from the car. He carried it along the same grassy slope where Peabody had gone, but soon veered left toward the water and climbed the steps to the little footbridge that crossed the river where it spilled into the lake. Lights from town were reflected in the lake, but the bridge was in near-darkness and we could just see Newman's silhouette. I never saw him drop the parcel, but we all saw the splash.

"Shit," I said, "there went the laptop."

Ray said, "You want us to—"

"No. Let it play out."

The outline of Reese Newman's confident shoulders moved back across the bridge toward us, but when he stepped down onto the grass he was lost in the shadows. He reappeared under the tall light at the lake end of the parking lot, walked to the van and got in the driver's side. He lit a cigar, rolled down the window and sat comfortably with his arm on the sill, smoking and flicking his ashes onto the asphalt. While he smoked, Hanenberger stepped out of an alley and

moved obliquely across the grass to the right of us, keeping the picnic shelter between him and the Honda. He walked into the shadow
at the south end of the shelter and disappeared.

"Al's here," Darrell said.

"I see him. Casey and Green are in the trees near the playground,"
Ray said.

When Newman's cigar was about half gone, an indistinct shape
began to bob around in the middle of the lake, noticeable mostly as
a dark spot in the middle of all the lights that were being reflected
out there now. As it drew close enough to catch the light from the
parking lot, it began to look a lot like James Peabody, sitting in the
water.

"What the hell's he doing out there?" Darrell said.

Ray said, "He's got one of those paddleboats from the rental
place." We watched as he paddled his little square watercraft to
shore, hopped out and pulled it up onto the beach. His head and
shoulders grew a torso and legs as he walked up the slope toward the
parking lot, startling some sleepy geese. When he was almost onto
the asphalt, Reese Newman stepped out of the van and knocked the
fire off his cigar.

They met at the back door of the van. Reese opened it, and they
slid a long roll of what looked like carpet partway out. They each
took a side, lifted it out with some difficulty, and began to carry it
awkwardly toward the boat.

"Okay," Ray said into the mike, "slow and easy, Rosie." The four
of us moved quietly with our weapons held close to our sides. We
skirted the parking lot on the darker side. Hanenberger moved out
of the shadow of the picnic shelter and fell in behind us. Our feet
made no sound on the grass and they were grunting, working hard to
hang onto their load, so we were almost on top of them before they
noticed us.

Peabody yelled, "What—!" and dropped his side of the bundle. Newman started to swear at him, caught a glimpse of some movement and whirled to face us, dropping his side too. Peabody started to run, but Newman hadn't seen our weapons and took us for muggers; he pulled an old Colt out of his jacket and even started to cock it. Then he saw five Glocks aimed at his upper torso, dropped the gun and said, "Oh, don't—" as Casey and Green knocked him down. Hanenburger was already kneeling on James Peabody, handcuffing him.

A small sound came out of the bundle they had dropped. It was carpet, rolled with the hemp backing on the outside, wrapped in a tarp and bound with clothesline. Some of the knots in the line had come loose, and the tarp was sliding off the carpet.

So even in the poor light that came across the slope from the parking lot, we could all see the white hand that slid out of the bundle.

23

Kylee wasn't a Scotch drinker, fortunately. Nor did she take tranquilizers, so Peabody and Newman had done her no serious harm with the one roofie they had managed to slip into her soda. She had refused even that, at first, she recalled for us later, but Reese had said, chuckling, "Better take it, Kylee, you got a tough problem here and a pair of real dunderheads to explain it to, so it's gonna be thirsty work."

She sipped a Diet Coke while she opened the spreadsheet on James Peabody's PC, the one he kept at the bank, and showed him how to set up a balance sheet and title it so it could be retrieved easily, steps she remembered teaching him several months ago and that he seemed to understand perfectly well at the time.

She was pondering that and beginning to feel distinctly uneasy about exactly what the three of them were doing in the bank after closing, with this measly little problem that could certainly have waited till tomorrow. And then after no time had apparently passed she woke up in Crystal Lake Park, rolled up in a rug with a lot of cops around her and a siren wailing nearby, feeling clear-headed and totally confused at the same time.

Rosie rode with her in the ambulance. Kylee kept saying she was fine but then insisting she had to close out the PC before she could leave and asking, why was it dark?

"We're just going to get you checked to make sure," Rosie said, holding her hand while the paramedics got ready to load the gurney. "Those bozos dropped you pretty hard." She tossed Darrell the keys to the Crown Vic as she climbed into the ambulance, saying, "Hey, grab my purse for me, will you?"

Darrell came running with it, saying, "Jesus God, Rosie, I think I'll let the weight training go and just carry your purse around for a while."

Rosie told us gleefully later how she won her fight with the resident in the ER who declared that Kylee Mundt's vital signs were fine and she should go home and sleep it off. Rosie flashed her badge and called victim's services and the head nurse at the battered women's shelter and finally the coroner. The first two supported her opinions by phone, but Pokey came downtown right away and described in detail what an overdose of roofies had done to the victim he had on a slab in the morgue. So Kylee got the closely monitored night in the hospital she kept saying she didn't need, and was soon sleeping soundly.

And just in case her kidnappers had confederates around we didn't know about yet, Rosie stood guard at her door until Darrell came down at midnight and relieved her. She was back at five in the morning with a tall latte and a prune Danish for him, sent him home for a nap before work and phoned me at seven for an okay to stick with Kylee till she checked out. Rosie was energized.

"Well, I mean, how often do you get to have this much fun?" she asked us all, around the conference table when we met there Friday. "That look on those dirty little date-rapers' faces when we caught them at the boat was worth a week's pay, wasn't it?" She kept calling them date-rapers even though all the evidence clearly indicated that the kidnappers were focused entirely on disposing of Kylee Mundt's body, not having fun with it.

The rest of us were downtown most of the night, explaining to Peabody and Newman how much shit hits the fan when you're caught trying to murder a female employee. They tried bluffing and outrage, of course; Reese Newman even said once, "I take umbrage at your suggestion," which led Darrell Betts to ask, later, "Why did he want to take a bridge?"

For James Peabody, of course, it was awkward to have the attorney who should have been riding to his rescue getting booked into the pokey alongside him. But he went on believing for some time, no doubt from force of habit, that if he kept his cool, preserved his usual pose of polite and humorous but nonetheless impermeable superiority, in the end we would see that because of who he was we would have to let him go.

"I know you're just doing your jobs," he said more than once with wonderful forbearance, "but please try to understand, I have meetings all day tomorrow—" He would look at his watch, shrug helplessly and sigh.

Acquaintances, happy to pile on in later interviews, assured us he had always had a Teflon shell that shed any unpleasantness. He had finessed flunking out of Harvard by treating it as a colossal prank, amusing friends at dinner tables for years afterward with stories about the glorious parties that kept him from doing any studying there. He had been brave and noble about the meltdown of the family fortune a few years later, glossing over the significant help he had given his father in squandering their assets. And when he escaped going to work by quickly marrying new wealth, he was clever enough to claim to be "over the moon" with love.

But even after a lifetime of graceful dodging and wasting and mooching, James Peabody's famous cool began to crack a little when he found himself getting fingerprinted in a cement room under fluorescent light. And stripping naked in front of the indifferent eyes of a jailor, replacing his well-made clothes with an orange cotton jumpsuit that bagged in the seat—he hated that part so much it almost made him gag.

We Mirandized the bejeezus out of them. Reese Newman declared with heavy contempt that he was quite familiar with the law, thank you very much, adding that before he was done he hoped to acquaint us with a few of its features that we seemed to have forgotten.

The chief was back downtown by then, worried about the high profiles. He asked us, "You absolutely certain you got both their asses in a sling?"

"They were carrying a girl full of roofies," I said, "wrapped in a rug. Seven of us saw it."

"Carrying her toward a boat in a lake," Ray said.

"Where they just drowned her laptop," Darrell said.

Something close to a smile crossed McCafferty's face. "Does sound like sufficient grounds for arrest, all right." He rubbed his big red face and thought hard. "Comes to conviction, my money's still on his law firm. But that's Milo's problem."

A senior member of Newman and Stringfellow, Jason Stringfellow himself, appeared within minutes of Reese's call. Expecting to do some perfunctory vouching and take his partner home from what he assumed was a drunken misadventure, he was indignant almost to the point of apoplexy to find Reese already fingerprinted and wearing prison fatigues.

Milo was on board by then, clicking his ballpoint to near-destruction and looking greatly in need of an antacid. Going up against Rutherford's biggest money pile made him nearly speechless with dread, which made things easier, in a way; he kept his mouth shut and listened while Ray and I told Stringfellow about the girl full of roofies in the rug.

We described the laptop our divers were certainly going to find in the lake in the morning, and the cement blocks we had found in the Honda, wrapped in burlap with little hooks attached, for weighting down the girl in the rug.

"Just luck she wasn't dead," Ray said. "In fact she was coming around as they carried her to the boat, but I guess they figured they could make it to the middle of the lake before she woke up enough to cause them any serious trouble."

"That's pure supposition," Stringfellow said, in his courtroom voice.

"You want to give us an alternate theory of why they'd slip her a Mickey and wrap her up like a bundle of laundry?" Ray asked him. "You feel like convincing a grand jury your guys were just playing a prank?"

"I'm only saying that prudence would suggest you be very sure of your facts," he said, "before you start accusing two prominent community leaders—"

"You're right, we don't have all the goods on these prominent leaders yet," I said, "and we won't until we talk to Kylee Mundt about what was on that laptop that they were so anxious to destroy. Fortunately the medics at the hospital are saying she should be fine by morning. Or is she still in danger of dirty tricks, by the way? How many more members of your firm are involved in this?"

"None! My God, I can vouch for every—" He stopped, aware that he would have said the same thing about Reese until a few minutes ago. It was interesting to watch as he began to evaluate the damage this night's business might inflict on his firm. He was a small gray man I would ordinarily not consider interesting, but his shrewdness began to show as we talked. He certainly didn't look like a thug, but then neither did Reese Newman.

"I need to confer with my clients," Stringfellow said, looking a little drained under the overhead lights but showing steady nerves.

"Of course," I said, and arranged a quiet room for them.

Milo said, "You notice he isn't calling Reese his partner anymore?"

Stringfellow's perfectly polished black leather briefcase went out the door of the jail a half hour later and never returned. By Thursday morning, the two suspects were being represented by journeyman lawyers from a small start-up firm to which Newman and Stringfellow often referred nuisance accounts.

Ray and I watched two of them entering the jail, uneasy guys in gray suits and plain ties. They did family practice as a rule, not criminal law, and they looked as if they were wondering if they were breaking into the big time or sinking themselves in a slime pit. "Something keeps bothering me," Ray said. "You ever have a feeling you're almost remembering something but you can't quite get a grip on it?"

"Plenty of times," I said. "Leave it alone and it'll come to you."

"I would if I could," he said.

We went and found Bo Dooley then and walked with him into the chief's office, to explain what we wanted to do that day and why.

Frank punished the springs on his chair, kicked his desk and pulled his nose. Finally he asked me, "Aren't you moving kind of fast?"

"It's today or never, for Elizabeth. We have to get to her before she finds out what's happened to her father. The rest of what we want Kylee to do can wait a day or two, if she doesn't feel strong enough yet, but I want her to call Elizabeth right away."

"Kylee's okay? You checked on her?"

"Just talked to Rosie. She says Kylee's full of piss and vinegar. Her mother called and wanted to come up, but Kylee said, 'Stay put, I'll be home in a couple of hours.'"

"But you're gonna talk to her about the phone call first."

"I'm going up there now if you say it's okay. Ray and Bo will get everything ready."

"Well—Bo, how do you feel about this?"

"Like a narc who wants to hear his chief say if this goes sour it won't be my ass hung out to dry."

"Uh-*huh*. Well, that's plain enough, I guess." McCafferty fixed Dooley in his blue-laser stare and said, "Tell me some of the ways it might go sour."

"She's a Peabody, which is the same as being an Aldrich."

"We got her daddy and her attorney in jail."

"We haven't got the whole friggin' firm in jail. And the Aldriches can hire every lawyer in town if they want to."

"True." He looked at me. "You sure you've thought this through?"

"Chief, Roger's dead and Dale Trogstad won't talk to anybody. Kylee knows some of what her brother did but she doesn't know it all. Elizabeth's up to her eyeballs in this whole dirty business we've been working on so long—she helped steal the guns and antiques, she knew about the kidnapping and she went to LaCrosse in Shelley's car. I think she counts on hiding behind her family and their attorney; she knows they may get mad at her but they'll keep her out of sight if they can. This morning that system's disabled and we have this little window of opportunity."

The chief chewed on his back teeth a while, squinting at the corner of his office. He restacked a pile of papers till all the edges matched, picked up all the pens on his desk and put them back in their mug. The numbers on my watch flipped from 8:10 to 8:11. I began to itch. Finally he said, "Okay, go ahead."

Bo said, "Chief—"

"All right, yes, Bo, I'll stand behind you. Don't I always?" He elected not to wait for an answer to that before he turned to me and said, solemnly, "Proceed with caution."

"Trust me," I said, and got out before he commented on that. In ten minutes, I was at Methodist Hospital, where I found Kylee Mundt looking rested and enjoying breakfast.

I asked her, "Do you feel up to making a phone call?"

"Sure," Kylee said, "I feel up to anything. I guess that's thanks to you, isn't it? I'm still a little bit vague on the details."

"We just did our job," I said, "and got lucky. They were getting ready to drown you, though, Kylee, we're sure about that."

"Rosie told me." She sipped her coffee. "Boy, this tastes good. I figured out something since I woke up," she said. She blinked her eyes rapidly and I thought, *Oh no, she's going to cry again,* but she swallowed, took another bite of bacon and said, "The only way Mr. Newman could have known I was coming home yesterday afternoon was if Mama told him." She chewed thoughtfully. "Everybody's been working me, haven't they?"

"Looks that way, doesn't it?" I said.

"Well, I'm done being the designated victim," Kylee said. "Mama's going to have to find another slave." She drained her cup and said, "I wonder how you get more coffee?"

"I'll get it," Rosie said, and went out with the pot looking happy.

Kylee listened while I explained the phone call I wanted.

"I'll do it," she said, "but it might not work. She turns her phone off a lot."

But a shortage of meth had jerked Elizabeth Peabody out of her usual torpor; she answered on the first ring. Kylee apologized politely for the "glitch in the system" that had delayed her usual shipment of "medicine," but said service would resume today.

"I won't be able to deliver it, though," she said. "I have to help Mama with the arrangements for Roger's funeral."

Elizabeth wasted no time on condolences. "What time will it be in the box?" she said.

"Ten o'clock," Kylee said, and was rewarded with a sharp click on the line.

"Good job," I said. "Now, do you feel up to talking about your laptop?"

"Sure. What about it?"

"They threw your laptop in the lake. Do you know why?"

"I think so. I'm not an accountant. I just fed in the numbers the way Mr. Newman told me to do it. But judging by how hard it was to get those accounts to balance—you know, I can show you easier than I can tell you."

"How? All your equipment's in the water, isn't it?"

"Well—" She grew a grim little smile. "Last spring when I started feeling uneasy about that job, I ran off an extra set of discs. And I've been keeping them up to date."

"But didn't the person who picked up your computer get those? Your uncle said—"

She shook her head. "He couldn't have given them my extra set, he didn't know about them." She looked at Rosie. "We could go get them. They're in my uncle's toolshed, taped to the wall behind the snowblower."

Rosie beamed like a proud aunt and said, "Does Kylee rock or what?"

A brief bureaucratic tussle followed because the hospital that had not wanted to admit Kylee the night before now declared that it could not check her out without a release from an attending physician. Asked how to find one of those, we were told they were all on rounds but one would be here "as soon as possible."

I left Rosie having fun with that problem, went back to the station and sent her a car. Then I called Milo quickly, before I could talk myself out of it. He had predicted disasters for all of us before he went home last night, insisting that no good ever came of "messing with the royals."

"Okay," he said, "you got a good point about the girl full of roofies in the rug, but you watched this guy in court, Jake. You know if he makes up his mind to it he can convince a jury that getting carried around in a piece of carpet is a cure for the clap." Milo's defeat in the Niemeyer case had made him more risk-averse than ever.

He cheered up when I told him what Kylee was bringing to town. A plain little temp-sec placed in jeopardy—okay, maybe even assaulted—when the alleged jeopardizers and assaulters were two rich men whose clout made his butt pucker with anxiety, that sounded like something he'd like to make go away. But a spreadsheet from the computer those two prominent men had dropped into the lake in the dark, a jury could get its teeth into that. Better still, if Kylee was really bringing him evidence of funny business with the accounts, he could take that to the jail one day soon and reach a very nice plea agreement that wouldn't even have to go to trial.

"But you know, Jake—" he got back into worry mode just in time, before a little stroke of luck could lure him into foolhardy optimism "—even though they're Kylee's discs, they're Newman's records. Be sure you get a warrant."

"Maddox is at the courthouse now, waiting for one. We'll need a CPA, though, probably, to help us figure it out. You know any?"

"I know a boatload," he said, "but listen, Chrissie got an accounting degree while she was in law school. Why don't we have her take a look at these discs first?"

"What else is Chrissie good at? Brain surgery?"

"I wouldn't be at all surprised. When, uh—"

"This afternoon, probably, I'll call you." I hung up and walked across the hall to Kevin Evjan's office. I could tell from his pleasant, unconcerned greeting that no one had told him about last night's arrests, so I sat down in front of his desk and told him about pouncing on Peabody and Newman and saving Kylee Mundt's life. It was not the best ten minutes I ever spent with him; his admiration of Peabody's style died hard. But I needed him to handle the regular nine A.M. press briefing for me, and in case any rumors had leaked I had to be sure he knew enough not to get blindsided by a question.

"We're not releasing anything about either one of them yet," I said, and made my third attempt to explain the sting we were preparing for Elizabeth Peabody. He stared at me as if I'd brought a basket of snakes into his office and said he thought it was the worst idea he'd heard all summer. I thanked him for his input and hurried out to get going on it.

24

Parked among the battered clunkers sagging along the curbs on North Fourth, the sleek little forest green BMW convertible might as well have been wearing a banner that said, "Steal me." The girl who pulled the keys out of the ignition and strode across the street looked better suited to the neighborhood. Thin and deathly pale, she wore a halter top that barely contained her bosom and ended four inches above her navel, and hiphugger shorts that didn't quite cover her buttocks. Her hair was cut in a ragged punk shag like Cyndi Lauper on her spazziest day, and dyed the color of raspberries. Many gold ornaments pierced her ears and nose and navel.

I'd never seen her before, and all her school photos had been from ninth grade or earlier, but I was sure she was Elizabeth Peabody. Despite her best efforts to conceal it, she showed a strong resemblance to her mother, especially in the elegance with which she moved and turned her head. I looked at Ray and raised my eyebrows and he nodded.

We were two doors north of Kylee's place, crouched in the back

244 | ELIZABETH GUNN

of the old brown Dodge so the front seat would look empty in case any alert meth-heads got concerned. But our tacky van looked right at home on the skuzzy street, and for all Elizabeth Peabody seemed to notice it or care, we could have been sitting on the hood eating foot-longs.

She climbed the two steps to the porch and opened the screen door, bent to unlock the padlock on the wooden box and lifted the lid. We had verified every detail of the package with Iron Man LeFever, and it must have looked right to her, because she lifted it out with no hesitation, took her key out of the padlock and dropped the padlock into the box. Elizabeth Peabody didn't replace padlocks; somebody else did that.

As soon as she had the package in her hand and was turning around, Bo opened the back door of the van and hopped out with Darrell right behind him. They walked together toward the rear of the BMW. Ray and I waited till Elizabeth came down the steps and crossed the sidewalk. Then we got out the side door of the van and walked along the curb toward her.

A car approached from the south, moving north along our side of the street. Most jaywalkers would have waited for it to pass, but Elizabeth stepped boldly off the curb and walked in front of it, forcing it to slow down. She got a North End salute for that, a blast from the car horn and a shouted obscenity. Her poise was absolute; she didn't flinch or change pace. Ray and I waited for the car to pass us before we stepped off the curb behind her. She was at the midpoint in the street, shaking out her car keys, getting ready to open the door of the convertible, when Bo and Darrell stepped between her and her car.

Every molecule of her body must have been crying out for the satisfaction waiting in the package she was carrying, and for a couple of seconds as she stopped and brought her arms up in front of her, desperation showed in her face. Then hot rage boiled up, and as she turned and saw Ray coming up behind her she swung the hand that held the keys. Ray ducked just in time—the keys were aimed at his eyes—and Bo stepped in behind Elizabeth, clamped one hand on her trapezius muscle and another in her tangled hair, and forced her to her knees.

Darrell cuffed her hands behind her back. Ray walked back to the Dodge and called the blue-and-white that was waiting, and Casey pulled around the corner and parked at the curb beside us.

I squatted on the pavement in front of her, held my shield a foot from her eyes and said, "I'm Captain Jake Hines of the Rutherford Police Department. We're all investigators, and we need to talk to you. Do you want to help yourself now and cooperate, or do I have to arrest you?"

"Isn't that what you're doing?"

"Not yet."

"Then why are my hands tied?" Her face was full of hate.

"Because you're fighting." I told Darrell, "Go ahead, pat her down."

His look said plainly that I must be joking, but when I just nodded, he reluctantly ran his hands over the few scraps of fabric on her mostly exposed body. When he reached her hips, his expression changed and he said, "Stand her up."

I stood up and put my wallet away, nodded to Bo and put my hands on her upper arms. He tugged a little on her hair to get her started, and together we lifted the girl till she was standing between us. Darrell slid his hand into the cargo pocket of her skimpy shorts and brought out a dinky little handgun.

"Well, looky here, a Beretta," he said.

A car turned into the street at the north end of the block and rolled toward us. Elizabeth screamed in a shrew's voice, "Can we please get out of this fucking street?" She was enraged by the sight of the gun in Darrell's hand, and looking for a way to put us in the wrong. But Casey stepped out of the squad in his uniform and motioned the car around us.

I waited until it had passed and said, "We have all the evidence we need to put you in jail. Is that where you want to be?" Her eyes were like her mother's, though not quite as blue. "Is it?"

"No, shit no!" She turned her head to look down at Bo's hand on her shoulder. "He's hurting me."

"Then do yourself a favor, Elizabeth. Calm down and make up your mind to cooperate so we can get off this street and go someplace more comfortable."

A terrible look, of greed and impotent rage, contorted her face as she looked down at the package on the asphalt. She was so obsessed by the pleasure it had almost given her, she could think of nothing else. I looked at Bo again and at that moment she spit in my face. Bo gave me a sad little smile, took his hand off her shoulder and clamped it on her left arm. He put her none too gently into Casey's squad and got in beside her.

Darrell drove the Dodge back downtown, saying, "Boy, she's a tiger, ain't she?" as I wiped spit off my face.

"She's a tweaker, that's all," I said. He stayed close behind Casey's squad and pulled up beside him behind the station. I got out and walked with Bo and Elizabeth as he took her up the back elevator and along the hall to his cubicle.

Bo said, "Probably best if you leave us alone for a few minutes, and let us get acquainted." He had a list of what LeFever and Sean both said she'd been getting, and he wanted to see if she was ready to give him a similar list, or even one that resembled it in any way. "No use wasting time on her if all she's going to do is lie."

He put her in the extra chair in his cubicle, stepped outside and said, "If I see she won't talk unless we put her in a cell for a while, then you and the chief better have another chat and decide if you want to go forward with this." He was grim and cold, doing his job but making sure I knew how dubious he felt.

"Okay," I said. "Call me when you want me."

Darrell walked down the hall, stopped at Bo's doorway and said, "Okay, the Dodge is back in the garage, Casey's gonna run me back over there to get her BMW. You want this checked into evidence or—" He held up the parcel Elizabeth had dropped, and stared at her in surprise when she burst out crying.

"I'll take it," Bo said, grimmer than ever, and stuffed the package in one of his drawers. "Give us some room here for a while, huh?"

"What did I do?" Darrell asked me, walking away.

"Nothing. She's just jumpy; she needs a fix."

"I *know* that. But why is Bo mad?"

"He isn't mad at you. He thinks going after users is a mistake."

"I thought we all thought that. Why are we?"

"I took a notion. After you get her car back here will you write up the incident report?"

"It's not an arrest yet, right?"

"That's correct." He went off down the hall rattling her keys, happy as long as nobody was blaming him for anything.

Ray was in his office, talking on the phone. I stood outside his glass wall and he waved me in, put his call on hold and said, "This is Rosie. They got the discs. They're on the way in. You want them here, right?"

"Let me talk to her, will you? And listen to what I say to her, please, because I never got time to tell you this." I told Rosie about Chrissie's accounting degree. "So take Kylee and the discs to Milo's office. Get some lunch first. It might be a long afternoon."

"But productive, I bet." Rosie sounded cheerful. "Kylee seems pretty sure about this."

"Good. Call as soon as you know anything." I handed the phone back to Ray.

"Milo hired himself a winner, huh? Milo needs one if anybody does. It's never been clear to me—what do you expect to find on those discs?"

"I don't know but it must be fairly interesting if two guys are willing to kill their steno over it."

"Uh-huh." He hit the side of his own head and then unreasonably began to look blissfully happy, an expression so rare on Ray Bailey I watched it with awe. "I just remembered what was bothering me!"

"What?"

"James Peabody's voice. Now why did what you said make me—oh, I guess because it was about killing. Isn't it funny how that works?"

"How what works?"

"Memory. Never mind, just listen. The way Peabody talks . . . it's unusual in this part of the country, isn't it? So of course he tried to disguise it the day he made that anonymous phone call. That's why I said his voice was weird. But now that I think of it, that was him on the phone all right, only trying to sound like somebody else."

"I'll be damned. But why would he do that?"

"Because he wanted Benny to take the fall."

"Why, though?" His phone rang.

"Bailey. Yes, we did. No, not yet. Jake's right here. The chief," he said, passing the phone.

"Did you pick up the Peabody girl?"

"Yes."

"But you haven't arrested her, right? You're just talking?"

"That's right."

"Okay. The crime reporter at the paper gave Kevin a real going-over about last night's arrest records. Apparently some rumors hit the street about Peabody and Newman, so now he's hot to know and he's got the rest of the media sniffing the trail too. How soon will we be ready to release something?"

"Well, we've got Elizabeth up here, so . . . anytime, I guess. We could go ahead and say we're 'holding them on charges of false imprisonment,' okay with you?"

"Uh . . . yeah. That'll work. How you coming with a motive for attempted murder?"

"Coming right along."

"Hell you say." He banged things around on his desk for a few seconds and said, "Still sounds so damn crazy . . . what's 'right along' mean? Next week, next year?"

"Would later today suit you?"

There was a silence during which he breathed heavily into the mouthpiece. Finally he said, "You're not running headlong into a swamp full of shit, are you?"

"No, I'm following procedure where it leads me—excuse me, Frank, I gotta go." There was an awful racket coming from the hall. Bo was standing in Ray's doorway, and for once he looked anxious to talk.

25

"Soon as she quit crying she started saying she had to call her father. I asked her why and she said, 'So he'll come and clear all this up, so I can go home.' " Bo peered through Ray's glass wall toward his cubicle. "This morning while we were waiting for her in the back of the Dodge we talked about when to tell her we'd arrested her father and you said, 'Let's use it when it will do the most good.' So I decided to use it then." He pulled a couple of tissues out of a box, wiped sweat off his face and blew his nose. "You hear the noise? She's coming unglued. She was sure her daddy would fix everything. Now that she knows he can't, she's scared of the pain she knows is coming and she's begging for help."

"She never suggested calling her mother?"

"No. You ready to do some business?"

"You bet. Bring her in my office, huh?" I turned to Ray. "We have to talk about the drug deliveries first. But if she holds up long enough, maybe you could ask her to confirm that Dale and Roger killed Shelley Gleason, huh?"

"Right. So you want me to stay out for a while?"

"Yeah. I'll call you when we're ready."

"Maybe Kevin can talk to her about the burglaries too, huh?"

"Right," I said, watching Bo start Elizabeth toward my office. "Tell him to be ready to do that, will you?"

Bo put her in a chair, asked if she was comfortable, got her a glass of water. His manner toward her had changed; he seemed protective now, almost fatherly.

Which was understandable, because Elizabeth Peabody looked like somebody who just found a bear in the cellar. Shaking, flushed and sweating, she kept licking her swollen lips, which were so dried out they stuck together whenever she stopped talking. Her eyes rolled sideways occasionally, as if she was trying to see who was behind her.

"We've been talking about the drugs in the package," Bo said, "about how much Elizabeth has been using. Tell Jake, will you?" he said, bending toward her like a parent encouraging a child at a school pageant, "how you increased the weekly order."

"I was getting, like, fourteen twists of crystal a week?" She had the high voice and standard teenage delivery, rushes of blurred words with question marks in the pauses. "Enough for two a day. But after a while it seemed like that wasn't enough. So I said I want more? But Daddy said no, more would be dangerous." She had pulled her right foot up in the chair with her, hugging her leg to keep it there, and now she bent her head and rubbed her cheek thoughtfully against her knee.

"Your father approved of your drug use?"

"Well—" She picked at a scab on the inside of her leg, frowning "—he kind of went along with it because it was the easiest way for him to get his coke."

"Ten dime bags every week," Bo said. "That's in the package too."

"So your father was paying for all this?" I asked her.

"Yes."

"Who did the ordering?"

"Daddy did." She said it the way she might have said, "Daddy got the tickets for our trip to Hilo."

"I see. And you took out your share when Kylee brought it, is that it, and gave him the rest?"

"Uh-huh. That's how Roger and I got the idea for how to get more meth. Roger said 'Wise up, Izzy, if you get the package first, how's he gonna know? Just take out the extra and give him what you always do.' "

"Wouldn't he know when he had to pay?"

"Oh, well, Roger asked around and found our dealer? So then he, like, made his own deal."

"How did that work?"

"He paid cash in advance whenever we wanted an extra delivery. But it still all came in the same package."

"So Kylee didn't know?"

"Kylee?" Elizabeth's sad face took on a livelier expression, of pure contempt. "Kylee is too unbelievably stupid to know *anything.*" She made an impatient noise and flounced in her chair. "Roger said work work work, that's all Kylee knows. Like some dorky slave."

"Uh-*huh.* And you and Roger got the cash by stealing things out of your own and your neighbors' houses, is that right?"

"Well . . . yes." She was scratching the inside of her left arm now, and a place behind her right ear, raising welts where the itch was worst.

"And you sold the things on eBay?"

"Usually. When we could find the, you know, proof of provenance? Otherwise Roger knew a fence." I began to see how the synergy must have worked in this unlikely alliance. She was a tweaker but she was also Nelson Aldrich's granddaughter, so she had access to wealth and knew things other teenagers didn't know, like the best way in and out of fine houses, and the practicalities of dealing in antiques. He was a boring layabout but he had connections in the thuggish netherworld of crime that she enjoyed, and he was willing to help her pursue her addictions.

"But after Roger went to prison," I said, "your source of extra meth kind of dried up, did it?"

"Yes." She sniffed and jiggled impatiently. "I drank a lot of vodka and it helped some at first but it's kind of like meth, you know? You keep wanting more." She turned her vapid, self-pitying face toward Bo. "I'm starting to feel real bad."

"I understand," he said. "Can you just sit tight a minute while I talk to Captain Hines out here? Then we'll get you some help."

We walked along the hall a few steps and stood outside the open door of Kevin's office, where the whir of his printer and the hum of LeeAnn's copy machine covered our voices. I asked Bo, "What about the roofies? Roger said she used—"

"We'll get to that next, but that'll have to be the last question. She's gonna be sick as hell before long and I want to get her to South Central before we have a screaming nut on our hands."

"The drunk tank? I don't think she—"

"They've got some beds for junkies now; they can keep her stable overnight till I talk to her mother and see how she wants to—" He was facing the east end of the hall and his face began to register surprise and concern. The buzzer on the door next to the lobby had just sounded and then the chief came walking toward us in the hall, his head bent attentively toward Helen Peabody's bright blue eyes.

"—A reporter from the newspaper," she was saying, "and I told him I didn't know anything but he wouldn't stop asking questions—"

"Why don't we go in my office?" the chief said.

"All right, and I was hoping maybe Kevin . . . uh," she looked at the card she was carrying, "Kevin Ev-jann?" The sound of his name being mispronounced reached Kevin through the white noise of work around him. I saw him raise his head, and heard Helen Peabody's voice going on, "—was so helpful about the guns we lost, so I thought if you could just ask him to—"

Kevin was out in the hall by then, smiling all over his handsome face, delighted that the elegant lady was asking for him. Moving toward her with his hand out, he said, "Mrs. Peabody, how can I help you?"

A crash sounded in my office as Elizabeth knocked over her chair. She charged out the door screaming, "Get that bitch out of here! Don't let her near me!"

Helen Peabody, reaching to shake Kevin's hand, stopped and turned her shocked face toward her daughter. "Elizabeth, what on earth—"

Elizabeth pointed at her mother and yelled, "Don't you touch me! I'm going to kill you if you ever come near me again!"

Mrs. Peabody reached both arms toward the hysterical girl, begging, "Don't, Elizabeth, please darling—" and took a step toward her in the crowded hall.

"No! I mean it!" Elizabeth ran away from her as far as LeeAnn's desk, where she snatched something out of a mugful of pencils there. She tipped over the pencil jar and the wire basket next to it; papers and pencils flew off the desk and around the hall. Elizabeth turned to confront her mother who was following her with outstretched, beseeching arms.

Elizabeth's white hand raised a pair of orange-handled scissors and came down in a great arc toward her mother. A red stain blossomed on Mrs. Peabody's white linen jacket. She cried out in pain and then, for a while, it seemed as if everybody in the building was yelling.

26

"**She actually stabbed her** own mother?" Rosie asked at the Friday afternoon meeting.

"As best she could with those hobby-shop scissors," Kevin said. "Good thing we didn't see fit to get you a good pair, LeeAnn."

"Some of your transcriptions are going to be a little late," LeeAnn said. "I'm still picking rubber bands out of the light fixtures." She smiled, though. Her part in Elizabeth Peabody's meltdown, even if inadvertant, had carved out a place for LeeAnn in the investigative division; no longer the new girl, she was part of the lore now, one of the guys.

"So," Rosie said, "is Mama hurt bad?"

"Mrs. Peabody only got a little nick in the shoulder," Kevin said, "but that perfect Chanel suit is ruined."

The chief gave Kevin a look that said real men don't know the names of dress designers, and moved on to his major bitch. "Four of you in the team that brought that girl in here and none of you noticed she was flipping out? Jesus, Bo, didn't they mention that problem in Drug Interdiction 101?"

"Fine," Bo said, "blame the narc."

"I'm not saying only you, Jake should've known—"

"What happened to your big guarantee about backing me up? Jake dreams up this cockamamie scheme and you tell me I have to go along with it. Now you want me to take the fall? I don't think so."

"Oh, sit down," the chief said. "Why do you always have to take everything so personal? Of course I'll back you up. I'm just saying you should all think ahead more." He punished his chair legs and the carpet, uneasy without the comfort of his own big desk and the familiar things he bangs around on it. "Let's move along; we have a lot of ground to cover. Beginning with, Kevin, did you say you knew this Beretta was missing? Why didn't you write it up?"

"Mrs. Peabody didn't want to report it because she didn't want her father upset again, and she thought he might have misplaced it himself."

"So you said you'd do what?"

"Keep my eye peeled for it."

"Oh, that's good." He looked disgusted at Kevin for a change. "Will you show me in the training manual where it tells you how to peel your eye?"

Kevin waved his hands. "She's Mrs. Peabody. She's used to getting what she wants."

"Fine. So we revise police procedure to please the rich lady and it turns out her daughter has the damn gun and is planning to ambush her with it. So you confiscate the gun and she goes after her with a pair of scissors. In the police station." Everybody winced.

Except Bo, who said, "No."

"No what?"

"She wasn't planning to shoot her mother. She intended to kill her grandfather."

"Her grandfather? *Nelson Aldrich?* Why would she do that?"

"He's been molesting her since she was in the ninth grade."

"Oh, Jesus." The chief has a little rocking motion he falls into when he has to talk about something he hates. His big silhouette crossed my line of peripheral vision twice before he said, "I'm almost afraid to ask this next part. Is there some connection between this and these roofies you all keep talking about?"

"Looks like it," Bo said.

"Aw, shit. Grandpa was giving her roofies?"

Bo looked at me. I said, "It's a little worse than that, Chief."

Frank got his lost-in-the-sewer look. "What could possibly be worse?"

"Her mother gave them to her."

"*What?*"

"The first time Aldrich molested Elizabeth," Bo said, his voice as dry as dead leaves, "she was thirteen. He picked a time when everybody was out of the house and told her, 'This is what girls are for.' At first she was ashamed to say anything, but finally she went to her mother and told her what was happening and her mother said, 'Boppo does everything for all of us. Don't you think you can do this one little thing for him?' Apparently he's been abusing the mother since she was just a child and she's convinced herself it's just a friendly thing to do for dear old Dad."

"Doormats," Rosie said fiercely. "What ails women anyway?"

"Mrs. Peabody bought birth control pills and showed her how to use them," Bo said, "but as Elizabeth got more into booze and drugs she got careless. So sometime in sophomore year she got pregnant, and her mother arranged for an abortion."

"Roger Mundt tried to tell me about that, the last time I saw him," I said, "but he ran out of steam before he could finish the story."

"Elizabeth complained to Roger about her grandfather while they were in detox together," Bo said, "and he started telling her she didn't have to take that crap if she didn't want to."

"Roger only believed in the exploitation of women when he was doing it," I said.

"I guess. Anyway Elizabeth started to fight off the old man," Bo said, "so Mrs. Peabody turned to Reese Newman. The family fixer. He got her the Rohypnol so she could keep Elizabeth quiet."

"You sure about this? He admits to procuring her roofies?"

"He's a lawyer; he doesn't admit to anything, not even the time of day. But his dealer was Iron Man LeFever, and he gave me dates and amounts, pretty close."

"Reese Newman is the name Sean left off his customer list," I said.

"Some lawyer. He actually conspired in Elizabeth's abuse?"

"Well, maybe not in so many words. Mrs. Peabody tried to tell us she had the pills because some of her friends told her they were good for migraines. She may have told Newman the same thing. Anyway she owns the money tree, so he wouldn't have questioned her too closely."

"God Almighty. All the grown-ups around her were helping this kid destroy herself?"

"But not all in the same way," Bo said. "Different parts of the family had different secrets. Elizabeth says Daddy didn't know about the roofies. He was buying her meth because it was the easiest way for him to get his cocaine. And Mummy didn't know about the meth. You'd think she must have known about her husband's co- caine use, but maybe not. That big house seems to offer everybody plenty of privacy."

The chief said, "But Mrs. Peabody and her father must have had . . . conversations—"

"Don't go there," I said, "you don't want to know."

"Well, but we'll have to, when we—" He tapped on the table a couple of times, sat still a minute and said, "Goodamn hard to decide who we ought to charge first with what, huh?"

"Sexual abuse is the hardest thing of all to prosecute," Ray said, coming out of his note-taking silence. "Why not start with the money?"

"Which money?" The hot word worked its magic once again; the whole crew quit brooding over the evil in the world and sat up straight.

"Rosie, how far have you gotten with those discs?" Ray said.

"Far enough to be sure Peabody and Newman have been robbing the foundation blind." Rosie began flipping through a pile of notes. "I wish you could have seen Kylee and Chrissie going through those records, guys. Kylee would say, 'Well, I always wondered why he made me put this account in here and then take it out over here,' and Chrissie would go pointing and clicking along that trail with happy little cries."

"They made withdrawals that the board hadn't authorized?"

"In spades. Sometimes Newman got one set of requisitions signed by the board and then kited the amounts on a second set with copied signatures. He must have used that skill to send the note to Kylee's uncle, by the way. Other times he got a project approved with an estimate, but the finished job always came in costing more. He may have had a couple of contractors getting a slice for helping with phoney bills."

"And Peabody's in on it too? His own family's money?"

"His wife's family. Aldrich never settled any money on Peabody, so I guess he decided to get some the old-fashioned way—by stealing it."

"Where are they hiding the loot?"

"There's a bank in Philadelphia that gets a lot of checks, and another one in Chicago. Chrissie figures those are just way stations and the final repositories are maybe in the Caymans. Or Switzerland? Anyway she's sure we can prove the two of them have been pulling a massive swindle, isn't that fun?"

"Delightful," the chief said. "Milo's getting help from a CPA?"

"Squads of them. I don't think I've ever seen him so happy. Every time he thinks about nailing Reese Newman's hide to the wall he wants to burst into song."

"I get it about Reese Newman," I said. "He's got spendy tastes. But James Peabody already has everything money can buy. I wonder why he needed to tap the till?"

Rosie's face grew a mean little smirk. "It looks like he found something to buy that he figured his wife wouldn't sign for. Her name is Moira and she lives in a tony high-rise near Water Tower Place in Chicago."

"You know this because money goes there—?"

"Every month. After journeys to a fake charity in Detroit and an equally phoney construction company in Grand Rapids, Michigan. These guys have been working pretty hard."

"But not as hard as we will, I suppose," the chief said, "by the time we get this all sorted out." He glanced at his watch and said, "Does that about cover this week's disasters?"

"I guess, but there's one piece of good news," I said.

"Hell you say. What?"

"About an hour ago I got proof Reese Newman killed Benny Niemeyer."

"Got from where?"

"From the Bureau of Criminal Apprehension, a.k.a. my girl-friend. By the time I got home Wednesday night—it was really Thursday morning—while we ate breakfast I was telling Trudy about these big cheeses in jail that tried to drown their temp-sec, and I started wondering if maybe they could have done Benny too."

"You never said you were thinking about that," Ray said. He looked a little miffed.

"Well, it sounded too damn crazy. But thinking about all the bad stuff these guys seemed to be into, I said, 'Haven't you always said BCA could expedite when it was a matter of solving a homicide?'"

"And she did it?"

"Indeed, she did. That smart lady went to work and moved us up in the queue. She did a superior job of swabbing that skateboard, and she found two places, down along the sides, where the killer must have held onto it with sweaty hands. Good old sweat, these days it's just as good as blood."

"She found some DNA?"

"Yeah. And it's so neat the way it all came together. Until this week the DNA she got out of that sweat wouldn't have matched anything on file, but because Newman and Peabody had just been arrested for carrying a girl in a rug, we'd sent their blood for DNA testing too. So she moved that to the front of the line too, and there it was, a perfect match between Newman's sweat and Newman's blood."

"Shee. Sounds like a book by Winston Churchill."

"Doesn't it?"

"But listen, that's crazy," Ray said. "Why would the guy who defended Benny Niemeyer turn around and kill him?"

"Well." Bo cleared his throat. "I can make an educated guess about that. Elizabeth said that time they drove to LaCrosse and rented motel rooms, Benny heard her and Roger talking about the extra meth in their drug deliveries, how they had to be careful to get it out before her father came to get his coke. And Benny started saying, 'Oh boy, I bet I could blackmail your daddy about his drug use. What a great source of cash that would be.' They both yelled at him to shut up and mind his own business, but he just laughed."

"But you think he may have tried it?"

"I think what he probably did, once he got arrested, is try to use what he knew to get money out of Peabody for his defense."

"I think so too," I said, "and Peabody told Newman they had a problem."

"Aw, Jake, that sounds pretty far-fetched," the chief said.

"Well, but think about what was going on that Benny didn't know about," I said. "Peabody and Newman were sacking the foundation. That was the big payoff, and they couldn't afford to have anybody poking through their affairs while they did it."

"You think that's why Newman volunteered the pro bono defense?"

"And then did his best not to defend him," I said. "Now that I think about it, he didn't challenge our evidence that Benny knew where the body was, till the judge prodded him into it. He let a couple of Chrissie's statements go by that he should have objected to, and he put on no defense witnesses at all. Milo thought he was being clever, but now I realize he must have been trying to throw the case."

"But Benny got acquitted anyway," Ray said, "because we just didn't have enough on him."

"Because he didn't *do* it," I said. "It's enough to make you think, if it's too damn hard to convict a guy, you maybe ought to consider that he might not be guilty."

"That's a pretty radical suggestion," the chief said. "You must be one of these tree-hugging liberals I hear so much about." He drummed with his fingers. "You think when their blackmailer beat the Gleason charge they decided they had to get him off the street?"

"Yes. I'll never be able to prove this, Chief, but I think Newman was responsible for Roger's death inside the prison, and he meant to get Benny in there and take care of him the same way."

"You think Peabody was in on it too?"

"Stands to reason he was. We might get some evidence he was present in the skateboard pit. The hair and fiber guy at BCA found a couple of threads caught in the skateboard wheels, and Trudy says they look like they might have come from a madras jacket. So I subpoenaed all the clothes in Peabody's closet."

"Oh, can I deliver them?" Kevin asked. "It's the closest I'll ever get to a Savile Row suit."

"Boy, Kevin," Darrell said, "you sure talk funny sometimes."

27

"We have to talk," Trudy said Saturday morning.

"Okay," I said, from behind the paper. The lead story on the sports page of the *St. Paul Pioneer-Press* was about the US women's soccer team, and featured that great shot of Brandi Chastain in her sports bra, swinging her T-shirt in triumph.

I took another sip of coffee, debating which weekend games to set up on the VCR. This thing with the Cubs and the Sox in Chicago—

A hand came down from somewhere and mashed my newspaper into an accordion fold. "I mean the kind of talk where you actually listen," she said.

"Jesus, woman," I said, "don't you think I get enough violence at work?" I folded the paper neatly and laid it beside my coffee cup. "Okay, talk. But please, whatever you do don't cry on me, okay? I think I've watched enough women crying this week to last me for the rest of my life."

She gave me a level-eyed look. "Poor poor Jake Hines. You lead a very tough life, don't you?"

"I didn't say—"

"So much responsibility, such an exhausting load to carry."

"Is reading the paper such a—"

"And you're the only one who has all these burdens, aren't you? It's just a shame the way you have to tote the whole load."

"I know perfectly well you do more than your share of—"

"Between your job and the farming and the work on this house you're just run ragged, aren't you? And we're still nowhere near done with fixing up this place."

"What's that got to do with—"

"And the money's so tight, and there's still another whole summer ahead of us with that great big garden. So I just don't see," she had quit looking at me and was no longer making any sense at all, as far as I could tell. She was drifting away on her own cloud of woe, twisting a paper napkin into confetti, saying, "I don't see how we could take on one more thing, do you?"

"Trudy, what do you want?"

"It's not what I want," she said. "It's what I've got." Her lips had begun to tremble. She was seriously upset about something and now, sure enough by Jesus, she was going to cry.

"Oh, please, Trudy, come on now." I wanted her to keep her tears on the inside of her head and enjoy this bright summer morning with me, do some work in the garden and maybe goof off this afternoon. And I was sure there was a way, some magic words if I could just think of them, to bring her around. I got up and went around the table, still talking; I leaned over her chair and began nibbling on her ear and kissing her neck. "Whatever it is we can work it out—you know we can. Be my sweetheart and don't cry and I'll do anything—"

"Jake—"

"I want whatever you want—you know that. We'll just talk it through; together we can figure it out—"

"Oh, Jake, for God's sake—" she pushed me away and jumped out of her chair, "will you just shut up a minute and listen to me?"

See, you try to give them all the sympathy in the world and you still get put in the wrong. "Fine." I walked stiffly back to my chair and sat down.

"It's just that I—maybe I should have taken care of this myself and not said anything but I thought—" She sat down again and folded her hands on the table. "I thought you had a right to say what you think."

"Which I would certainly be glad to do," I said, making it clear that I was not glad at all, "if I could just figure out what in the holy living hell you're talking about."

"Good." She picked up a fork and slammed it down again. "Okay. Here it is." She gave me a kind of edge-of-the-cliff look and began talking very fast. "With all this working in the garden I got, I guess I got tired, and kind of careless about taking my pills for a while, and yesterday when I thought about it I went out and bought one of those pregnancy kits and the damn thing came out blue." She watched me then, the way a fox watches a henhouse, as I sat staring back at her with my mouth open while happiness flooded through me like mind candy. "But I know it's not the right time for us and I'll take care of it—don't worry. You don't have to do anything except help me figure out the money, only I thought I ought to tell you first."

"First before what?"

"Well, first before I make arrangements to have an abor—"

"No, now, stop, wait—" I jumped up and reached her side of the table in two steps, knelt down by her and put my arms around her. "Trudy, oh sweetheart, oh, please please please say you'll have our baby. Why would you think you ought to—oh, please, Trudy. Is it because I'm not white? Are you afraid of what people will say?"

"What a terrible thing to say to me! I never even thought of such a thing. Jake, are you crying?"

"Well, then, are you afraid because we're not married?" I found a napkin in her lap and mopped at my face. "We can *get* married. What's hard about that? It only takes a few minutes—people do it all the time!"

"You *are* crying." She lifted my face up and laughed at me, but she had tears on her cheeks too. "You said you couldn't stand any more crying and now you're doing it yourself. What kind of a deal is that?"

"I said I couldn't stand to have you do it. When I do it, it feels pretty good." We held onto each other, crying and laughing. "Will you do it? Please, will you? I'll help you. I'll be right there the whole time and I'll do anything—"

"Are you sure? Because it's really nuts, Jake. We're not ready for this at all—"

"I'm ready," I said. "I've been ready ever since I met you. I've been dreaming about this for years."

"Oh, Jake, you crazy fool." We did some more hugging and crying and laughing. Finally she said, in a small voice, "You really think we can swing it somehow? Is it right to have a baby when we're so broke?"

"Broke is just a temporary condition. We'll work our way out of it. I'll do some extra shifts, be a security guard at rock concerts and stuff like that. All that matters is, are you willing to do it? You have to do the hard part."

"It's not hard; it's exciting." She thought a minute. "I love my job, though. And I don't see how we could manage if I quit."

"Why would you quit? You're good at your job and you keep getting better. Look what you did for Rutherford just this summer— saved our bacon time after time. Anyway, I just happen to know the best day-care provider in southeast Minnesota." I began to feel as if balloons were attaching themselves to my body. "How soon can I tell Maxine?"

"Oh, not for three months. Well, two, anyway." She laughed, watching my face. "I know, it's hard to think of waiting, isn't it?" She did some hiccuppy laughing and finally said, "Oh well," and got up and put her cup in the sink. "I guess we better quit laughing and crying and get out there in that garden."

It took me quite a while to get organized. I was too happy to keep my mind on the carrots. I kept trotting to the other end of the row to ask Trudy questions, like, "How soon are you going to get some of those tops with pleats in the front? I've always wanted to see how you'd look in one of those."

"Jeez, let's not hurry that part. You'll be plenty sick of those before we're done."

"I won't," I said, "I'm going to love it all." I went back to weeding, but before long Trudy's garden clogs appeared beside the beets.

"Listen," she said, as I stood up. "Was that a proposal I heard back there in the kitchen? Because if it was I accept."

"Absolutely," I said. "Wait, I'll do you another one." I got down on my knees between the beets and the leaf lettuce. "Please, Trudy Hanson, will you marry me and have babies with me and go deep in debt and stay with me till my teeth fall out? Please?"

"You don't make it sound very attractive." She giggled. "Is becoming a father going to turn you into some kind of a worry-wart?"

I put on my best Alfred E. Neuman face and said, "What, me worry? Hell, woman, optimism is my middle name!"

"Well, hey, time you had one." She laughed some more; she was giddy too.

"Mrs. Jake Optimism Hines, how does that sound to you?"

"Oh, I love it!" She hooted up at the sky. "I'll have cards printed up!"

We finally got serious long enough to pick four baskets of produce for the Sullivan families, and then Trudy said, "The rest of these weeds aren't going anyplace; let's give 'em a break for the rest of the day." So we picked two perfect tomatoes and carried them into our tumbledown kitchen for lunch. We had a pig in the poke and a bun in the oven, and we needed all the vitamins we could get.